The power he had over her now was terrifying.

How had she strayed so far from her course? Her behavior had been reckless, irresponsible. She had leapt into the fire, oblivious to the consequences. What had happened to her strength of will and determination?

She had boasted about wanting a predictable man. But she had tempted the Fates with her dictates, and they had laughed, giving her the very thing she feared most—a man of mystery.

But against the magic of his touch, she was helpless. Each time she closed her eyes and thought of him standing before her, tanned, strong and glorious in his manhood, she could feel his hands gliding over her flesh, his lips teasing hers, his tongue stroking her. She could taste him, feel him throbbing deep inside her.

And even as she raged against it, her body ached for fulfillment....

Dear Reader,

Welcome to Silhouette **Special Edition** ... welcome to romance. Each month Silhouette **Special Edition** publishes six novels with you in mind—stories of love and life, tales that you can identify with—romance with that little "something special" added in.

And this month is no exception to the rule. May 1991 brings *No Quarter Given* by Lindsay McKenna—the first in the thrilling WOMEN OF GLORY series. Don't miss more of this compelling collection coming in June and July. Stories by wonderful writers Curtiss Ann Matlock, Tracy Sinclair, Sherryl Woods, Diana Stuart and Lorraine Carroll (with her first **Special Edition**!) round out this merry month.

In each Silhouette **Special Edition**, we're dedicated to bringing you the romances that you dream about—the type of stories that delight as well as bring a tear to the eye. And that's what Silhouette **Special Edition** is all about—special books by special authors for special readers!

I hope you enjoy this book and all of the stories to come.

Sincerely,

Tara Gavin
Senior Editor

LORRAINE CARROLL
Lead with Your Heart

Silhouette Special Edition

Published by Silhouette Books New York

America's Publisher of Contemporary Romance

To Joe, Matt and Danny, the special men in my life;
and
to Joy, whose help and friendship
made this book possible

SILHOUETTE BOOKS
300 East 42nd St., New York, N.Y. 10017

LEAD WITH YOUR HEART

ISBN: 0-373-09670-4

First Silhouette Books printing May 1991

Printed in the U.S.A.

LORRAINE CARROLL

traces her dream of becoming a novelist back to the seventh grade, when she penned a teenage romance/action adventure story for a writing assignment. To the teacher who had unknowingly planted the seeds of commitment in her, Lorraine gives thanks.

Lorraine has moved around a bit—from Columbus, Ohio, where she was born and raised, to Germany, Connecticut, Louisiana and Mississippi, where she currently resides. She has been married over twenty years to the "world's most perfect husband," and has two sons. When she finds time, she plays the piano and sews.

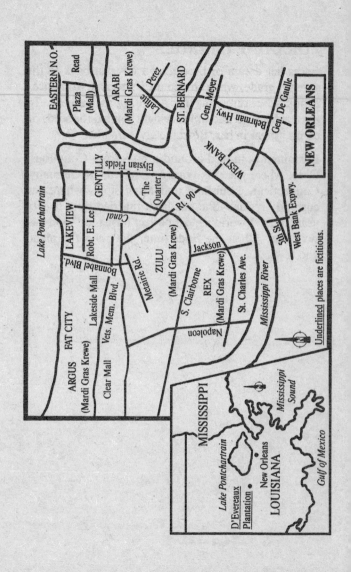

NEW ORLEANS

Underlined places are fictitious.

EASTERN N.O.

Read

Plaza (Mall)

ARABI (Mardi Gras Krewe)

Lafitte

Perez

ST. BERNARD

Gen. Meyer

Gen. De Gaulle

Behrman Hwy.

WEST BANK

Elysian Fields

GENTILLY

The Quarter

Rt. 90

5th St.

West Bank Expwy.

Lake Pontchartrain

LAKEVIEW

Canal

Robt. E. Lee

Bonnabel Blvd.

Metairie Rd.

ZULU (Mardi Gras Krewe)

S. Clairborne

Jackson

REX (Mardi Gras Krewe)

St. Charles Ave.

Mississippi River

ARGUS (Mardi Gras Krewe)

FAT CITY

Lakeside Mall

Vets. Mem. Blvd.

Clear Mall

Napoleon

MISSISSIPPI

Mississippi Sound

LOUISIANA

Lake Pontchartrain

D'Evereaux Plantation

New Orleans

Gulf of Mexico

Chapter One

It hardly seemed like a day for a funeral. The sky was a brilliant blue, and the sun beating down through the atmosphere had sent the temperature in New Orleans to its normal late-summer high of ninety-five. Kenley Farrell stepped from her small gray car and was met with a soft breeze that stirred the humid air, carrying the delicate scent of magnolias intermingled with the musty smell of the mighty Mississippi. It was a day more suited to a lazy ride on the river or a comfy seat in a wicker swing than a visit to a cemetery.

Briefly Kenley allowed her thoughts to be distracted by the eerie beauty of the New Orleans burial grounds. Sitting five feet below sea level, the city had been forced to bury its dead above ground. The resulting collections of grotesque tombs and gothic crypts lined row upon row had come to be known as "cities of the dead." A faint smile moved the corner of her mouth. There was something fascinatingly macabre about these places that never failed to stir her imagination.

"Are you coming, kiddo?"

Kenley blinked and looked at her passenger and co-worker, Alva Guidroz, who was waiting patiently for her on the other side of the car. Quickly she joined her friend on the grassy easement and followed the mourners along the path toward the grave site.

New Orleans in August was a steam bath. The air was as thick as corn syrup, and Kenley could already feel the peplum on her navy blue dress going limp and beads of perspiration forming on her upper lip. It didn't really matter, though. She was here to pay her respects to a kind and generous benefactor of the city.

Seth Crawford's death had saddened all of New Orleans. Kenley had first met the owner of Crawford Plastics six months before when he'd purchased the one hundred acres adjacent to his plastics plant in Mossville, twenty miles upriver from New Orleans. In the center of the land stood a 150-year-old plantation home called D'Evereaux. The heirs, cousins Sam Keenan and Jake Edwards, had bickered for over thirty years as to the best method of restoring the home. As a result, nothing had been done and the plantation had steadily deteriorated, exposed to the brutal Louisiana climate.

As administrator of the Crescent City Preservation Society, Kenley kept abreast of the sale and acquisition of historic properties in south Louisiana, with an eye toward their restoration. When Seth Crawford bought the property, she immediately approached him about preservation.

Walking silently along the narrow path to the ornate tomb near the end of the grass alley she smiled, remembering her first meeting with the spry old gentleman. He had been most receptive to her ideas; his enthusiasm and devotion to preserving New Orleans's historic past rivaled her own. She would miss him, and the knowledge that he was without family to mourn his passing saddened her greatly.

After his wife's death twelve years earlier, Seth had moved his company headquarters from Columbus, Ohio, to New Orleans. With the oil boom in full swing his processing plant in Mossville became the most profitable of all CP facilities. Seth had quickly adopted New Orleans, aligning himself with the cause most near and dear to the people here—preservation. His generosity had garnered him the respect and admiration of the whole city. The fact that he had chosen to be buried here rather than back in Ohio spoke volumes about his own feelings.

As the mourners pressed in among the closely built crypts, Kenley realized she was totally surrounded by people. Alva's shoulder touched hers as the crowd eased closer to the grave. A thin film of sweat appeared on her face and she glanced around anxiously, her blue eyes widening. Everywhere she looked people were moving in, cutting off what little air there was. It became difficult to breathe. "Alva, I'll wait for you back at the car," she said suddenly.

"For heaven's sake, why?" she asked, looking at her friend curiously.

"It's too hot. All these people." Kenley tried to think up a logical excuse, but it was so hot and it was so hard to draw breath. "It must have been breakfast," she stammered, putting a hand to her throat.

"What did you have to eat?"

"Nothing. I should have eaten. I just need air." She turned and began to push her way through the crowd, leaving Alva with a look of puzzlement on her face.

Breaking free, Kenley took a deep breath and felt herself relax. She was grateful that she'd been at the end of the procession instead of in the middle. Otherwise... Pushing that thought firmly aside, she took several more deep breaths. It felt cooler here away from the press of humanity. She smiled to herself and walked slowly back toward the road, stopping in the shadow of a vault whose rusted iron fence and roof ornaments attested to its age.

She turned her eyes back toward the grave and the coffin that was being carried toward it, wondering what would become of Crawford Plastics now. Would one of the vice presidents step forward to assume command? Or had Seth made other provisions for his business.

And what would his death mean for D'Evereaux? Had he left instructions for the restoration? Would the matter be settled quickly or held up in probate? Would he keep his promise to her and the society? A rush of warmth filled her cheeks and she felt ashamed of herself for thinking about D'Evereaux at a time like this.

Kenley watched the mourners bow their heads in prayer and did likewise, distracted momentarily by the sound of an approaching car. Its powerful engine rumbled loudly in the warm, still air, and the tires grinding on loose gravel seemed a thoughtless intrusion into the reverent setting.

Frowning in disapproval, she had barely turned her attention back to the funeral when the faint rustle of shoes upon dry grass reached her ears, and she fought the urge to turn and glare at the intruder. The squeak of soft leather soles drew closer, moving with slow, deliberate steps. A shadow, long and foreboding in this city of the dead, cast itself in front of the encroaching stranger. Kenley stiffened, and her heart seemed to freeze in her chest.

In spite of her determination not to, her eyes darted to the left as a tall, dark-haired man drew even with her. He stopped, slowly turning his face in her direction. Something in his posture, the angle at which he held his head, sent a chill up Kenley's spine.

He was tall, broad-shouldered and imposing, exuding an aura of power and authority that was both frightening and stimulating. Here was a man who knew who he was and precisely where he was going. When he spoke, he probably expected people to listen. But underlying the commanding presence ran something more powerful, more basic—a raw, primitive masculinity so potent, so forceful it was almost carnal.

Dark glasses obscured his eyes, cutting across his temple and disappearing into thick, dark hair that hugged his ears. His features were strong, a combination of planes and angles that, even partially hidden, added up to handsome—a long straight nose, a forehead that was high and wide though softened by the strands of black hair that hung over it. A rugged bronze complexion accentuated his high cheekbones. The mouth was sensuous and firm, the jaw tapered and sharp, and lips full and pulled slightly to one side as if in amusement or possibly mockery.

Kenley stood motionless, spellbound by the savage masculinity he broadcast. Then subtly she sensed a change. Even though his eyes were masked, she felt them upon her now, reaching across the short distance between them and touching her, evaluating, making her shiver despite the sultry atmosphere. Something tightened in the pit of her stomach, her lips parting ever so slightly. She felt him peeling away her cover, undressing her boldly, expertly, then going beyond the flesh and seeing into her heart and the farthest recesses of her mind, stimulating areas of her subconscious she'd never known existed.

Transfixed by some unseen force, her mind filled with illicit thoughts and unnamed desires. She was powerless to stop them and helpless beneath his intimate scrutiny. Her heart pounded violently in her chest and her blood sparked, surging through her veins like wildfire.

He didn't smile, didn't acknowledge her presence in any way, yet he seemed to hold her in place with the sheer force of his will. Then slowly, his assessment apparently complete, he moved away.

The encounter lasted only a few seconds, but Kenley felt totally exposed—as if in that one moment the stranger had laid open her very soul. It was a most disturbing experience, and she found herself unable to shake his spell. Her eyes followed him as he continued on his slow, deliberate way toward the grave. He moved gracefully, with athletic control, as though he commanded each muscle and tendon individually. There was a nonchalance to his gait that was arrogant, bordering on rude.

The black suit he wore called attention to his maleness, draping his broad shoulders and tapering down abruptly to narrow hips. The fabric skimmed his thighs as he moved, suggesting a strength in the long legs beneath.

Mesmerized, she watched until he stopped near the fringe of the crowd. Not until that moment did she realize she'd been holding her breath. Raggedly she sighed, releasing the pent-up tension, surprised to discover she was quaking.

Thoroughly disquieted, Kenley turned away from the crypts and closed her eyes, breathing deeply, determined to calm her shattered nerves. This was ridiculous, she chided herself after her heart rate slowed and respiration eased. A strange man passed her in the cemetery and she reacted as if a ghost had suddenly materialized. She really needed to curb her overactive imagination.

With her composure safely in place once more, Kenley returned her attention to the service, only to find that it had concluded. With no family to comfort or console, the mourners quietly and quickly began to disperse. Kenley's attention was inexorably drawn back to the stranger. He hung back from the others, then, when he alone remained, he stepped forward and extended his hand to the minister. Kenley was too far away to hear what was being said, but she could see from the expression on Reverend Bouchard's face that the man's words were a surprise to him. Curious, she started forward only to be frozen in her tracks when the stranger turned suddenly and pinned her with a stare. It was almost as if he'd sensed her eyes upon him. But before she could react, he looked away and Alva was standing at her side.

"Can you believe that?" she asked, her voice filled with awe.

"Believe what?" Kenley asked, unable to tear her eyes from the man's back.

"Didn't you hear what he said?"

"Who?" she replied, finally shifting her attention to her friend. "What who said?"

"That man over there. He walked up to Reverend Bouchard and introduced himself as the new owner of Crawford Plastics."

Kenley's eyes narrowed. "What?"

"Yep. Says his name is Blane Crawford and claims he's Seth's son."

Blane Crawford looked over his shoulder directly at the young woman he'd noticed upon his arrival. His instincts were correct; she was staring at him.

When he'd stepped out of his car into a blast furnace, he'd wondered how the people here could tolerate such an oppressive climate. It was then he saw her. She stood in profile, dressed in navy and white—a cool, crisp oasis in a sea of heat and humidity. The sun was shining on her hair, glinting copper and gold. The rich brown tresses were swept up on her head, but several tiny curling strands had escaped, kissing her slender neck and shoulders. The dress hugged an enchantingly feminine form, emphasizing womanly curves that begged to be held.

His footsteps slowed, his senses captivated by the vision before him. He was melting under the intense sun, and rivulets of sweat were running down his back, dampening his shirt. Yet when he stopped beside her, she looked completely calm and serene, untouched by any of it. She glanced in his direction, and he found himself looking at the largest blue eyes he'd ever seen. Surprisingly, they were filled with mild irritation.

Curious, he looked at her more closely. There was intelligence and a healthy measure of self-confidence behind the blue eyes. He'd started to smile when he noticed a subtle change in her expression. He stared, fascinated by the rapid succession of emotions that were clearly visible on her delicate features—first surprise, then wonderment followed by a trace of desire, then finally a flicker of fear. She looked vulnerable, and he felt a ridiculous desire to go to her and hold her in his arms, assuring her that everything would be all right.

Then suddenly he remembered where he was and why he was here. Reluctantly he wrested his attention from the woman and continued on. He waited patiently as the mourners drifted off, then he spoke briefly with the minister. The hair on the back of his neck tingled, and it was then he turned his head to find the woman watching him. The knowledge pleased him greatly. He held her gaze briefly, then turned away, a sardonic smile on his lips. His curiosity about her would have to wait. Right now he had other matters on his mind.

He quietly stepped forward, gazing down at his father's tomb. A sense of loneliness swelled inside him, followed by regret and a profound feeling of loss. His mind was a jumble of darting, unconnected thoughts—some good, some bad, some too painful to dwell on. He let them swirl freely around in his head until one finally emerged above the others: his bewilderment at having Crawford Plastics thrust upon him. He'd gotten out of his dad's business long ago and had no desire to return. He had his own concerns, his own line of work now. Not that his father had ever agreed with or understood his calling. Seth Crawford had labeled him ungrateful, told him he was shirking responsibility and accused him of turning his back on his family and honest work to "throw in with crooks and crackpots."

Blane had to smile at that. His dad had never been able to accept the fact that his own son was one of those so-called crackpots. At least he'd proven his father wrong there. Although his business had gotten off to an inauspicious start, it had eventually thrived, a fact that had galled the elder Crawford for the last decade.

Now he found himself saddled with Crawford Plastics once again, and like it or not, his life would have to be put on pause until he settled the estate. With any luck he'd be able to accomplish that in a couple of weeks and get out, but somehow he didn't think it would be that easy. Gently he let his fingers trace the name newly engraved on the granite plaque. "Why did you do it, Dad?" he asked softly. "You knew how I felt." He let his hand drop to his side and closed his eyes for a long moment. When he opened them again, they were filled with tears. Silently he turned, noting that the woman had vanished.

He realized with profound disappointment that he'd probably never see her again.

Kenley's mind was spinning, trying to digest the shocking news about Blane Crawford. She maneuvered her car through the streets by habit and instinct. "I thought Seth Crawford had no family," she questioned Alva.

"That's what we all thought. Word around the building was that he was alone. He never talked about anyone, least of all a grown son."

Kenley shook her head. "Where did this guy come from, and why the big secret?"

Alva shrugged. "Beats me. Black sheep, perhaps? Maybe the old coot disowned him."

"That doesn't sound like the Seth Crawford I knew," Kenley pointed out thoughtfully.

"Honey, there was a lot about Mr. Crawford you probably didn't know. You only saw one side of the man. He could have had a whole other side to him none of us suspected."

Kenley's hand gripped the steering wheel tightly. She couldn't argue with that point. Hadn't she learned firsthand about the hidden aspects of a person's life? She was barely fifteen when her father's true characteristics had been revealed. "I suppose. But if he disowned him, then why is he here now?"

"I don't know. All I know is that he struts up to Reverend Bouchard and introduces himself as Blane Crawford, Seth's only son. The good reverend was a bit taken aback, I can tell you."

"Maybe he's only here for the funeral," Kenley speculated.

"I doubt it. He made a point of telling the reverend he was the new owner of Crawford Plastics. He'll probably take over the whole thing now. Unless..." Alva said mysteriously, "What if he's really a spy from a rival company? Or an FBI agent looking into illegal business practices? Maybe he's not Blane Crawford but some con man trying to scam the inheritance."

The smile on Kenley's face was incredulous. "And I thought I had a wild imagination. FBI? Con man on the take?"

Slightly offended, Alva pressed her lips together in a thin line. "Aren't you even curious? Aren't you intrigued by this guy?"

Kenley was careful to keep her eyes trained directly ahead. "Not particularly. I'm only concerned about what effect this will have on the future of D'Evereaux." She steered the car to a halt in front of Alva's ultramodern condominium.

Alva sighed and opened the car door. "One of these days you're going to regret all this devotion to inanimate objects."

Kenley didn't even bother to ask what she meant by the remark. Alva was always spouting warnings about what she deemed Kenley's obsessive devotion to her work. "I'll see you Monday morning, Alva."

With an affectionate smile, she watched as her friend walked toward her front door. Alva had been her most valued asset since Kenley had come to New Orleans five years before. The widow of a prominent businessman, Alva had been a longtime volunteer to the society. When the group decided to hire a professional preservationist to administer its holdings, Alva had offered to show the new kid the ropes. The friendship between the two women had formed instantly and resulted in Alva taking over the position of full-time associate.

Pulling back into the flow of Saturday traffic, Kenley had to admit that she couldn't kid herself any longer. She was intensely curious about Blane Crawford and more than a little uneasy about his sudden appearance.

Why hadn't Seth spoken of his son? Most fathers were openly boastful of their male children. Was Alva right? Was Blane the black sheep? She remembered her strange encounter with the man at the cemetery and bit her lower lip. He had seemed threatening, dangerous. Not at all like his genial parent.

Kenley's mouth felt dry, and the humidity seemed to be seeping into the car despite the air conditioner. Pulling into a fast-food restaurant, she turned toward the drive-through and ordered a diet cola. Once more in the flow of traffic, her thoughts reverted to Blane Crawford. If he had been disowned, then why was he here? To stake his claim? To cause trouble? She had no doubt that he was fully capable of that. There had been a steeliness to him, something hard and determined.

What if he was the new owner of Crawford Plastics? What would that mean to her? To the future of D'Evereaux?

She wished now for a more tangible commitment to save the house than just Seth's verbal promise. It had seemed to her on several occasions that he was dragging his feet on the matter, but then she would remind herself that these things took time. Rarely was the fate of an historic landmark settled quickly. Often it took months or years of legal finagling. She was fortunate that Seth Crawford had agreed so promptly. It was only the manner in which he would contribute that had taken time. They had looked into endowments as well as setting up a foundation to oversee the restoration, but neither had proved a viable solution. Finally the day before he died, Seth had decided to donate the entire thing to the Crescent City Preservation Society. The only problem was that she still had only the promise of a well-intentioned old man.

Her thoughts were still jumbled when she pulled up in front of her French Quarter town house. With a lift of her chin, she decided to put all the speculations aside. She would have the answers soon enough. After all, the worst it could mean to her was that she'd have to start over, convince Blane Crawford that D'Evereaux had to be saved, and confront him with his father's promise of donation and force him to honor that commitment.

She saw again the imposing figure of Blane Crawford, and she knew that forcing him to do anything would be impossible. He was a man who would do what he pleased, and she doubted if he was accustomed to letting anything stand in his way. Her next thought both angered and surprised her. She found herself wondering what he looked like behind those dark glasses.

Chapter Two

After the funeral Blane took refuge in the paneled library at the back of his father's palatial Victorian home in the Garden District. In the few days since his arrival, he'd found himself retreating here more and more often. Of the seventeen rooms in the old mansion, this was the only one in which he felt comfortable. The others, even the room he'd taken as his own, felt more like a museum than a home. At least here he felt free to kick back and put his feet on the furniture if he so desired.

One bright spot in the unwelcome situation was that he liked New Orleans. Perhaps this time he'd have a chance to get to know the city. His last trip had been made under the gun, and he'd seen little more than an abandoned building and a hotel room.

His father had loved it here, and despite their differences of opinion Blane had been anxious to see what it was about New Orleans that had engendered such devotion. Maybe by understanding that he would also gain some insight into his father and his reasons for leaving him a company he didn't want.

Blane took a sip from the chunky mug he held, and grimaced. The coffee was cold. After placing it on a nearby table, he absently paced across the room, stopping in front of the large multipaned window that dominated the rear wall and afforded a magnificent view of the lavishly landscaped garden beyond. Immediately outside the library at the corner of the house stood a huge magnolia tree, and Blane focused on one of the auburn leaves as it drifted gracefully to the ground. It brought to mind an image of the woman he'd seen at the cemetery. Even if he could find her again, there was little time in his hectic schedule for personal relationships. And then if all went well he'd be moving on, back to his own business and a life-style that was ill-suited to a permanent address.

A strange feeling of sadness touched him. For a moment he allowed himself to imagine a life with roots and enduring emotional ties to one very special person. Then with a muttered curse he yanked his thoughts back to more practical matters, such as settling his father's affairs as quickly and as easily as possible.

Wednesday morning, esconced in the downtown offices of Crawford Plastics, Blane was forced to accept the bitter knowledge that no quick or easy solution would be possible. Sitting behind the broad desk, he ran his hands through his dark hair. He'd been sorting through his father's affairs, trying to make some sense of it all, yet so far he'd made little headway. His father's files were a shambles and his correspondence either missing or incomplete. Crawford Plastics was in serious financial trouble and because of that he had been forced to implement some severe policy changes at the board meeting Monday. Not that any of this surprised him. He had argued fiercely in favor of updating facilities while his father held to the belief that what worked in the past would continue to work in the future. It gave

Blane no particular satisfaction to be proved right. It was becoming clear, however, that rectifying the situation would require a commitment of several years. Something Blane wasn't sure he was willing to make.

A tour of the processing plant upriver in Mossville the day before had left Blane discouraged and wondering if Crawford Plastics was worth all the time, money and effort needed to restore it to a profitable business. He'd never wanted to run this company, and now the responsibility settled upon his shoulders like an anchor. He felt stone-walled. Each time he decided on a course of action, a new obstacle would present itself and he'd have to start all over again. For two cents, he'd let the damn thing fall into bankruptcy. But then his conscience would call to him and he would relent. He might not be happy with the situation, but he owed it to his dad and to himself to try.

Leaning back in his chair, he rubbed his temple, wondering if there were any aspirins around. Dealing with his father's business never failed to give birth to one hell of a headache. He was contemplating the old adage "some things never change," when Dave entered. "Go away. I don't want any more bad news today."

"Okay." Dave shrugged, perching on the edge of Blane's desk. "How about interesting news, then?"

Blane looked up, his eyebrows nearly touching when he frowned. "It had better be interesting. Or you're fired."

"You can't fire me. I'm irreplaceable. You said so yourself."

"I said you were *irrepressible*," Blane corrected. David Kesler had been his right-hand man since Blane had left Crawford Plastics and started his own business nearly fifteen years before. Part accountant, part advisor and sometime rescuer, Dave could always be counted on to provide whatever Blane needed.

Among his other jobs, Dave often served as PR man for Blane's organization. His open, friendly face and gregarious nature had smoothed the way for many of their proj-

ects. With his shock of sandy hair, smiling green eyes and
fun-loving personality, he was a valuable asset in their line
of work. Dave put people at ease. He was a good listener. It
was easy for people to talk to him, to trust him with their
problems and to confide their secrets. That fact more than
any other had made their work much easier—and profitable—for everyone.

"Well—" he shrugged "—it seems you and your dad
weren't as far apart in your business philosophies as you
thought." Blane's eyes narrowed. "Remember the idea you
had last night about building a new plant and renovating the
old one?"

"Yes, and after seeing the plant I'm more convinced than
ever that's the way to go."

"So was your dad." Dave's eyebrows bobbed up and
down in pleasure. He handed Blane several thick folders.
"Feasibility studies on construction of a new plant and
renovation of the present facility."

Taking the files, Blane started leafing through them.
"Verdict?"

"Well, the report from the consulting firm said full steam
ahead. It'll take me a week or so to study it more thoroughly, of course, but they must have been very positive for
your dad to purchase that land."

Blane looked up sharply. "What land?"

"The property next to the plant up there in Mossville.
Over a hundred acres of prime commercial real estate."

Blane rubbed his temple thoughtfully. It was an unusual
move for his extremely conservative father. "He was really
serious about this expansion?"

"Oh, yeah," Dave answered firmly. "He'd had the blue-
prints filed and was accepting bids from construction companies. But for some reason he dropped the project about
two months ago."

"Why?"

"Money, I'm sure. He used his last available capital to buy the land. There weren't too many options left to him. I guess he realized that and gave up on the idea."

Cocking his head, Blane fingered a dark folder on the desk. "What do you know about a place called D'Evereaux?" he asked.

Dave shook his head. "Nothing. Oh no, wait. Is that the old plantation on that property?"

"I found this in the desk drawer." He handed the slim folder to his friend. "Seems my father once again caved in to his philanthropic habit. From those papers it looks like he was trying to help this woman, Miss—uh . . ."

"Farrell," Dave provided.

"To restore the old house. You know her?"

"No, but I know of her. Her secretary has called our secretary four times so far this week and once this morning wanting to talk to you about that house. As if we don't have enough on our minds."

Blane grunted in response.

"You don't think your dad would scrap the expansion project just to save an old house, do you?"

A wry smile moved the corner of Blane's mouth. "In a minute. Only I can't figure what he planned to use for money."

"Beats me. Let me check with the legal guys. Maybe they know something."

While Dave used the phone, Blane took the opportunity to finish looking through his father's desk. He pulled open the last drawer on the left and stared with unbelieving eyes at the object on top. In a small silver frame was a picture of himself taken about fifteen years ago. His mind struggled to comprehend the discovery as he lifted the photograph for a closer look. Seth Crawford had never been a sentimental man. He never mixed family and business. Yet here in his desk drawer was a picture of his only son. A warmth spread through Blane as he held the photo, and his eyes burned. Maybe, just maybe, his father had forgiven him after all.

"Well, looks like you were right," Dave said as he hung up the phone. "The boys in legal say your dad asked them to look into setting up a foundation to restore the old plantation. Then last week he sent them a memo asking them to draw up transfer of title to the society instead."

"Was anything signed?"

"No. Apparently your dad couldn't make up his mind on just what he wanted to do. There were lots of papers drawn up on a couple of ideas, but nothing was ever taken out of the legal department and none of it was signed."

Lacing his fingers together, Blane rested his head on his hands. "What could he have been thinking of? Scrapping plans to revitalize Crawford Plastics in favor of saving some prehistoric mausoleum."

"I think the term is antebellum," Dave commented, only to receive an icy glare from his friend.

"What about this Farrell person?"

"She's a persistent old gal." He laughed. "She's the administrator with one of the historical societies or something. She saves these old places for a living. And from what Mrs. Pohl says, she's *real* determined to meet with you."

A smile eased the frown on Blane's face. Finally, a small problem that he could deal with quickly and easily. "Tell Mrs. Pohl to grant the old lady's wish. I'll see her as soon as possible," Blane announced.

"That won't be hard. Their offices are right down the hall here."

"Good. Then get her here pronto."

Dave rose and headed for the door. "In that case, I'm outta here. I can picture the old broad now. Skinny, stooped, with a prune face. The only passion in her dried-up life is saving old relics like herself."

Blane tried not to smile, but he had to admit that Dave's image perfectly matched his own. In any event, he'd be gentle but firm with the lady. Nothing would stand in the way of his plan to save Crawford Plastics—especially some moldering old mansion.

* * *

Kenley knew the moment she awoke that it was going to be one of those days. Traffic was bumper-to-bumper and the humidity factor rivaled the temperature as she drove to work Wednesday morning. Since the funeral Saturday her mind had been nagged with concern over the future of D'Evereaux. In addition, the bizarre encounter with Blane Crawford at the cemetery had replayed ceaselessly in her mind, and as a result sleep had been fitful and plagued with dreams. Yet even there she couldn't escape the unsettling image of Blane Crawford. He hovered in the back of her mind, a presence both frightening and intriguing. She couldn't determine which disturbed her more.

This preoccupation with Mr. Crawford had only been compounded by a general state of chaos at work. Like a line of dominoes, everything she touched this week had fallen apart. Today she'd overslept, then realized she'd forgotten to set her automatic coffee maker. The newspaper was late and there was a tropical depression forming in the Gulf. By the time she arrived at her small offices in the Ellison Building on Canal Street she felt limp and irritable. It came as no surprise to find Alva waiting by the door wearing her customary scowl.

Kenley held up her hand and sailed past. "I don't want to hear it. Just handle it yourself. I'm going to be in conference with some aspirin and a cup of coffee all morning."

"Oh no, you aren't. You've been summoned to meet the new man at Crawford Plastics."

"Mr. Crawford wants to see me now?" Kenley asked, setting her briefcase on her desk.

"Pronto." Alva nodded. "I told them you'd be right over."

"Has he made his decision? Is he going to donate the land?" she asked eagerly.

"Didn't say, didn't ask," Alva replied bluntly.

"Wonderful," Kenley muttered sarcastically. "I'm not prepared. I wasn't expecting to see him right away. I don't have a proper presentation ready. I don't know what he'll want to see, what methods he'd like to consider." She picked up her purse and looked at Alva. "I've got to plead my case in front of a man I've never met and whose intentions are a complete mystery to me." Just like his very existence, she noted mentally.

A small knot of tension formed at the center of Kenley's chest, swelling rapidly and seeming to lodge in her throat. She struggled to stay calm and master the anxiety that was choking her. She had to be strong. This was what she'd waited for. She couldn't collapse just because it had come without warning. Taking a long, deep breath to force the air into her lungs, Kenley hoped Alva hadn't noticed her momentary weakness.

Alva's smile was gentle. "You don't need anything but your own enthusiasm and determination. You've done it before."

Kenley lowered her eyes. But I didn't have a downward trend in my confidence factor then, she wanted to say. "Yes, I know. But I wanted it to be on my terms."

"Life doesn't always play on our terms."

So she had noticed. It seemed as if the past few months of her life had been adhering firmly to everyone else's terms—a situation Kenley hoped to change. "Well, maybe this is a good sign. At least D'Evereaux is at the top of his list."

Alva snorted. "Which one? The 'to proceed' or the 'to cancel'?"

Kenley glanced up at her as she snapped the fasteners on her briefcase shut. "You know something I don't?"

"Maybe."

"Such as?"

"Such as, he's ordered an immediate wage and hiring freeze, a ten-percent cut in commission to salesmen, a step-up on accounts receivable and the probable elimination of certain products that are no longer cost effective. He's also ordering a complete audit of the company books and a reevaluation of product lines and production procedures."

Kenley stared at her friend, total amazement reflected on her face. "Where do you hear this stuff? You sound like you're quoting from the minutes of the last board meeting."

Alva shrugged. "It wasn't a direct quote, but close." When she saw Kenley was still staring at her, she added defensively. "I know a lot of people in this building. Some of them just happen to work for Crawford Plastics."

"And like to gossip," Kenley added with a smirk. "Well, wish me luck," she said as she headed for the door. Out in the hallway she lifted her head and walked confidently toward the main office of Crawford Plastics, ignoring the nervous ache in her stomach. She tried not to think about the massive amount of work that would be involved if she was forced to start from scratch with Mr. Crawford. Several steps toward preservation had already been taken, based upon the elder Crawford's verbal promises. Now those might be in jeopardy as well. Staunchly she reminded herself that she had faced greater obstacles in the past. Blane Crawford was only one minor businessman. She'd fought her cases before state senators, governors and corporate heads. How difficult could this man be? His intimidating presence at the cemetery filled her mind, and her heart fluttered wildly with anxiety.

Edith Pohl, secretary and longtime fixture at CP, ushered Kenley in promptly upon her arrival. Taking a deep breath she pushed open the heavy door, mentally bolstering her confidence with each step. She noticed a subtle change in the large office the moment she stepped inside. Nothing had been moved. The antique rosewood desk still stood in front of the expansive windows that provided a spectacular view of Canal Street below, and the other small groupings of tables and chairs were in their customary positions along with the credenza and the various planters. Seth's office had always been impressive, but today it seemed imposing as well.

She saw him then, standing in front of the bookcase that covered the far wall. He was replacing a binder on the shelf, his back to her. The light beige suit he wore highlighted the breadth of his shoulders and the lean masculine lines of his frame. Even under the fabric of his suit, Kenley could see the controlled strength in the muscles. Abruptly she recalled her reason for being in his office. "Mr. Crawford," she said in a firm business tone, "I understand you wanted to see me."

Slowly he turned and she found herself looking into the most beautiful brown eyes she'd ever seen. She watched as they widened slightly when he saw her. A look of puzzlement passed over his strong features, then the corners of his mouth moved. It wasn't quite a smile. "You're Miss Farrell?"

"Yes, I'm Kenley Farrell," she said, extending her hand. Blane stood calmly looking at her. His suit coat was unbuttoned, and he brushed it back with his hands, resting his splayed fingers on his hips. "I'm with the Crescent City Preservation Society." She felt flustered again, off-balance, the same way she'd felt in the cemetery. What was it about this man that unsettled her so?

He started toward her, his eyes leaving hers briefly to skid up and down her length. She felt a warmth in her veins as she watched him. There was something positively erotic in the way he moved. She had the fleeting impression he was stalking her for the kill. She'd convinced herself that his strange effect upon her before was pure imagination, but now it was happening again.

His eyes fused with hers as he came nearer. She forced herself not to jump when their hands touched, but was still powerless to stop the tremors that rocketed through her.

He stood so close she could smell the male scent of him, tangy and sharp. His virility seemed to surround her. He was taller than she remembered, over six feet, and much more attractive. His hair was nearly coal-black, thick, with a hint of a wave that looked as if it would curl riotously if left to its own devices. But it had been styled to control the waves, combed back from his face in a deceptively casual fashion. She could see the lines on his forehead and the deep crevices running between his nose and mouth, but it was his eyes that held her full attention. They were even more beautiful than she'd first thought. Deep-set and large under dark brows, they were framed with long, thick lashes, the kind any woman would kill for. The term "bedroom eyes" had surely been coined just for him. There was also an intelligence in the warm brown eyes—knowing but not cynical.

His hand held hers easily, gently, but Kenley could feel the strength in the long fingers. His palm was warm and dry, and unwilling to release her own. She tugged slightly and he let go.

"I feel as if we already know each other," he said quietly.

Kenley flushed, recalling the sensation of being undressed by his eyes. She quickly recovered. "May I extend my sympathies? Your father will be greatly missed by everyone in New Orleans."

There was a slight pause before he answered. "Thank you. Won't you be seated, Miss Farrell?" He motioned her to the chair. "I appreciate your promptness and I apologize for summoning you so hurriedly, but the state of my father's affairs has forced me to make decisions rapidly."

As Blane eased himself down behind the desk, Kenley noticed how much smaller the huge chair appeared. The elder Crawford had always seemed to be swallowed up by the leather upholstery and polished wood. In contrast, his son filled out the piece of furniture most nicely. His shoulders nearly reached from side to side, and his dark head just topped the high rounded back. He looked almost despotic behind the desk. She realized with a start that Blane was still staring at her. "Is something wrong?"

"Forgive me, Miss Farrell, but you're not exactly what I expected."

There was an amused curve to his mouth that softened the dark eyes to amber. It was a struggle to recall why she was here. "Oh? What did you expect?"

Blane leaned back in the chair, long fingers loosely entwined. "Someone older, more prim and much less attractive."

"Sorry to disappoint you," she replied stiffly, trying to ignore the way his deep voice vibrated on each nerve.

"Not at all." He inclined his head, and his eyes held an odd glint.

Kenley was beginning to rethink her campaign. This might be a much more difficult task than she'd imagined. But she was determined not to back down.

"Actually, Mr. Crawford, I'm glad you moved so quickly on this matter. I'm very anxious to have D'Evereaux's fate decided."

Did she imagine it, or had his eyes turned suddenly from warm and friendly to cool and hard? She continued, "Your father was most supportive toward restoring the plantation. He was a great patron of historic New Orleans. I'm sure you're aware of his many philanthropic gestures to the city and surrounding areas."

The muscles in Blane's jaws flexed, and his eyes stared past her now.

"I met with your father just a few days before he died, and we discussed a variety of preliminary steps that could be taken to facilitate restoration." Kenley felt as if her words were falling on deaf ears.

"Just what exactly did my father promise you, Miss Farrell?"

Momentarily taken aback, Kenley frowned. "It was all in the file—the memos about the land, obligations of CCPS once title was transferred. . . ."

Blane reached over to pick up the folder marked "D'EVEREAUX" and held it up. "This is all I have on the house, Miss Farrell."

Kenley couldn't help but notice how slim the green folder was. Her own file on the plantation was at least an inch thick and overflowing with data. "I don't understand. I gave your father copies of everything."

Blane tossed the file on the desk and flipped it open, pulling out three small sheets of paper. "A brief description of the architectural style of the house. A letter from you urging restoration and pledging assistance from your society. A form letter detailing the history and past track record of the Crescent Society."

Kenley leaned forward, puzzled. "I don't understand. There should be nearly six months of correspondence in that file."

Blane spread his hands in a submissive gesture. "This is all I have."

"There's got to be a mistake," Kenley said earnestly. "We discussed every aspect of the plantation, every detail. I met with your father on this over a dozen times. Are you sure you haven't misplaced the rest of the papers? Or perhaps you haven't found the correct file."

Blane's eyebrows arched. "There is that possibility, I suppose. I still have a great many things to go through." His tone was icy.

"I'm positive it will turn up. I was careful to send him copies of everything concerning D'Evereaux. He was so interested, so enthusiastic about the project. And so very generous."

"Too generous," Blane said softly, so softly that Kenley wasn't certain she'd heard him.

"I beg your pardon?"

"Miss Farrell, my father liked to give away money. He was always pledging to one worthy cause or another."

"There's nothing wrong in supporting charities," she said defensively.

"No, because he usually had a solid financial base to work from. But he hadn't counted on the sudden drop in the price of oil, nor the market crash a few years ago. He suffered a severe setback on both occasions. The point is, whether or not I locate another file on this house is really of no importance.''

Kenley felt a stab of fear. ''What do you mean?''

''Crawford Plastics is now my responsibility, and it's up to me to see that the first order of business here is just that—business. Getting involved in a sideline, one that would take great amounts of time and money, would not be in the best interest of the company at the moment.''

Kenley's combative nature took hold. ''Involved? Mr. Crawford, your father was very involved in this endeavor. But rest assured you needn't take on that responsibility. My society is perfectly capable of restoring the house without your lifting so much as a hammer or a nail. All we need is the land and the house that your father agreed to donate. Once we have clear title we'll not bother you further on the matter.''

Blane's head snapped up. ''Donate? Is that what he promised you?''

Kenley flinched slightly at the steel in his voice. ''Yes. He said he'd decided not to expand his plant in Mossville and that he would sign the hundred acres and house over to us. It's all in the file.'' She remembered the nearly empty folder. ''Or it should be.''

''Do you have any formal documentation to substantiate this agreement?''

Kenley didn't want to let him know so quickly that she had only Seth's verbal commitment on D'Evereaux. ''It should have been started, yes.'' She ignored the twinge of guilt. After all, she reasoned, Seth had said he'd ''get right on it with the boys from legal.'' ''We were supposed to meet the morning he died to go over the legalities. Perhaps you should talk with your attorneys.''

His eyebrows rose. ''Perhaps. But if my father promised to donate that property, then I'm afraid I won't be able to honor his commitment.''

''But you must. I have his word on it.''

"But not mine. I have better use for that land, and unless I can turn up written confirmation of my father's intentions to save this house, I'm afraid you have no claim."

Kenley was consumed with fury and chewed her tongue in an attempt to maintain control. "Mr. Crawford, I don't think you appreciate the situation. Your father and I had already started preliminary work. Some commitments have been made. The society has already contracted for a thorough inspection of the house. I've made arrangements with a restoration architect for a detailed survey of the entire structure."

Blane leaned back in his chair. "I'm very sorry, but I won't authorize those things until I have some proof of my father's intentions."

"What possible harm could it do for a couple of architects to walk through the house and assess the reconstruction?"

"None, Miss Farrell, and I don't disbelieve you. It's entirely in character for my father to get involved in saving some old relic of the past. However, sometimes he allowed his love of the past to blind him to more pressing and practical concerns of the present. It's a question of priorities, Miss Farrell, and my first priority is the well-being of Crawford Plastics, not my father's hobbies."

"Priorities!" Kenley rose from the chair and leaned across the desk. "Priorities means learning, education. Preservation of our past *is* a priority in southern Louisiana, Mr. Crawford. It's who we are. It's a commitment the people of New Orleans and Baton Rouge made nearly sixty years ago. We believe in the value of the past, and Louisiana is a living schoolroom of history, a time machine to the Civil War and the early settlement of our country. New Orleans isn't a cold, impersonal museum. It's vital and alive. People work and play on these historic streets. They suffer and die in the old buildings. There's a wealth of knowledge about people, architecture and life in the 1700s and 1800s. We are determined to preserve our heritage. Too much has already been lost forever to companies and men who saw no value in preserving one old opera house or a grand hotel, and the generations that followed were the losers.

"Priorities? If you mean money, then consider this. Louisiana brings in millions annually from tourism—tourism based upon the very thing you're so quick to dismiss. Plantations, the French Quarter, Acadian Village and the Garden District. D'Evereaux is part of that. She deserves to live on, to be saved as a valuable piece of history, and to take her place in Louisiana's tradition."

Blane was overwhelmed by the passion in Kenley Farrell. He'd caught a glimpse of her vulnerability that day in the cemetery, but there had been no hint to the depth of her emotions. Her eyes were aglow now with an inner fire, her face flushed with a warm pink light as she pleaded her case. He could see the rapid rise and fall of her breasts as she bent toward him, her blue silk blouse caressing every enticing curve. Her delicate, soft lips were decorated with deep dimples on each side that teased him adorably. He was tempted to kiss her right then and there just to see the reaction in her incredibly blue eyes. He was even tempted to do as she asked and sign the house over to her, no questions asked. But reality couldn't be ignored so easily.

"I appreciate what you've said. But the bottom line is I have only your word for all this."

Kenley jerked erect. "Are you calling me a liar?"

"Certainly not. But I am saying I'm not prepared to simply hand you one hundred acres of valuable property without something more substantial than the desire of a pretty woman."

She had the impression he was mocking her. "Your father agreed to donate that land, and my being a woman had nothing to do with it. Are you aware that in Louisiana a verbal agreement is as binding as any document?"

If she intended to bluff him, it didn't work. "Only if you have a witness to the conversation. Do you?"

Kenley had to admit a loss of points on this matter. Her meetings with Seth had always involved just the two of them. They would sit and discuss the details and possibilities for hours, undisturbed. "No. But I have the data that passed between us. That should clearly show you his intentions. I'll be most happy to duplicate my files on D'Evereaux. It will take a couple of days."

"I'd appreciate it," he said, rising. "However, I doubt if it will change my mind, at least as far as donation is concerned. I don't think that will be possible under any circumstances."

"If I understand you correctly, you have no interest in saving D'Evereaux at all."

"To be honest, no. I see no value in saving one more old house." He crossed his arms over his chest. "However, I don't want to be unfair. Send me your data and I'll look it over carefully."

"No promises."

"None."

"Your mind is closed?"

"Not at all. But I must warn you again that my priorities are toward the company."

"And what about the architects? May I proceed with that end of things?"

Blane uncrossed his arms and put his hands at his hips. "I think it best to call a moratorium until we can reach a fair and equitable settlement."

"It's already been scheduled."

"Then cancel," he said sharply. He leaned against the desk, softening somewhat. "Think of the practicality. You won't be spending money on something that will be a waste of time." Blane could see the fire gathering in her eyes again and smiled inwardly. This lady had spunk. Then his conscience pricked him. He didn't need to come off like such a cold bastard, but he did enjoy watching the sparks in her eyes. "Miss Farrell, I've been placed in a very difficult position. I've been saddled with a job that was not of my choosing. My own endeavors have had to be tabled until I can straighten out my father's estate. Why don't we postpone any final decisions on D'Evereaux for a few weeks? Perhaps the missing file will turn up. Once I have a clearer picture of the situation here, maybe I'll be in a better position to discuss your request.''

The conversation was at an end. Kenley knew when to press her advantage and when to bide her time. Picking up her briefcase, she looked him in the eye. ''I hope you don't make the mistake of treating this problem lightly, Mr. Crawford. The citizens of New Orleans have been known to join forces when a landmark is threatened. They can prove a formidable adversary.''

''Is that your job—to spur the natives into action?''

''Sometimes.''

''Are you always successful?''

''Let's just say I have a very good track record.''

''I can be very obstinate, Miss Farrell.''

''I've persuaded more obstinate people than you.''

He grinned laconically. ''You undoubtedly won them over with your charm.''

Kenley stiffened. ''No. My abilities.''

''Ah,'' he drawled, ''a feminist.''

''An individual. They overlooked the fact that I'm a woman.''

He leaned toward her, his eyes piercing her with his gaze. ''Something I could never do, Miss Farrell.''

His response left her momentarily nonplussed, but she recovered quickly. ''I'm afraid you'll have to, Mr. Crawford. Good day.'' With all the pride and confidence she could gather, she turned and walked out.

Blane grinned and watched the door shut behind his lovely visitor. The lady had thrown down her delicate gauntlet. She was determined to see this old plantation home was preserved. It might be interesting to watch her try.

Chapter Three

Kenley marched back to her office seething with anger and determination. There was no trace of indecision in her posture, no hint of sagging confidence in the set of her jaw. Her blue eyes were steely as she shoved open the door of CCPS and pointed a finger at Alva. "Pull out the D'Evereaux file and bring it and yourself into my office." She strode past and into her small room, unaware of the scowl on Alva's face.

Kenley pulled off her linen jacket and sat down, reaching for the phone. She was deep in conversation when Alva walked in. "I'm sorry, Mr. Martin, but Mr. Crawford refuses to give his permission for an assessment of D'Evereaux at this time.... Yes, I know what the elder Mr. Crawford agreed to, but the property belongs to his son now and he has other plans for it.... Of course, I understand the money is nonrefundable.... Yes, I will.... Fine, thank you." She banged the receiver back into place and looked up at her friend.

"I take it Mr. Blane Crawford was less than receptive to your idea."

"Receptive?" Kenley scoffed. "He was downright antagonistic. He sees no purpose in saving one more old house. He all but accused me of lying about his father donating the land. Then he tried to tell me I didn't understand the priorities involved."

Alva rested a hand on her hip, frowning. "What about the files? Didn't he read all the correspondence between you and the old man?"

"That was the same question I had for the new owner. Seems the only file he could locate had just three small pieces of paper in it. He claimed it was all he could find on the house. If you ask me, he didn't look very hard."

Alva tapped the thick folder she'd just placed on Kenley's desk. "Daddy Crawford should have had a file every bit as thick as this."

"I know," she said, eyes snapping. "But his son obviously has no intention of honoring his father's promises."

"What are you going to do?"

Kenley placed the palms of her hands on the desktop and pushed herself erect. Her face was a study in determination. "I'm going to show the cold-blooded Mr. Crawford how things are done in New Orleans. I warned him that the people here don't like it when landmarks are threatened."

"How did he take to it?" Alva asked warily.

"To what?"

"Being threatened. He strikes me as the type that might fight back."

"I didn't threaten him," she corrected looking away. "I challenged him."

Alva looked skeptical. "With what? You and I both know that Seth Crawford never legally committed himself to donating that land."

"He said it was in the works, that he'd talked to his attorneys," Kenley pointed out quickly. "There's a good chance that something was signed. I've got all the notes he sent where he clearly stated his intentions.''

"You're grasping."

"Then I'll try other tactics." She began pacing the small office as she spoke. "I'll appeal to his sense of honor. His father's memory. Something. I'll fight dirty if I have to, but I *will* save that house."

"Okay," Alva said, "but first things first."

At the grim expression on her friend's face Kenley asked, "Now what? I've only been gone an hour. What could possibly have happened in that amount of time?"

"Plenty. The electric company shut off the power at The Cottage, which means there's no air-conditioning, and the guides are threatening to go home if it isn't turned on soon. Two gardeners at Avondale quit and took a few tools with them as severance pay, and now the grass is as high as an elephant's—well, you get the picture."

Kenley groaned and leaned back in her leather chair. "Go on."

"Our illustrious president, Mrs. C. J. Arcenault, called and wanted to know if you'd talked with Mr. Crawford about D'Evereaux and if not, why not. She would like a decision ASAP so they can make plans for the restoration."

Kenley fought to stay in control of the chaos that seemed to be descending on her from all sides. She'd barely had time to deal with Blane Crawford's indifference toward D'Evereaux, and now all these other problems were escalating. Masking her anxiety, she kept her eyes fixed on the surface of the desk, willing herself to make the necessary decisions.

Finally she lifted her head and started giving directions. "Okay, first get me a cup of coffee. Then get hold of Southern Landscaping and have them send some people out to Avondale to at least cut the grass and pick up. Then call Marc Blacet at the classifieds and get an ad put in the paper. And you'd better call Joy at the employment agency and see if she has any leads.

"Get the electric company on the phone. I know I paid that bill the same time I paid the others. And if Mrs. Arcenault calls again, stall her. I'll deal with her later."

"Done. You want the rest?"

Kenley gaped at her associate. "What else could there be?"

"The lease-renewal form hasn't arrived yet," she announced, fixing her glasses more firmly on her nose.

"That's odd. It's up in little over a week. It's not like Dr. Ristelli to forget. Perhaps you'd better call him."

"I did," Alva drawled. "He's either not in, can't come to the phone, or the secretary will get back to me."

The glare on Alva's face suggested questionable motives afoot, but Kenley chose to ignore them for now. "Well, keep trying. I'm sure there's a logical explanation. Dr. Ristelli promised us these offices for as long as we needed them, and he's always been prompt in the past."

Alva grumbled under her breath and left the room as Kenley tried not to think of the implications of the tardy lease form.

The small suite of offices was the generous gift of one of the society's more affluent patrons, Dr. Michael Ristelli. Though far from the opulence of many offices in the building, they were more than adequate for the administrative needs of the Crescent City Preservation Society, and his generosity had enabled the group to channel more funds directly into preservation.

"Oh, and Pam won't be in today." Alva shouted from the outer office. "Her youngest has the chicken pox." Although a part-time employee, Pam Cobb did enough work for three people.

"Don't we have some volunteers coming in today?" she called back hopefully.

"Nope. The Junior League arts-and-crafts show opened today at the Rivergate."

"Wonderful," Kenley muttered sourly under her breath.

"And..." Alva drawled, appearing in the doorway again.

Kenley lifted her hands in surrender. "Go ahead. I can take it."

"I doubt it. The new brochures for The Raymond House arrived."

"Oh, good." She perked up slightly. At least something was going right today.

"Oh, bad," Alva countered quickly, gesturing her to the outer room.

Kenley rose and walked behind her, stopping at Alva's worktable and pulling out a stack of slick, colorful brochures. It only took a glance to see the pamphlets were all wrong. "They were supposed to be trifold, not bifold," she wailed. "And the pictures are too dark." She flipped through the glossy paper. "How are people supposed to find the house? There's no map. The hours aren't listed either, and they didn't mention the bed-and-breakfast options or the restaurant. I don't believe this," she growled, tossing the paper down with a snap. "Get that man on the phone *now*."

"Already tried. Not in."

Jamming her hands into her skirt pockets, Kenley chewed her lip, trying to get her frustration under control. She knew from experience that the only way to sort out this tangle was to tackle one snag at a time. But right now it all seemed more than she could handle in one day.

"Here's your coffee," Alva said quietly.

"Thanks." Kenley took the hot mug and returned to her office, dropping into her chair. After a quick sip of coffee she reached for the phone, only to discover that she was incapable of lifting it from the cradle as the mounting pressure rushed through her again. She felt overwhelmed by all the problems, all the petty decisions. What used to be viewed as challenges to overcome had lately turned into sheer escarpments that taxed all her abilities to climb. The adrenaline that used to carry her through had dried up, leaving her strangely discontented. Somewhere, the immense satisfaction she usually derived from her job had vanished.

For the past several months she'd felt out of sync with her world. Her interest in almost everything had been dropping. Only D'Evereaux had captured her imagination, and now even that had been put on the shelf.

She fought a childish urge to run and hide, to find someone to take care of the problems, to take care of her. Her conscience wouldn't allow her to embrace that notion for more than a few seconds without feeling guilty. Besides, she knew that running away solved nothing. The problems would still be there when she returned. A few more sips of coffee eased her tensions, and once more she reached for the phone. This time she picked it up and dialed.

It was late afternoon when Alva came and stood in front of Kenley's desk again. "It's nice to see the old enthusiasm back in your eyes," she said softly. "I was beginning to worry about you."

Kenley tried to hide her surprise at Alva's words. She'd been so certain that she had concealed her discontent from those around her. "I don't know what you're talking about."

"Don't you now?" Her voice held a note of affection. "It was obvious to anyone who knew you that you were off your feed. I figured it was one of two things. Either you were fed up with your job, or else you were in need of a little romance in your life." She leaned closer. "A little male stimulation."

"Oh, for heaven's sake," she snapped, setting her jaw in annoyance. Alva's comment had brought a picture of Blane to her mind. "Why does everyone assume that a woman's not complete until she has a man in her life? I'm perfectly content as I am. I enjoy my job, I have a lovely home, and I'm financially secure. Why do I need a man in the picture?"

Alva clutched a stack of folders to her chest and inclined her head toward Kenley. "Because nature decreed that a man and a woman should be together. No matter how hard you protest, no matter how loudly the feminists scream, it's a fact of life and you can't escape it any more than you can escape breathing." Alva made her pronouncement as if the final and definitive word had been spoken, then straightened and looked down her nose at Kenley.

"That is an obsolete way of thinking."

"Out of fashion, perhaps, but not obsolete," Alva countered.

"You're wrong. Dead wrong." She held up a hand in defense. "I lead a very satisfying existence. And as for romance, I have all I need, thank you," she replied, dismissing Alva's observations. "I get more than enough working with these old houses. What's more romantic than exploring old plantation homes?"

"Exploring a handsome man."

Again Blane Crawford flashed through her mind setting Kenley's teeth on edge. A look of disgust crossed her face. "I'm surrounded by the romance of New Orleans from daylight to dusk. *Besides,*" she added forcefully when she saw Alva gearing up for another assault, "who says romance has to be the man-woman kind? It can mean the romance of adventure, of discovery, the romance of the sea, or the romance of legends like Robin Hood and Zorro." She'd no sooner uttered those names when Blane's face flooded her mind. Angrily Kenley snatched up a set of files, only to be struck dumb by Alva's next comment.

"Seems to me Blane Crawford might be just your type."

Was the woman a mind reader in addition to being a gossip?

"He's strong, good-looking and sexy as the devil."

"Granted," Kenley agreed in icy tones. "He's also an arrogant, self-satisfied, tunnel-visioned business shark, without an ounce of compassion in his blood. Then there's the matter of his sudden, unexplained appearance. Seth dies and up pops a long-lost, never-before-mentioned son who steps in to take over Crawford Plastics, bringing along a lot of questions and very few answers. No," she said with a little shake of her head, "he is definitely not my type. Any relationship I have will be based on truth, openness and honesty."

"Honesty shmonesty." Alva scoffed. "Personally I think you're obsessed with it. But look, kiddo. I saw this guy Saturday, remember? He is a certified hunk! If you're smart, you'll go out and get yourself a slinky dress—something that shows a lot of leg—then go over there to his office and bat your baby blues at him." She winked. "You'll save your house."

Blue eyes turned stormy. "That's disgusting."

"Not at all. It's using your business assets. Too bad I'm not a few years younger or I'd offer to head your campaign myself." She grinned lecherously and amended that. "On second thought, I'll go anyway. Maybe he has a thing for older women."

"Alva, for heaven's sake. You're a mature woman," Kenley scolded.

"Mature, yes. Dead, no."

"He's just a man." She hoped her voice didn't sound as false to her friend as it did to her own ears.

"Honey, if that's just a man, then Helen of Troy was just a woman. Aren't you interested even a little in the tidbits I've uncovered from the CP steno pool?"

"No."

"Then I assume you've already seen this?"

Kenley took the business section of the *Times-Picayune* her associate handed her. "The paper was late this morning." There on the front page was a picture and small article about Blane stepping into his father's shoes as new owner of Crawford Plastics. It gave a brief biography—barely more than his birthplace and college—along with some vague references to his "personal" business interests. Kenley studied the photograph of Blane, noting that it didn't do him justice. It didn't reveal the angular jaw, the thick waves of his hair, nor the straight line of his nose. The only feature in keeping with the real man was the eyes. Even in the shaded newsprint, his eyes seemed to have a life of their own, holding some secret knowledge, something amusing and mysterious and very sensual. But the picture failed to show the color of his eyes, that beautiful warm sable hue so in keeping with his swarthy complexion and dark hair. At the cemetery she had sensed his gaze upon her but had attributed the idea to her imagination. But after their meeting this morning, she couldn't dismiss the feeling so easily. There was something behind those eyes, something eerie, as if he could see completely through her. The direction of her thoughts shocked her, and she felt a warmth creeping up her neck. She stiffened. This was ridiculous. She'd spent barely an hour with the man. "It's hardly an in-depth biography," she snapped, tossing the paper on her desk. "There's an awful lot left out."

"Yeah, like for instance, he's divorced."

"How do you know that?" Kenley mentally kicked herself for asking so quickly.

Alva leaned forward, smirking. "I've been doing a little detective work on Mr. Crawford. I figured you're too noble to pry into his life, so I thought I'd do it for you."

"Alva, it's none of our business," Kenley scolded. But despite herself, she couldn't stifle her intense curiosity. As much as she hated it, where Blane was concerned, she was every bit as nosy as Alva. "What else did you find out?" She held up a warning finger to forestall the "I told you so" that she knew was coming.

"Actually, no one knows much about him. I found out he was born and raised in Ohio, graduated from Ohio State. Which as it turns out I could have learned from the paper. I did find out that he dropped out of sight for a couple of years."

"You mean he disappeared?"

Alva shrugged. "No one knows where he was. But then he showed up again and went to work for daddy in the main office of CP in Columbus. A year later he left to start his own business."

Kenley's mind was filled with questions, but only one seemed important at the moment. "Married? When?"

"I'm not sure, but apparently it was a good while back and it didn't last very long."

It had never occurred to her that Blane might have been married at one time, though there was absolutely no reason for her to be surprised. She realized suddenly that she was under the intense scrutiny of her friend. Tossing her head nonchalantly, she replied lightly, "Lots of people have been married and divorced. It doesn't mean anything." Kenley picked up the stack of mail, ostensibly studying the contents and hoping Alva would take the hint. She should have known better.

"I suppose. But what about those years he was missing? Where do you think he was?" Alva speculated.

Kenley's patience was at an end. She didn't care at all for the topic of discussion, and besides, it had taken a decidedly uncomfortable turn. "Alva, we still have a ton of work to do, and I think it's time we got busy." Alva opened her mouth to continue her arguments, but Kenley silenced her with a glare. She also pushed the nagging image of Blane Crawford firmly to the farthest recesses of her mind. "Now, here's what I want you to do first."

Kenley Farrell's challenge seemed to echo in Blane's head the rest of the day. Propping his feet up on the desk, he rested his head against his fingertips, marveling again at his good fortune. The situation read like a plot from an old movie: man admires woman from afar and she miraculously turns up in his life a few days later. At least now he knew who she was. Kenley. Her name was almost musical.

He'd been stopped cold with shock when he saw her standing in his office. He was only vaguely aware of her introducing herself, and when her name finally registered, he was even more surprised. This was Kenley Farrell? This was the determined preservationist out to save the old plantation? His gaze had been riveted upon her, unable to believe what he was seeing. She'd spoken again, and he'd started toward her, thanking the Fates for delivering this intriguing bit of femininity to his doorstep. His eyes left hers and made a quick tour. She was shorter than he remembered. Softer, too. He detected curves under the oversized white jacket she wore, and the blue blouse matched her eyes. He thought he saw some uncertainty in their depths, but if he did, it was fleeting. She looked like a fresh summer day. The white suit heightened her chestnut hair. She wore it up again, but the same little tendrils escaped to hang teasingly about her face. Then he was standing in front of her, and his hand reached out and clasped hers. The contact jolted him from his stunned state. Her small fingers were soft and slightly damp and fluttered nervously in his grasp. The knowledge pleased him, and he found that he liked the feel of her hand in his, liked the fragrance of magnolias that floated around her. She gently pulled free, and he heard himself babble something insane. She responded, but it took a moment for his mind to register that she was offering sympathy.

Automatically he motioned her to be seated, his mind taking note of every movement. He didn't realize he was staring until she asked if something was wrong. He'd been tempted to answer truthfully, to tell her that nothing was wrong. He was just more pleased than he could express at her reappearance.

After overcoming his initial surprise, he'd spent the rest of the time studying her—discreetly, he hoped.

She'd seemed to be bolstering her confidence throughout the conversation, though she masked it well. It had been a puzzling thing to watch. Her physical actions were precise, her speech firm and businesslike, but her eyes struggled to meet his and he saw a trace of apprehension in them from time to time. He didn't flatter himself to think that he was responsible. He had the distinct impression she was used to dealing with all types of men.

But when she thought her house was threatened, all traces of hesitancy vanished. She became an impassioned angel, a crusader and a temptress.

And she had tempted him. He longed to unleash the passion he'd seen in a more intimate setting. He wanted to explore the source of the fire in her eyes and the flush in her cheeks—cheeks that he ached to caress. He'd been so overwhelmed by her intensity that he'd had to fight every second to keep his mind on business.

As a result he'd come off sounding like a heartless bastard, regarding the old plantation. He'd have to apologize. Not that it would change his decision, but perhaps they could work out another arrangement.

He rose and walked to the window, leaning against the frame, one hand on his hip. Maybe they could also work out a personal arrangement. It had been a long time since he'd been this drawn to a woman. His job kept him on the run, never in one place long enough to form any lasting attachments. The women he did meet were either clients and off-limits or business contacts he found efficient, capable and totally uninspiring.

He realized that up until today he really hadn't cared. There had been no desire for a woman to share his life. Two bad relationships in a man's past made for a lousy track record. He had no desire to get emotionally involved with anyone. But something about Kenley was different. He wanted to know more about her, and found he was looking forward to thrashing out the differences between them and spending time in her company. Anything serious was, of course, out of the question but a short-term association, a casual friendship, wasn't beyond the realm of possibility.

He recalled the proud lift of her determined chin as she left him and found that his resentment at being saddled with Crawford Plastics had eased, the prospect of rebuilding it feeling more like a challenge than a punishment. Perhaps, just perhaps, his father had done him an unexpected favor.

Turning from the window, Blane's expression softened with affection as Dave strolled up to his desk. "Go ahead, hit me with your best shot. I can take it," he said good-naturedly. When his friend didn't respond with his usual smart remark, Blane eyed him more closely. "What's up?"

"The reporters are starting to call. One in particular is giving Edith a hard time."

Blane gritted his teeth and shoved the folder in front of him across the slick surface of his broad desk. "So handle it. That's your job."

"I thought I had. I gave them the standard bio. But..." He shrugged eloquently.

"That's all they're going to get. Crawford Plastics will issue press releases as the need arises."

"You know that's not what they want to know about."

"Then tell them I'm only here for the funeral and to settle my father's affairs, both personal and those involving CP."

"While we're on the subject, just what do you plan to do about your own business?" Dave pointed out. "Who's going to run that while you're dabbling in the fascinating world of plastic."

"It'll run itself."

Dave rolled his eyes.

"We have a lot of skilled, competent people in the organization," Blane reminded him. "They can maintain the status quo until we get our hands back into things. We could even use the New Orleans setup as the home office and run the organization from here until I'm done. I'll check in once a week, and you can coordinate."

Grimacing, Dave crossed his arms over his chest. "You make it sound so simple."

Blane positioned his large chair and sat down, thoughtfully rubbing his temple with two fingers. "No, not simple, but I've got to try."

"I knew it. I knew it." Dave glanced heavenward. "You're on a guilt trip. You're really gonna stay here in one place for God knows how long and play industrial tycoon?"

"If I have to." Dark eyes challenged Dave's skeptical look.

"Blane, your dad is gone. If you couldn't make amends for the past while he was alive, what makes you think you can now?"

"I'm not sure I can. But I won't be able to live with myself if I don't at least make the effort."

With a sigh of resignation Dave muttered, "You're the boss."

Kenley managed to avoid Blane Crawford for two days, but with their offices on the same floor it was inevitable that she would run into him sooner or later. The next time they met, however, she would be prepared. In the meantime, she kept busy copying the D'Evereaux file, contacting key people and apprising them of the status of the plantation. She spoke with Mrs. Arcenault and warned her there might be a fight to save the old home. To Kenley's dismay, the president of the society was not very supportive. Apparently she was not anxious to get involved in any long-term battles over D'Evereaux. The society's funds were limited, and donations had fallen off sharply of late. She'd not been too pleased about the recent administrative problems, either. Still she vowed to do all she could if—and she had stressed the if—Mr. Crawford would agree to donate the house and land. But as Kenley knew only too well, Mr. Crawford had refused, rather adamantly at that. Kenley's job now was to find a way to change his mind. But how did one go about changing the mind of a man made of stone? Kenley tried yet again to draw some comparison between father and son. Seth had been so congenial and outgoing. Blane, on the other hand, seemed cold and remote. It was difficult to believe they were even related.

By late afternoon Kenley was more than anxious to go home, so she dismissed Alva and Pam early, then locked up and headed for the elevator. When it arrived it was nearly full, and she opted to take the stairs instead.

At the second floor she reached for the door marked "GARAGE."

"Allow me."

She recognized the voice instantly, that deep resonant timbre that seemed to ripple across her skin. She froze and looked over her shoulder into the piercing brown eyes of Blane Crawford. His face was only inches away, his chest touching her shoulder. His arm stretched across her waist, holding the handle on the steel door, effectively trapping her between it and his body. He towered over her, making her feel small and insignificant.

Kenley opened her mouth to protest, when the dark eyes suddenly warmed and a smile played about the corners of his mouth. She caught a glimpse of white teeth, then he leaned closer, his lips so close she could feel his breath on her cheek. For a moment she thought he was going to kiss her, and her mouth trembled. She was shocked to realize she wasn't wholly averse to the idea. His nearness, the total maleness of him, sent her mind racing into unfamiliar territory. She fought the urge to touch his face, to smooth the tiny laugh lines around his eyes, to stir the few gray hairs near his ear, and to run her fingers over the soft, smooth surface of his lips. Her heartbeat quickened, and a spark of desire filled her blood. She wanted to succumb to the heady warmth that emanated from him, wrapping around her gently, almost protectively. She felt a flicker of fear in her stomach and savagely wrenched her eyes from his. They probed too deeply, saw too much. Things he had no right to see.

Blane must have sensed her dilemma. He pulled back slightly, and there was amusement in his voice. "I'm sorry if I startled you, but I've been anxious to talk to you."

"Oh? I had the impression you didn't want to discuss D'Evereaux at all." Kenley felt her indignation wrapping around her like a piece of armor. "That *is* what you want to talk about isn't it, Mr. Crawford?'' Bravely she squared her shoulders and stared straight into his eyes. They seemed to be mocking her, but she ignored it.

"Actually, I merely wanted to apologize."

His comment was so unexpected that her indignation burst like a balloon. "Excuse me?"

Blane released the door handle and stepped back. "I was preoccupied the other day, Miss Farrell. Inheriting Crawford Plastics came as a shock to me, and untangling all the loose ends has been difficult. I'm afraid I was less than civil. I didn't mean to sound so unsympathetic toward your cause. I hope you'll forgive me."

Kenley was momentarily speechless. It was the second time he'd stolen her thunder and left her feeling adrift. "Y-yes, of course," she stammered for lack of anything better to say. "I should have realized you had other things on your mind besides saving D'Evereaux."

Blane reached behind her now and opened the door, gesturing her through. She stopped on the other side and asked, "Does this mean you've changed your mind?"

He shoved his hands in his pants pockets and looked down at her, an amused smirk on his lips.

"Let's just say the jury is still out until I have more data to examine. Such as your own file on D'Evereaux."

"It should be ready on Monday." She smiled at him, but she wasn't at all sure why.

"Fine. Are you parked nearby?"

Kenley pointed toward the far aisle. As they walked she pondered this new aspect of Blane Crawford. He was more approachable today, less intimidating—almost friendly. A far cry from the ominous specter he'd seemed at the cemetery. It gave her courage a boost. "You know, you came as quite a shock to everyone here."

"So I understand. It shouldn't have been such a surprise, though."

"Oh? The long-lost son suddenly appears out of nowhere."

Blane glanced at her, his one eyebrow arched quizzically. "Hardly long-lost. I've been around."

"Your father has been here for ten years and no one even knew you existed," she persisted, wondering how far she could push him on this.

"It's really not that strange. Tell me, do all your business associates know about your parents, your brothers and sisters and your old boyfriends?"

"Of course not."

He touched his fingers to his chest and grinned. "Then why should I be that big a surprise?"

"Probably because your presence here was so unexpected."

He stopped and looked down at her. "Unexpected *and* unwelcome?"

Kenley shrugged. "For some of us."

"I'm sorry if I upset your plans." He made the word *plans* sound more like *schemes*.

"It's only a temporary setback."

"You sound very positive for someone in your position."

Kenley felt the old fighting instinct beginning to stir. "In my position?"

He nodded. "I hold all the cards. I have the land and the house, and you have—what do you have, Miss Farrell?"

Kenley gritted her teeth. She'd been a fool to think this man was anything other than ruthless and hard. He was merely toying with her. "What I have, Mr. Crawford, is the city of New Orleans on my side, the backing of the National Register if need be, and the support of state officials if it comes to that. You can't just come in here and destroy a piece of local history and not expect to account to someone for your actions."

Blane watched the sparks leap into Kenley's eyes the same as they had in his office. Her cheeks flushed softly as her anger blossomed. He'd deliberately goaded her just to see if the fires were still there, if her impassioned plea the other day was part of her campaign—or a true and delightful part of her personality. He grinned inwardly now. Kenley Farrell was for real.

His conscience stung, and he held up a hand in mild defense. "I'm not out to destroy anything, Miss Farrell. I'm simply not making any decisions now. Later, when I've had time to look over the situation more carefully, then perhaps we can work something out."

"Time is what this is all about," she said earnestly. "The longer that house is left untended, the more difficult and costly the restoration becomes. Wind and weather can't be turned on and off like a TV set. They're relentless. They eat away at the roof, the walls, the wooden floors and the mortar, the wrought iron and the plaster. D'Evereaux is dying every day."

Blane's dark eyes narrowed slightly. Kenley was determined. But so was he. "Crawford Plastics is dying as well, Miss Farrell. Time is my enemy, too. If I don't get this company back on its feet, then all my father's work will be lost. I appreciate that the house is of some value architecturally, but—"

"You really don't understand, do you?" Kenley interrupted.

Blane ignored her and continued, mildly irritated that she was refusing to see the larger issue. "I have a business to run and people who depend upon the success of that business for their livelihood. I have a moral obligation to those people. Putting food on the tables of the people of New Orleans is far more important than one of your pet projects."

"Pet projects?" Kenley set her jaw, eyes blazing. "Your father didn't think of it as a pet project. He thought of it as a gift. He loved this city and loved its people. He gave them a helping hand whenever he could—provided neighborhood parks so the inner-city children could have a place to play, helped build the new wing at Charity Hospital, and did his best toward education by helping to keep historic New Orleans alive for future generations."

"How long had you known my father?" he asked, leaning against Kenley's car.

Kenley blinked at the deft change in subject. He always came at her from a direction she wasn't expecting. "Officially we met six months ago when he bought D'Evereaux. Before that I'd seen him at various charity affairs. Why?"

Crossing his arms over his chest, he stared over her head for a long moment before speaking. "My grandfather started Crawford Plastics in 1895 in Ohio. He was a second-generation immigrant who clawed his way up the ladder of success through hard work and determination and against the tide of public opinion. Do you have any idea what the world thought of plastic back then? It was a joke, a fad. It was viewed with the same skepticism that TV and space travel were later on. But he believed in it and kept battling the odds until he won. When my father took over, CP had become a thriving business with processing plants in six major cities."

He took a measured breath and continued. "My father had his good points, Ms. Farrell, but he was not a good businessman. He lacked the hard edge, the ability to take risks that's vital in keeping a company growing and profitable. But he loved the business, so he tried to make up for his lack by giving CP a public image of concern and caring. His philanthropic gestures were a way of accomplishing that. But because of his altruistic nature and a nearsighted approach to progress, there's very little left of the company today. I intend to put Crawford Plastics back on its feet and the plant in Mossville is the first step. I owe it to my grandfather and my father."

Kenley's antagonism had faded steadily as Blane had talked. Perhaps she was being a bit narrow-minded herself. "I don't fault you for wanting to save your family business, Mr. Crawford. But must it be at the expense of a landmark? I can't stress enough the dedication, the profound support your father gave us toward saving D'Evereaux."

Blane rested his hand on his hips, exhaling slowly. His tongue worked furiously against the back of his teeth. He remembered a time when he'd needed his father's support, but the cause hadn't been a very popular one, so his father had slammed the door in his face, refusing to get involved. He'd said there was nothing to be gained. Blane looked back at Kenley. "I have a more practical nature. Have you looked at the unemployment rate in New Orleans lately? It's rising every day. The longer this oil recession drags on, the more businesses have to shut down. If I can expand this plant, I can put over a thousand people back to work. If I update the present facility, six hundred more jobs will be created." He paused to take a breath. "I realize that Crawford Plastics alone won't end unemployment in this city, but it's a hell of a lot more practical than donating parks and renovating one more relic from the past, something my father was never able to see."

"In your opinion," Kenley stated bluntly.

"You don't trust my opinion of my own father?"

"Sometimes it's difficult to really know and understand a relative. Our judgment is hampered by emotional ties."

Blane had the distinct feeling Kenley was speaking from personal experience, and he filed that thought away to inspect later. "True. But just because a man presents a certain image to the outside world doesn't mean he's that way with his family. We all have two faces. A public and a private one."

Kenley flinched reflexively. Just like her dad. One day the devoted husband and loving father and the next... And then there was Russ. Oh yes, she was only too familiar with the many faces a man could have. "Your father was always very open and honest with me," she said quietly.

"Right," Blane smiled sardonically. "That's why you never heard of me."

"Our relationship was professional," she said defensively, lifting her chin. "Based upon a mutual goal. We never talked about personal things. But I find it strange that a man never mentions a grown son, even in passing."

"And I find it strange that someone with as much emotion and commitment to a cause cannot understand that the people of New Orleans need jobs, not another showplace. Tell me, why are you so determined to save this house?"

"I've already told you," she replied quickly.

"No," he said firmly, shaking his head. "There's something about this house, something personal."

Kenley felt as if he'd reached in and touched her soul. What had she said that gave her away? How could he even suspect that D'Evereaux had become her lifeline, the only thing she could focus on without feeling overwhelmed. He was waiting for her answer. What could she say? "It's unique...rare...the only one..." she faltered unable to pinpoint a valid reason other than her affection for the plantation. She was not, however going to admit that to him.

Squaring her shoulders she met his curious gaze unwaveringly. "There's more than one way to solve a problem, Mr. Crawford. I think you've made it clear where the battle lines are, and we are definitely on opposite sides."

"I don't want to be on opposite sides," he said quietly.

Kenley couldn't help but be stunned by the sudden change. The brown eyes were warm again and compelling. She felt her footing slipping away. His rapid switches from unmovable adversary to sympathetic charmer were unnerving. Kenley could deal easily with known facts and a direct course of action. It was the unforeseen obstacles that threw her well-ordered world into turmoil. She prided herself on her ability to plan ahead, to skillfully anticipate obstacles and lay practical, logical detours around them.

Blane Crawford, however, was an obstacle she hadn't figured on. She didn't like his sudden and mysterious appearance in New Orleans, she didn't like his mysterious past, and most of all, she didn't like his mysterious effect upon her.

"I'm really not the enemy here." He spoke softly, deliberately.

"Aren't you?" She wanted to sound firm, but her words came out as a breathless whisper.

"I don't want to be."

Kenley puzzled over his comment all the way home.

Chapter Four

Kenley was exhausted. It was after seven o'clock on Friday evening and everyone had gone home. She should be at home, too, curled up in front of the TV with a romantic old film on the VCR, sipping a cool iced tea as the ceiling fan slowly stirred the air. It was a nice picture, but an even better one, she decided as she stood and stretched, would be to go directly to bed.

Stacking the day's correspondence at the corner of her desk, she puzzled over the continued absence of the new lease. What if it didn't come? What if Dr. Ristelli was no longer in a position to donate the space? There wasn't room in her small town house to hold all the files, let alone three employees. Could they find another patron willing to pick up the tab or donate space elsewhere? Could their budget support the rent on a smaller place out in Metairie?

The questions seemed endless. And pointless. Here she was, anticipating trouble before it had even occurred. The lease would probably be in tomorrow's mail. End of problem.

Gathering up the reports she'd finished, she carried them to the filing cabinet and slipped them into the appropriate folder. She shoved the rest of the items on her desk into her briefcase and picked up her purse.

As she turned out the lights and walked through the outer office, she was struck by the emptiness of the small rooms—not much different from the place she called home. Suddenly she didn't want to go there, either. Not alone. Briefly she allowed herself to fantasize about someone waiting for her at home. Someone who would smile warmly, lovingly, when she came through the door, who would open his arms and enfold her, chasing away all the day's problems and the fatigue. His nearness and love would put everything into proper perspective.

They could share the day's events over dinner, snuggle up on the sofa to talk, watch TV or read the paper—all those wonderfully ordinary things married people did together.

Kenley closed her eyes, envisioning the homey scene—herself curled comfortably in one corner of the sofa, her hand reaching over to gently stroke the back of Blane's neck.

Her eyes snapped open. Good heavens, where were these thoughts coming from, all of a sudden? She'd always liked living alone and valued her independence. Her life was well-ordered, structured, uncluttered. There was no need to complicate things with a relationship. And why did Blane Crawford continually invade her thoughts? Obviously, she must be more tired than she realized. He would never fit into such a domestic picture, especially not in her life. She wished she could put him out of her mind, but for some reason she couldn't explain, he had carved out a niche for himself and stubbornly refused to budge.

She'd been unable to shake the memory of his nearness at the garage door yesterday. She'd been denying his attractiveness from the beginning, but was now forced to admit he had a definite effect upon her—an effect she strongly resented. Kenley prided herself on being immune to the flirtatious ways of most men, particularly the ones with good looks and charm. She had a vast reservoir of experience to draw from when dealing with that type. Her father had been a charmer, with a silver tongue and a winsome smile that made you believe in fairy tales. Russ had been devastatingly handsome, with an ego to match. Thanks to them, she'd learned how to look behind the beguiling facade to their hidden motives—to undermine the credibility of women and keep them dependent on a man's needs.

Blane Crawford, however, was different from the usual handsome male she'd encountered. She couldn't figure him out. One minute he was the very image of a hard, unfeeling businessman, and the next he was warm and friendly. At no time, however, had there been a hint of the usual macho aura that seemed to be an integral part of other men such as Blane. It was almost as if he didn't realize he was attractive to women.

The only consistent factor about Mr. Blane Crawford was that he kept her off guard, and that was definitely a negative aspect in her book. The fact that he was a mystery was even more disturbing. She was leery of men with shadowy pasts. It had been her experience that those shadows eventually came forth to destroy the present.

Even Blane had acknowledged the fact that everyone wore two faces. He'd been referring to his father, but was that all? Was he hinting that he wore another face, as well? And if so, was he like Seth, the charming but conservative businessman who had settled for less? Or was he like his grandfather, a hard-edged risk taker who got what he wanted?

As she walked toward the elevator, she tried not to think of Blane as a man but as an opponent, someone who stood in the way of something she wanted—D'Evereaux. It was easier to think clearly when Blane Crawford was a faceless someone, rather than a tall, virile, sensuous man whose sexuality was lethal.

There it was again—intimate thoughts of Blane. How she hated herself for being so weak-willed. He was only a man, after all. She was reacting like some frail heroine swooning and palpitating at the mention of his name. That thought sent a new wave of self-loathing through her and she smacked the elevator button in retaliation.

"I think all you need to do is touch it. That usually works for me."

Kenley cringed inwardly at the sound of Blane's voice. He had the most disturbing knack of materializing at the worst possible moments. Why couldn't she run into him when she was fresh, confident, in control and primarily *not* thinking about him? She refused to look at him and merely acknowledged his presence with a slight twist of her head. She didn't want him to see her with her defenses down. However, the best defense... "You really shouldn't sneak up on people, Mr. Crawford. You might not like the reactions you get."

Blane glanced down at the thick carpet that covered the hallway. "Sneak? I merely walked to the elevator. I'm sorry if I startled you. Next time I'll whistle or maybe toss a hand grenade in front of me."

She could hear the teasing in his voice. There was no graceful way to end her cold-shoulder act now without looking like a bubbleheaded ninny impressed with his charms. She was afraid to smile; it might shatter the aloofness she was struggling to maintain. "That would be safer," she finally replied, keeping her gaze fixed on the elevator, afraid to read the look in his dark eyes at her rudeness.

"You're working late, too, I see."

"Yes," was her clipped reply. Did his voice have to sound so deep, so vibrant?

The elevator arrived. "Somehow that doesn't surprise me," he commented as he stepped into the car.

Kenley set her jaw and looked at him. There didn't seem to be a challenge in his words or his expression, only amusement. That irked her more than anything. "Meaning?" she asked icily.

Blane grinned as he held the door open. "Meaning you strike me as a woman who is dedicated to her work, no matter what the hour or the obstacle." He cocked his head to one side. "Are you coming?"

Kenley strode inside, wondering if he was the obstacle to which he referred. She really had to stop coming unglued whenever he was near. It was pointless, not to mention exhausting. She stood in the back, ignoring him as best she could. The doors closed but the car remained stationary. When she glanced over at him, he was looking at her quizzically. "Floor?"

Chagrined, she looked away and murmured, "P-3."

There was a moment of awkward silence as the car began to move, then Blane spoke. "I was looking through a tour book this afternoon. Did you know that there are thirty-five plantation homes in the corridor between New Orleans and Baton Rouge?"

"Yes."

"Several dozen more in St. Francisville and down around New Iberia?"

"And over one hundred in Natchez, Biloxi and Galveston," she added. "What's your point, Mr. Crawford?"

"With all those homes already restored and open, is one more really that important?"

Kenley's eyes darkened, and she favored him with an icy glare. "The banks of the Mississippi are lined with oil refineries and plastics plants much larger than yours. Is one more small company that important?"

The car slowed and Blane touched one finger to his forehead in a mock salute. "Touché."

When the elevator stopped, Kenley stepped forward, anxious to put some space between herself and Blane Crawford. But when the doors opened, it was not the broad corridor of the garage she saw but a blank, cold slab of concrete. Her blood instantly turned to ice in her veins and

an unbearable pressure descended upon her chest. For a
moment she thought she was going to pass out. Gulping in
a breath of air she tried to speak, but all that emerged was
"Oh, God," in a shaky whisper. She took a step backward
and bumped into Blane. He rested one hand on her shoulder and with his other hand reached over and pressed several buttons on the panel. The car refused to move.

"Looks like we're between floors," he stated calmly.

Kenley's heart rate accelerated, and she felt light-headed
and weak. The warmth of Blane's hand on her shoulder
created a new kind of fear. She wasn't alone. She mustn't
fall apart. Not now. Not with him. It was imperative she
maintain her composure. "That is rather obvious," she
snapped. "I hate these stupid things. You can never rely on
them. Have you tried all the buttons? Why won't it go?"
Wrapping her arms around her chest, she took refuge in the
back of the car, avoiding Blane's eyes.

Blane eyed her intently. A thin film of sweat had appeared on her face, and he could see by the throbbing in her
neck that she was frightened. He pressed the door button,
closing the steel partitions and blocking out the stark grey
walls of the elevator shaft. It seemed less alarming that way.
"Are you all right?"

"Yes, of course!" Kenley barked. "I just want out of
here. Can't you call for help or something?"

There was no ignoring the near hysteria in her voice now.
"There's no phone in the car. I did push the emergency
button."

"Well, push it again."

Calmly he reached over and depressed the red button once
again.

Kenley turned away. She knew she was behaving terribly,
but she was powerless to stop it. Her fear was mounting with
each second, as was her dread of being exposed. Dear God,
she was losing her mind. Better for Blane to think her rude
than guess the truth. He was looking at her closely now,
those dark eyes piercing her veneer of anger. She could feel

the fear swelling up inside, cutting off her air, pressing down on her chest like an anvil. "Why don't they do something?"

"They will," Blane answered. His voice was calm and measured, like a steady rock in a sea of turmoil, and Kenley felt herself inexorably drawn to it. "It'll take them a few minutes to check things out. We'll be safe until they get us going again."

"Safe? I'd hardly call hanging twelve stories up safe."

"We're only six, as near as I can figure."

"This isn't funny." How could he be so unperturbed about this?

"No, but it's not disastrous, either."

Clenching her fists she turned away. She refused to humiliate herself in front of this man. She couldn't let him see her weak and defeated. And he would see it. Those eyes were like radar, picking up every telltale emotion. If she didn't get control of herself, her image as a competent businesswoman would be ruined forever. How could she hope to negotiate with a hard man such as Blane if he'd seen her whimpering in fear. Why did it have to be him? Why couldn't she have been with someone else or even alone? No. Not that. Blane Crawford was preferable to being alone in this tiny, airless . . . She closed her eyes, gripping her sides tightly.

Blane pushed the emergency button once again and the car lurched. Kenley screamed and buried her face in the corner. All hope of staying rational vanished. A sob caught in her throat and escaped as a whimper—a mixture of fear and humiliation. Her chest was convulsing with heaving sobs, but her eyes remained dry. Even in her near hysterical state, she refused to let the tears come. Suddenly gentle hands grasped her shoulders and turned her around into a warm embrace.

The gesture broke the last remaining strands of self-control and she grabbed onto the front of Blane's jacket, burying her head in his chest. "Please get me out of here. Please. I want out of here. Please."

Blane held the quaking form tight against him, muttering soothing phrases and gently stroking her hair until she had calmed somewhat. When he spoke, he put all the reassurance at his disposal into his words. "It'll be all right. I promise. We'll be moving any moment. Come on, let's sit down. Try and get comfortable. Talk to me. It'll keep your mind occupied."

Her eyes were wide with fright, and he doubted if she was fully aware of what he was saying. He'd have to be very careful. One wrong word could set her off again. Slowly he urged her into a sitting position, her hand still gripping his like a vise. He eased himself down, slipping his free arm around her shoulders.

Blane's nearness and the steady sound of his voice slowly penetrated Kenley's rampant fear. Her heart rate slowed and she felt much of the panic beginning to subside.

"Better?"

Kenley nodded. His hand held hers firmly and his fingers rubbed against the back of her hand in a comforting way. "I'm sorry." The hot flush of embarrassment began to wash over her again as she realized what had happened.

"Nonsense. This isn't my idea of a good time, either, you know." His voice was gentle and soothing. "At least you aren't alone."

Kenley nodded, struck by the irony of his words. But she was overwhelmingly grateful that he was here. Blane was being so sweet and understanding; she'd never suspected him of being so compassionate.

"Tell me, is it elevators, in general, or all tight places that upset you?"

Kenley closed her eyes, unable to face him. It was such a stupid weakness, one she'd struggled to overcome for years. So far she had managed rather well, but today she'd totally lost control. It had slipped away like a handful of sand, something that was becoming an all-too-common occurrence lately. It scared the hell out of her.

"You don't have to answer," Blane said quietly. "We can talk about something else."

Opening her eyes, she took a deep breath. "All enclosed places." There was no point in false bravado now. Her worst fears had been realized.

"Do you know what caused it?"

"Yes." She tried to keep her voice from wavering. "I was playing hide-and-seek and used an old metal shed as a hiding place. When I pulled the door shut, it stuck or locked. Anyway, it was a good place to hide—no one found me for five hours. It was my own fault, and it's a childish reason to be so terrified now. I should know better."

Blane squeezed her hand gently. "Don't be so hard on yourself. Everyone is afraid of something."

Kenley turned and looked at him. She couldn't imagine Blane being afraid of anyone or anything. He seemed so strong, so confident. "Not you."

There was a hint of sadness in his eyes as he looked at her. "Me, too."

Kenley studied him more closely. "What are you afraid of?" she asked softly.

He hesitated a moment then replied, "I'm afraid of being alone."

His words touched her deeply. She looked into his eyes, which had softened with a new, unexpected vulnerability. Her heart seemed to open up. An unexplained sense of understanding passed between them. There was something else, too, something quiet and mystical, but she shied away from naming it. His hand came up and caressed the side of her face, and his touch felt warm and strong. He leaned close, drawn by the same unknown force that held her mesmerized. She watched his face drawing nearer. Her eyelids grew heavy, and her lips parted. Every nerve in her body was keyed for his kiss. Her heart pounded wildly in anticipation.

But then he pulled away, his thumb tapping her cheek lightly. "No," he whispered against her lips. "I won't take advantage of you when you're so vulnerable."

Kenley was totally bewildered, strangely disappointed and slightly embarrassed. She looked away and realized her real predicament again. For a few brief moments she'd forgotten where they were. "How long has it been?"

"Ten minutes."

It seemed like ten hours.

"So," Blane asked, keeping his tone light and casual, "just what exactly does the administrator for the Crescent City Preservation Society do? I've never run into one before and I'm curious."

"I, uh..." Kenley fought to focus her mind on his request but her fear kept getting in the way. "I...do a little of everything," she finally managed to reply.

"Ah," he drawled softly. "One of those superwomen I've read about, huh?"

She tried to smile but failed. "I...uh, administer the properties the society owns." Her mind struggled to complete the thought. "There are five of them."

"And what does that mean?" he asked quietly. "Besides striking fear in the hearts of industry heads in New Orleans, CP in particular."

She glanced at him and saw the teasing glint in his eyes.

"Fear?" she repeated with a hint of skepticism.

"Absolutely," he stated.

Taking a deep breath she rested her head against Blane's shoulder and tried to mentally list her many obligations. It was easier to think now, as long as she had something to occupy her mind and Blane to hang on to. "I pay bills, hire guides and maintenance people, locate restorationists, arrange benefits, solicit donations. I manage the other two employees, coordinate the volunteers, direct research and mailings. I keep tabs on the hotel and bar and watch for new sites to acquire. Now and then I do some lobbying and meet with the press and the legislature, if necessary. Sometimes I act as ambassador to other states in helping them start restoration programs—"

"Whoa, that's enough," he interrupted. "When do you find time for a private life?"

"I don't," she answered simply.

"No boyfriends, no fiancé?"

Kenley shook her head.

"No tall, dark and handsome prince has tried to sweep you off your feet and carry you off to his castle?"

"Once. But when we got to the castle he found another princess he liked better. It didn't matter." She shrugged. "I found out I didn't really want a prince, after all."

"Every woman wants a prince, so I'm told."

"Not me."

"What type do you want?" he asked softly, not certain that she would even answer him.

"I want someone predictable."

"Predictable?" His voice held a hint of amusement. "That's an unusual requirement for a partner. Do you have any particular reason for that trait?"

"I don't want any surprises in a relationship," she said firmly. "I want a man who is open, honest and totally truthful with me. Someone compassionate, gentle and dependable, who'll never let me down and always be there when I need him. He'll trust me implicitly and allow me to be my own person. No shackles, no complaints about my career. He'll be content with our relationship and not run off the first time something more appealing comes along. He'll be steadfast and loyal, someone who will be there at the end of the day for comfort and security."

"Have you considered getting a dog?"

Kenley turned and stared at him then her eyes softened and she smiled. "I'm sorry, I'm babbling."

"Good. You're supposed to. Talking will keep your mind off the situation. What you talk about doesn't matter." He shifted slightly, positioning her a little more securely in his arms. "Are you from New Orleans?" He felt her head move slightly against his chin.

"Virginia."

"How long have you been here?"

"Five years. Five years last, uh . . . June."

"You like it here?"

"Very much."

"Do you live nearby?" Might as well ask a few practical questions while he was at it.

"In the Quarter."

The mundane conversation was beginning to have the desired effect. Kenley felt calmer now, less terror-stricken. Blane's soothing voice and solid presence had eased her fear enough for her to realize he was asking all the questions. She had several of her own she'd like to ask. "My turn. Why don't you want to take over CP?"

"What gave you that idea?"

"You've mentioned it twice now. Once in your office and then again in the garage."

He hadn't counted on Kenley turning the tables on him. He would have to choose his words carefully. "I have my own business."

"Plastics?"

"No. I never liked plastics."

"You never worked for your dad?"

"For a few years at the main office in Ohio. That was before he moved the headquarters down here."

"Your father didn't approve of your leaving, did he?" He didn't answer right away, and Kenley suddenly remembered the wild suggestions Alva had presented. "Did he disown you?"

Blane frowned over at her. "Isn't that a bit melodramatic? No, he didn't disown me, but our relationship was strained for a long time. We made up years ago. But we were never close, not the way many fathers and sons are. It wasn't his way. We stayed in touch. But I understood his reasons for being angry with me. I let him down."

"Then why did he leave you CP if he knew you didn't want it?"

"I've asked myself that question a hundred times this last week. I don't know. It could have been just because I'm his only son, or maybe he hoped he would change my mind. Maybe it was a last-ditch attempt to change me."

"Maybe he felt you were the better businessman. Like your grandfather, and he wanted you to do what he couldn't—save Crawford Plastics."

"I doubt it. We never agreed on how to run the company. In fact we never understood one another. We existed on two entirely different wavelengths."

"If you're so unhappy, why don't you turn Crawford Plastics over to someone else, or sell it?"

Blane shook his head slowly. "As much as I'd like to, I can't do that. I turned my back on him once and shattered his dream. I won't let him down again. The least I can do is see that Crawford Plastics is put back on its feet and running smoothly. After that, well, I'll just have to wait and see."

Blane's vague explanation had set off warning bells in her head. "Just what sort of business are you in? Your father must have disapproved strongly if he cut the ties?" Abruptly a shadow passed between them. An invisible barrier that removed Blane from her as surely as if he'd walked out of the elevator.

Blane felt the old wounds of the past throbbing to life. He should have known better than to allow his interest in a woman to go beyond a casual curiosity. The questions had started already, and after that would come the sympathy, then the fascination, then either rejection or exploitation depending upon the woman. He couldn't deal with either one again. But Kenley was waiting for an answer. She wanted truth and openness, but he wasn't sure she was ready to hear it and he wasn't ready to tell it. His voice was low and laced with fatigue when he finally answered. "I guess you could say I'm a promoter."

Kenley craned her neck to look at him, but he was staring straight ahead and he looked tired. She knew she probably shouldn't press the issue, but something compelled her to ask. "A promoter of what?"

"Services," he said bluntly.

A strange tightness formed in her chest, not related to the terror she'd experienced before. "What sort of services?"

"The kind no one else can provide."

Kenley had opened her mouth to speak when the car suddenly jerked and then moved slowly downward. Blane helped Kenley to her feet, keeping her hand in his. "We're on our way again."

The realities of life came crashing down on her head with a vengeance, and she quickly retreated to safer territory. She retrieved her hand and avoided his gaze. There was no time to comment. The car stopped at the next floor and the doors slid quietly open. A maintenance man greeted them.

"You folks okay?"

"We're fine," Blane answered for them both.

"Just a few crossed wires. Nothing to worry about," he said, readjusting the cap on his head. "That elevator is the safest part of the building. She's okay now, if you want to try her again."

"No, I think we'll walk the rest of the way this time."

They descended the stairs in silence to parking level three. "If you'd like, I'll walk you to your car," Blane offered.

"No, thank you. I'm fine, really." She tried to smile, but didn't quite accomplish it.

Blane inclined his head, his eyes warm and friendly. "Don't worry, Miss Farrell. Your secret is safe with me."

Kenley glanced away, uncomfortable under his canvassing gaze. He'd seen her emotionally naked, defenseless and at the mercy of a senseless phobia, and he was gallantly offering to ignore the shameful flaw in her character.

"Are you sure there's nothing I can do for you?" he asked again.

She shook her head, bravely lifting her eyes to his face. "Really, I'll be fine."

"I could see you home."

Her heart skipped a beat. "No. I'll be all right."

"Well, if you're sure." He paused. "Goodbye."

"G'bye."

Kenley watched him start down the stairs to the next level of the garage, a wave of regret washing over her. Why had she lied to him? She wasn't fine, at all. She didn't want him to leave. She wanted him to stay with her, hold her. She wanted to feel the comfort of his arms, the reassurance of his fingers upon hers. "Mr. Crawford!" she heard herself shout. He stopped and looked back up at her from the stairwell. Now what should she say? Come home with me. Hold me. Make me feel safe again. "Thank you. For everything." The words were woefully inadequate.

His mouth curved upward, and even from this distance she could see the glint in his eyes. "My pleasure, Miss Farrell. Anytime you need me, just whistle." He turned and disappeared out of sight, the sound of his footsteps on the gritty stairs echoing faintly in the air.

Kenley felt more alone than she'd ever felt in her whole life.

Saturday morning dawned clear and bright. The intense heat of the past week had subsided enough to make the day pleasantly warm. It was Kenley's favorite type of weather, especially in the morning when the French Quarter was quiet and peaceful.

She rose early, feeling rested and content. She had anticipated having bad dreams, but none had materialized. Unfortunately there'd been no good dreams, either. After a refreshing shower, she dried and slipped into a pair of lace panties. She'd forgotten to bring her bra into the bathroom, so she slipped on the bright blue silk robe, wrapping it around her and looping the belt. The slick fabric felt cool and luxurious against her bare skin. After brushing the tangles out of her hair, she went downstairs to linger over coffee and the newspaper. It was an hour and three cups later when she opened the French doors of her second-floor studio and stepped out onto the balcony that overlooked Chartres Street below.

It had rained the night before and the cobblestone streets were shiny with the collected moisture. The old facades were still streaked with water, and the wrought-iron-trimmed balconies harbored small puddles that trickled over the edges and dripped down onto the sidewalks.

Near the end of her street Kenley could see Esplanade, the eastern boundary of the French Quarter. Beyond it lay Faubourg Marigny, a lesser-known but equally interesting historic district. This end of the Quarter was usually quiet. There were few shops or restaurants here, mainly homes with easy access to the French Market and freeway. Kenley's blue eyes grew dreamy. She loved New Orleans. It had a rhythm, a primal beat and a life of its own, unequaled anywhere else. There was an air of adventure tinged with naughtiness and a kind of savage romance in every fiber of the old city. The word "romance" caused images of Blane to materialize. It was becoming a habit, especially after yesterday's episode in the elevator.

She'd been forced to reevaluate her first impression of Blane Crawford. He wasn't quite the unfeeling business shark she'd assumed. There were obviously facets to his character that she had never considered. His compassion and understanding had been genuine. And despite her continued uneasiness at her embarrassing behavior, she was more indebted to him than she'd ever be able to express. She'd relived that warm, secure embrace a dozen times before falling asleep the previous night, and now she was beginning to think she might have been approaching Blane in the wrong way. Maybe her own blind desire to save D'Evereaux had erected barriers between herself and her goal. Perhaps it would be more beneficial to try a friendlier method, appeal to his sense of decency. Instead of coming at him like a lion, perhaps as a lamb she could win him over.

From down the street she heard a shrill whistle and looked up to see a man calling to his dog. The pair disappeared around the corner, and Kenley leaned against the juncture of the iron railing and smiled. Blane had told her to whistle if she needed him. Would it work? she wondered. It might be interesting to try. Kenley sipped her coffee, idly watching the street below. Cars lined the curb, and foot traffic was beginning to increase.

A man was walking up the banquette toward her building, his bright red shirt standing out against the surrounding gray bricks and concrete. He stopped in front of her gate below, and to her amazement she recognized Blane Crawford. He stood there a few moments as if undecided, and she was struck anew by his dark good looks and physical strength. He possessed the casual masculinity of a man who knows who he is and has nothing to prove.

As if he'd felt her scrutiny, he suddenly looked up, an appreciative grin on his handsome face. Kenley felt her pulse quicken. "Good morning. Should I recite from *Romeo and Juliet*?"

"Not unless you feel inspired," Kenley replied, her voice sounding a bit breathless in the morning air. Strange how easily the banter came to her lips now.

"I do."

His low-pitched voice churned deep in her stomach.

"What are you doing in this end of town?" she asked, hoping the loud pounding of her heart wasn't audible to his ears.

"I came to see how you were feeling after our adventure yesterday. May I come in?"

"Yes, of course. Give me a second and I'll buzz you in."

Quickly she retreated downstairs to the front door, pressing the electronic release on the gate at the end of her brick hallway. He was standing in front of her when she remembered that she was still wearing only panties and a robe—a very thin, silky robe. It was too late to run upstairs and change. She'd have to act casual about it and hope he didn't notice. Discreetly she tugged the blue silk more snugly around her waist as he smiled.

"Hello."

"Hello." Why was her pulse racing so?

"The lady of the balcony, I presume."

"Come on in."

Blane looked quizzically back at the narrow tunnel-like entrance he'd just passed through, then at the colorful garden that opened out at the opposite end. "Unusual."

Kenley smiled at his expression. "I'll bet you've never been inside a town house before. You have that look of astonishment on your face."

"No, I haven't. I wasn't expecting this."

"Let me show you." She stepped out into the walkway and led him to the courtyard. "Most French Quarter houses are like this. It's Spanish design, actually. The side of the house that faces the street is really the back. The courtyard was the focal point of the house, so all the rooms and balconies open onto it. Since most of the homes shared a common wall, it was a way of maintaining some privacy."

Blane tried to show the proper amount of interest, but all he could think of was the way Kenley looked. She was positively breathtaking. Her face was free of makeup, and her skin glowed with a new softness. Her dark hair hung nearly to her shoulders and was slightly damp. The drier strands were beginning to wave softly around her chin.

Although she tried to treat the fact casually, Blane was well aware that she wore little, if anything, beneath the silky blue robe. Technically it preserved her modesty well. Only her ankles, her forearms and the top of her collarbone were exposed. It was what the gown didn't reveal that was most provocative, sending a familiar warmth through his veins. The shimmering material hugged every rounded curve of Kenley's body. He had proof now of what he'd suspected. She had a luscious figure—delicate neck and shoulders, and small round breasts that stood proudly under the blue silk. He could almost see the pink rose tips, feel the softness in his hands. Her small waist gave way to rounded hips and curvaceous thighs and legs.

She was telling him something about the house, and he struggled to pay attention. There was a sweetness about her this morning, and he fought the urge to crush her to him and savor every morsel of that sweetness for himself. Instead, he attempted to prolong his stay. "Would you show me the rest of the house?"

Her blue eyes expressed surprise, but she granted his request and gave him the grand tour of the formal living room downstairs, the adjoining dining room and the large modern kitchen renovated to accommodate the conveniences of the 1990s. He admired her sunny courtyard with its shade tree, flowers and ironwork furniture with bright cushions. Upstairs she was less thorough. A peek into her bedroom with sitting room and a gesture at the bathroom, then she stepped into her studio. "And last but not least, the obligatory junk room."

Blane glanced around the studio. "This is where you work?"

"Yes. When I can."

"Where you escape."

"Escape? Hardly that."

"The rest of the house is all wrong."

"Wrong! I'll have you know I researched every detail. I've put a great deal of effort into making it an exact replica of a home of the period."

He watched her defenses go up as she tried to justify her decorating efforts. He wished she wouldn't jump to conclusions so quickly. "But it's not you," he said, stepping into the studio. It was open and airy, with rattan furniture and fabrics in fresh spring colors. "This room has your imprint all over it." She started, and he sensed a withdrawal. He was afraid she would ask him to leave. Instead she changed the subject.

"Would you care for a cup of coffee?"

"Yes, that would be very nice. Thank you."

He followed Kenley down to the courtyard, wondering how much longer he could resist the tempting sight of her. As she returned to the kitchen, he seated himself at the patio table and smiled. He had just added a new objective to his list: learning everything there was to know about Kenley Farrell.

Kenley moved around the kitchen automatically, preparing the coffee and trying to figure out how Blane Crawford could read her mind. She could still feel the shiver that touched her spine when he'd blatantly labeled the studio as her room. How did he know? She'd merely explained it as a junk room, yet he'd singled it out as *her* room. It was unnerving that this man, almost a stranger, had put his finger on the core of who she was.

Absently she tugged at the sash around her waist. She really should put something on. It was absolutely indecent entertaining an attractive man in her home with little more than a piece of blue silk draped around her. She'd felt his eyes on her, knew he could see every curve. She also knew she should feel embarrassed, even offended, but instead found herself feeling flattered and strangely excited. She'd never been a tease, but she wanted Blane to find her attractive and desirable. A small part of her said she was being naughty. A larger part said, so what?

Kenley carried the coffee tray out to the courtyard. Even in the dregs of summer, the patio was awash with color. Bright red begonias overflowed from hanging baskets under the balconies. The crape myrtle tree in the corner dripped lavender petals onto the brick floor, mingling with the pink and white petunias housed in terra-cotta pots. Blane was seated at the white iron table and gave her an appreciative glance when she sat down.

He fixed himself a cup of the fresh brew and leaned back. "Are you fully recovered?" He could see the question still made her uncomfortable.

"Yes. Thank you." She smiled. He really should wear red more often. It did wonderful things for his eyes.

"No bad dreams?"

"Not a flicker," she confessed. "I'm sure it was all due to your patience and understanding. I really am very grateful."

Blane smiled inwardly. He knew how much it cost her to say that. Kenley Farrell wasn't used to taking help from anyone, least of all an adversary. If he had anything to say about it, though, they wouldn't be on opposite sides of the fence for very long. "I assure you the pleasure was all mine. I don't often get to rescue lovely damsels in distress. The knights in shining armor always seem to beat me to it."

Kenley grinned. "You don't consider yourself a knight?"

"Hardly. Merely a humble villager struggling to do my small part day to day." He paused. "Miss Farrell—"

"Please, call me Kenley. It's silly to be so formal. After all, you know my horrible secret."

"Yes, I do," he drawled pointedly. "So tell me, how did you get into this business of saving and administrating historic landmarks? It seems a rather obscure occupation."

"It is. Very." She smiled. "It's not the kind of thing you can take courses for in college. I majored in history, with a minor in business and economics."

"Where was that? In Virginia?"

She nodded. "I suppose that's where I first got the bug. History is very much alive and well in the Old Dominion. Anyway, I started out working with a friend to try and preserve an old house that was slated to be destroyed. We gathered others, lined up volunteers and started our campaign."

"You won." His words were a statement, not a question.

"Yes, we did. I stayed around afterward and lent a hand with the bookkeeping, helped contact people about funds, and tracked down carpenters with the necessary skills. In general, I made myself useful."

"And that led to this job?" he asked, his eyes focused fully upon her.

"Not quite that easily. No, I helped save a few more buildings and historic areas. Even did a bit of lobbying here and there. Then one day I got involved with trying to save the waterfront district of Savannah. It was a near-impossible task. The preservationists were up in arms, but the businessmen had a strong hold on the city. I drew the unhappy job of mediator between the two. It wasn't an easy battle, but we won in the end."

"And you found yourself with a reputation."

Kenley nodded. "Of sorts. Mrs. Arcenault read about it and called me. She founded the CCPS and needed someone to administrate it."

"Is that common practice?"

"No. Most historical societies are manned by volunteers. But Mrs. Arcenault had been successful in saving two plantation homes—The Cottage and The Raymond House, as well as the old St. Nicholas Hotel. Maintaining all of them had become too much for her staff to handle. She needed a professional to oversee the business. I jumped at the chance."

"You've been successful since coming here."

"Very. We've added Avondale Plantation and Brackett's Tavern. It's a very satisfying job. Each house has its own set of problems and challenges just to keep it running and open to the public."

"You're used to doing things without help from anyone, aren't you?" he observed quietly.

"It shows?" she said with a faint smile. "I had to learn to be self-sufficient at an early age. I don't like depending on others."

"Because they usually disappoint you?" he guessed.

"Yes. Always."

Blane raised an eyebrow. "What about your family? Your parents?"

Kenley hid her discomfort by rearranging the creamer and sugar bowl on the table. "My parents are divorced. My mother died several years ago. I have a sister in Richmond, but we're not close." She smiled, determined to change the subject. "So you see, I survived the great elevator adventure with no serious aftereffects. Thank you again. It was very nice of you to check on me today."

Blane noted the fact that she had omitted any reference to her father and he couldn't help wondering if that was significant. "Well, I confess, I do have another reason for coming here. It's about D'Evereaux."

Kenley pressed her lips together, immediately defensive and very disappointed. Her good mood evaporated. She should have known his friendliness came with a price tag. He probably wanted her to back off, now that he'd been so solicitous. "I'm not going to change my mind, Mr. Crawford, no matter how helpful you were yesterday. I'm very grateful, but it doesn't change a thing."

Blane's eyes grew dark and his jawline hardened at her assumption. She was far too defensive, and he didn't know why. He'd already apologized for his earlier behavior. "I wanted to talk to you about joining forces."

"What do you mean?" There was a suspicious tone in her voice.

"I've been thinking. We've both approached this thing like bull terriers. I'm not overly thrilled with my new responsibilities, and you're not pleased with the unexpected turn of events, either. My father's death has put a major glitch in both our programs." His hand moved in a short gesture. "Perhaps the solution is to work together, not against each other."

Once again Blane had come at her out of left field. "Together?"

"I have several urgent matters to deal with first, but I intend to give D'Evereaux my full attention as soon as possible. All I ask is for you to be patient." He looked at her over the rim of his cup, and his eyes were smiling. "As difficult as that might be."

He was teasing again. His eyes had taken on that soft, warm quality she was coming to appreciate. "Well, we certainly aren't getting anywhere this way."

"I'll promise you this much, Kenley. I'll investigate every possible solution to save your house. Surely two bright, intelligent people like ourselves can come up with an answer that will satisfy both our dilemmas."

There was no mistaking the sincerity in his voice, and Kenley felt a warmth spread through her at the knowledge. She realized at that moment that she genuinely wanted to like this man. "I don't see why we need to continue to fight." Kenley looked into her coffee cup, unwilling to allow Blane to see her delight at his suggestion. This was, after all, still a business proposition. "Thank you. You're being very understanding."

"Well, now I hope you'll be understanding when I say I must be going. I have an appointment and I'm afraid I'm already late."

"Yes, of course."

"I wish I could tell you right now that I'll save your plantation, but unfortunately I can't."

She walked him to the gate and reached for the latch at the same moment he stretched out his hand, and his fingers brushed her arm. She jumped, the contact racing through her like fire. Turning, she found his face scant inches away and those soft, compelling eyes casting their spell, rendering her powerless.

His fingers rested under her chin, and he tilted it upward to receive his kiss. His mouth was firm and gentle, and he tasted her lips reverently, slowly. Kenley felt her strength fading away, her every nerve springing to vibrant life under his touch. He tasted her more fully, more demandingly, and Kenley parted her lips, understanding that in doing so she would be lost forever. His tongue slid between her teeth, probing, exploring. A delicious weakness came over her, and she was drowned in the wondrous taste of him.

His arms slipped around her neck, pulling her against the hard line of his body. Her breast throbbed against his chest, and she felt the heat of his desire through the thin folds of her robe. As if in a trance, she was unable to respond to his kiss, only able to relinquish herself to him totally. She was filled with a sudden, urgent desire, a powerful need, and realized that she would gladly give herself to him here and now if he should ask. The realization shocked her, but it didn't matter. His mouth devoured hers, and she'd never felt so beautiful, so happy, in her life.

When the moment ended, Kenley looked up into those penetrating dark eyes, eyes that were smiling gently.

Blane then glanced downward, and she followed his gaze, noticing that her robe had slipped off her shoulder. It seemed an unimportant detail.

Slowly he took the fabric between his fingers and returned it to its proper, modest place. "You didn't seem so vulnerable today," he said softly. Then he left.

Kenley stood in the shaded walkway long after she heard the gate shut behind him. She rested her palms against the cool brick, easing the heat that still lingered in her blood. She'd been anticipating that kiss, but was totally unprepared for her response. She hadn't expected to feel so glorious in his arms, so strangely right. Nor had she predicted the sudden need that had slammed into her. Kenley took a deep breath and walked back to the courtyard, lifting her face to the sun. Her heart rate was returning to normal, and she was able to think clearly again.

Was it possible? Could they work together to save D'Evereaux? He seemed very willing to try. It wouldn't hurt to be nice to the man who owned her house. Besides, after that kiss there was no more denying that she was strongly attracted to him.

But wouldn't that attraction create complications? Could she really ignore the strong feelings he aroused in her, and keep them from blurring the line between business and pleasure?

She wouldn't let them. After all, she was an adult and in control of her life and her emotions. She was perfectly capable of working closely with a man to whom she was attracted. She'd done it before. It was just a matter of keeping the proper perspective, and Blane was no different from any other man she'd come in contact with. Or was he?

Kenley spent the remainder of the weekend pondering that question. Thoughts of Blane and the memory of his kiss appeared at the most unexpected moments, like now. It was Sunday. As she was folding clothes from the dryer, the red socks in her hands reminded her of the red shirt he'd worn yesterday. It was a polo style, and the bands around the sleeves had been stretched over the muscles in his upper arms. The front was unbuttoned, and where the collar lay against his neck and throat, she could see the dark hairs on his chest. He'd looked so sinfully handsome.

She piled the red socks on the counter and pulled out a dish towel. What was it about Blane that intrigued her so? Yes, he was attractive, but she'd known other men who were more so. Yet when he appeared, her mind and body seemed to spring to life.

His kiss had left her scared and craving for more. Scared because one kiss shouldn't be able to shatter a lifetime of common sense. It shouldn't still haunt her, or stir longings she couldn't even name. The touch of one man's lips shouldn't make her feel so much a woman. But it did, and that explained the craving. No one else had left her feeling weak-kneed and helpless. The sensation was totally new and, she had to admit, enjoyable—too enjoyable. It was all so sudden and unexpected.

Kenley gave herself a mental shake and picked up the stack of clothes she'd folded. Topping the stairs, she paused at the studio door, chewing her lip when she remembered his uncanny perception regarding her studio. How had he known that it was her favorite room? What had he seen there that had given her secret away?

Suddenly she realized that it *was* a secret. The rest of the house was a reflection of the image she wanted to project to the world. The precise blending of furnishings and colors were meant to suggest class, breeding and elegance. When giving a tour of her home, she never included the studio. Yet with Blane she hadn't hesitated. Perhaps she had wanted him to see the real Kenley and gauge his reaction.

"This room is you," he'd said. How had he known? The room was open and airy with gaily colored curtains over the French doors, a blue love seat with comfy pillows, a large desk cluttered with papers, shelves lining one wall holding her extensive collection of books and magazines, and a large wicker fan chair with bright yellow cushions.

The rest was an odd assortment of personal things—a table from her mother, the signed and numbered print by Kendrick that Alva had given her, an old wrought-iron fireplace cover.

What had Blane thought when he'd looked in her studio? He hadn't appeared surprised, only as if he'd expected nothing else. He seemed to have some uncanny insight into who she really was, but she knew absolutely nothing about him except that he was determined to save his father's company, he was kind to hysterical women, and he was fatally attractive. Hardly enough to build a relationship on.

Besides, he was too evasive about himself, too hesitant to speak of his past. There were too many gaps, too many things unexplained. She'd made several attempts to uncover his life, given him every opportunity to be open and honest. Yet whenever the conversation turned toward his business or anything personal he closed her out. No, that wasn't exactly true. He had been frank with her about a few things. His feelings for his dad, the fact that he was afraid of being alone.

But were those things true or was he merely using them as a ploy to calm a woman on the verge of hysteria? She had felt him withdraw, fold in on himself when she asked him what sort of a business he had that would alienate him from his father? He had changed right before her eyes, wrapping an invisible cloak around himself. Was his business on the shady side? He had called himself a promoter of services, the kind no one else could provide. The implications were alarming, but regardless she couldn't bring herself to believe Blane was involved in anything illegal. But then what did that leave? If only he were more open with her.

Back to square one. Same old problem. Her judgment where men were concerned was lousy. She'd adored her father, worshiped him with the intensity and devotion only a child could have. But he had been living a lie and when the moment of truth arrived he left them all behind. And Russ, so charming, so attentive, so thoroughly self-serving. But had she learned her lesson? Apparently not, because here she was, following the same old patterns, getting emotionally involved with a man who wasn't quite what he seemed, a man who held more questions than answers. No, she decided with a little jerk of her head. Blane was the wrong man to be attracted to. Period. She strode to the bedroom and commenced putting her clean clothes away.

Chapter Five

The world was a soft, warm, comforting haze in which Kenley floated happily. She was surrounded by blue skies and fluffy white clouds. A gentle breeze ruffled her hair. Her feet walked across an emerald green carpet of grass and in the distance stood a gleaming pillared castle she knew instinctively was D'Evereaux. She smiled as she drew closer. The house had been reborn. Its facade was freed of blemishes, its windows sparkled with new glass, and its galleries were painted a pristine white. Some sixth sense told her that inside the house she would also find perfection. She floated onto the veranda and stopped. Standing in the shadows was a man, tall and dark, with burning black eyes. He wore red. Kenley felt his power reaching out to engulf her. He came closer, and she knew a mixture of fear and excitement. He reached out for her, his hand closing slowly around her throat. She opened her mouth to scream, when an insistent buzzing shattered the disturbing dream. She opened her eyes with a start, the sound of the alarm clock near her bed chasing away the last vestiges of her dream. Groggily she stretched out her hand and fumbled with the off switch, moaning wearily. She felt awful. Her sleep had been disrupted by dreams all night.

It was only seven in the morning, but the air was already sticky and warm. The humidity seeped into the house despite the air-conditioning and ceiling fans. It was going to be a scorcher of a day, with predicted highs in the upper nineties. Life in the Crescent City would be moving at a slow crawl today. It was the only way to survive the heat. Mentally she shoved herself into action, but her heart wasn't in it. Her morning tasks were performed with slow determination and little enthusiasm. She showered, fixed her hair and applied makeup, then moved to the closet and stared blindly at her wardrobe. The array of garments loomed before her eyes. The thought of putting on another business suit was depressing. She was tired of the constant need to look professional, to set an example, to fit the image. She wanted to let her hair down and take a day off. But there were too many responsibilities on her shoulders. If she didn't do it, who else would? Even her weekends were filled with social functions. Not the kind where she could relax and enjoy, but obligatory business affairs. Except for the morning Blane dropped by, she'd been busy every minute. "To hell with it," she growled caving in to her rebellious mood. Blindly she stuck out her hand and grasped the first thing her fingers came in contact with—a pair of linen slacks and silk blouse. Compromise.

The ride to the office was slow and irritating, and it only added to her frustration. It would have been quicker to walk, but the high humidity would have turned her into a damp mass of limp linen after the first block.

Arrival at the office was heralded by a summons from Mrs. Arcenault to come to her immediately, and after a brief check with Alva, Kenley was off again, battling the crosstown traffic this time.

It was afternoon when she returned to the small CCPS offices. Alva greeted her with such a look of doom that Kenley felt like turning around and going home. She dropped her purse on the older woman's desk and braced herself, stuck again by the contrast in the woman. Tall and stately, with a pleasant face and impeccably groomed figure, her elegant appearance was at odds with her pessimistic attitude. "All right, what now? Though I doubt you could make the day any worse than it already is."

"Don't count on it," Alva said. "Where would you like me to start?"

"At the beginning," she replied, crossing her arms over her chest.

"Okay. Then you'd better make plans to go furniture shopping, because Mrs. Virgil has completed renovations on her plantation home and the furniture she has so graciously been loaning out to us for The Raymond House will be moved to her home this weekend."

"But her house wasn't supposed to be finished for at least three more months."

"Seems she and hubby have split and she's moving in now, and she wants her furniture and antiques with her."

Kenley rested a hand behind her neck. "But I've not even begun to line up replacements. I can't show The Raymond House with empty rooms."

"There's always Mrs. Bueche's collection."

"Oh, please," she scoffed with a wave of her hand.

"Most of it is of the right period," Alva pointed out.

"But poor quality. You know as well as I do, Mrs. Bueche is dying to loan us that stuff so she can climb up another notch on the social ladder. It'll give her the edge in joining one of the older Mardi Gras Krewes."

"Do you have a choice?"

"I don't know. There's got to be someone somewhere who can loan us a few rooms of furniture. Surely one of the dealers in town could do better than Mrs. Bueche." She picked up her purse and started off. "I'll get on it right away."

"Well, you'll have to call from someplace other than here."

Kenley spun around. "What are you talking about?"

"Dr. Ristelli has decided he's no longer in a position to donate his suite for our use. He regrets that the lease has expired and he'll be unable to renew. He cites pressing financial obligations."

"How soon do we have to be out?" Kenley asked, coming back to the desk.

"Now. No later than the end of the week."

"A week? That's impossible. Where can we go?"

"I'll put out a few feelers. I was hoping you'd have some ideas."

Kenley shook her head. "None. And I doubt if our budget will be able to stand the addition of rent. Why didn't he give us some notice?"

"Well, it's just a rumor, but I suspect that Dr. Ristelli got himself involved in that land mess on the West Bank."

"Great," she said sarcastically. "This makes the day just perfect. Not one single thing has gone right since I got up."

"What did Mrs. Arcenault want?"

Pressing her fingers against her temples she tried to ease the throbbing ache that had begun. "She wanted to know about D'Evereaux, why nothing has been done. She wants to know when we expect Mr. Crawford to reach a decision. I tried to tell her Blane was busy with Crawford Plastics and that he'd promised to give D'Evereaux every consideration. She's unhappy with the lack of progress, and hinted rather strongly that if something isn't decided soon she may withdraw support from the project."

Alva leaned across the desk, eyeing Kenley quizzically. "Blane?"

The woman had pounced upon the name like a ravenous vulture. Kenley knew there was no way to cover up that something had happened between her and Crawford.

"We...talked over the weekend," she replied, doubtful that the evasive answer would pacify her nosy friend.

"Your place or his?"

Was that a leer she detected in Alva's eyes? "Mine."

"You seem to have changed tunes rather abruptly. Was his melody so persuasive?"

"Don't go reading too much into this. He helped me with a small problem last Friday, and as a result we decided to try and find a solution that was mutually beneficial to us both."

"You discussed this at your house?" Her expression was positively gleeful.

"Over coffee. In the courtyard."

Alva nodded. "And just how did you discuss it? Orally?"

Kenley sighed in disgust. The woman was impossible. "Alva, I need the financial records. Now." She turned and stomped into her office.

Kenley dropped into the chair behind her desk, hearing Alva humming happily to herself. The woman was worse than a mind reader. She seemed to instinctively know when Kenley had something to hide from her. She'd have to be very careful how she spoke about Blane in front of Alva from now on, or else the woman would have them married and on a honeymoon by next week. She flipped through her address file, picked up the phone and began making calls.

Blane rubbed his tired eyes and leaned back in his chair. Bending over the desk for the past two hours had made him stiff and sore. His intense concentration while poring over the stacks of data had created a tension at the base of his neck that was slowly creeping up his skull.

No matter how he looked at it, no matter how he rearranged the figures, the answer was still the same—Crawford Plastics was in serious trouble. He had to agree with his accountants: situation not hopeless but critical. If he didn't take steps immediately to correct the problem, there might not be a Crawford Plastics to worry about. And he owed it

to his father to at least see that the company was put back
on the road to recovery.

It was quiet in the office. All the other personnel had gone
home an hour ago—home to their families, their mort-
gaged houses, their budgeted incomes. It sounded wonderful. Stability, permanence, commitment. Those things
suddenly seemed very important to Blane.

He would be forty in a few months. It was time he put
down some roots. He was tired of running from one place
to the next. Tired of the strangers in his life, the starting over
in each new city with new obstacles and problems to overcome, then running off to start the process all over again
after a few months.

Spinning around in his chair, Blane stared out the huge
window at the city of New Orleans spread out below him.
He was beginning to think he could be happy here, given the
proper incentive. Resting two fingers against his temple, he
contemplated the most obvious incentive.

He was fascinated by Kenley, intrigued with her combination of independence and vulnerability. She'd called up
all his protective instincts in the elevator, something he'd
never felt before with a woman. Yvonne had been so accomplished, so serene and centered. She'd never needed his
support. Debbi had been attentive and flattered his ego and
stroked his male pride. But Kenley had touched some unknown part of him that he couldn't quite explain. He'd been
strongly attracted to her from the first moment she'd walked
into his office. No, he corrected quickly, at the cemetery. But
he hadn't realized how deeply his emotions were involved
until he had pulled her close and found that he didn't ever
want to let go. The knowledge surprised him.

He wanted to make her feel safe and loved, keep all the
fears and doubts out of her life. On a less noble plane, he
wanted to feel her against him, soft and supple, the sweetness of her curves molding to his. He wanted to bury his face
in the heady freshness of her shiny hair and taste her tempt-

ing lips for eternity. The memory of her in his arms had lingered in his mind all weekend.

He'd not been wholly truthful with her on Saturday. He had wanted to see if she was all right, and he had wanted to discuss their cooperation. But mainly he'd wanted to be near her again, to watch the endless play of emotions in her blue eyes, and maybe to catch a glimpse of the adorable dimples that decorated her inviting little mouth.

He'd been greatly relieved when his kiss hadn't been answered with a slap in the face. On the contrary, she had surrendered almost willingly to his embrace. But while she hadn't openly rejected his advances, she'd been wary of him. He'd have to be careful. Kenley was fiercely independent, and there was a shell around her heart that he didn't as yet understand. It probably had something to do with the prince she had eluded to and her desire for predictability.

He wished he could settle the plantation question in her favor and remove that obstacle. But he'd been over the reports a dozen times, and the answer always came up the same. He needed every penny and every inch of that land to get Crawford Plastics on its feet. Unless something new developed, D'Evereaux would have to go. He chewed the inside of his lip. This damn house was going to be a major bone of contention. It would spell the difference between having a relationship with Kenley and having none.

Who was he kidding? He was in no position to have emotional entanglements of any kind with anyone. Yet here he was thinking about something that was out of the question. He'd been feeling melancholy ever since his dad's funeral and this interest in Kenley was probably only an overflow from that. Death had a way of altering your perspective and clarifying the parameters of the human condition.

Frustrated, Blane rose and walked to the small table in the corner of his office and poured himself a cup of overly brewed coffee. It was bitter and hot. He swallowed the first gulp, tossing the rest into the small sink. Maybe there was still something in the files he could use to solve the problem. He'd promised Kenley he'd look into it. Now was as good a time as any.

Kenley hung up the phone with a bang. The day had been an absolute and total failure. No matter where she turned she found insurmountable obstacles. In the past few weeks her life had been coming unraveled piece by piece, and she felt powerless to halt the erosion. She'd always been able to plan ahead, foresee possible roadblocks and form sensible contingency plans. It was one of her fortes. Yet now she was trapped in a canyon so deep she couldn't see daylight, and there was no means of escape. She tried to pinpoint the beginning of this downward trend—when she had started to lose her grip, feel discontented and question the direction of her life—but failed.

Suddenly she found herself here, alone, facing problems that seemed unsolvable, feeling lost and incapable of making even the simplest of decisions. What was wrong with her? Why couldn't she function any longer?

For the first time in her life, Kenley felt totally defeated.

The tears rushed out in a flood. Unable to stop them, she put her head down on her arms and let them come, the hot tears falling wet upon her skin, sliding onto her desk and dampening the papers beneath. The situation seemed hopeless. Her life was coming apart at the seams, and she felt at the mercy of everyone else's whims.

"Kenley, are you all right?"

The deep voice cut through her weeping, and she raised her head. Through blurred vision she saw Blane standing in the doorway, and her heart sank. Did he have some sixth sense that was fine-tuned to her misery? Angry at having been caught crying, she snatched up a tissue paper and began dabbing furiously at her eyes. "I'm fine," she snapped. "It's just been a bad day."

Blane walked into the room, his hands resting easily in the pockets of his slacks. He wore dark gray pleated trousers that accentuated his long, lean lines. The crisp white shirt was rolled up at the sleeves, revealing strong masculine forearms covered with dark hair that tapered down to the back of his hands. The stark contrast between the white shirt and his olive skin made his already overpowering maleness even more pronounced.

By comparison, Kenley felt soggy and rumpled, and she knew her eyes were red and puffy from crying. Her common sense told her not to worry—after all, he'd seen her in worse shape than this the other day—but the feminine part of her wanted him to see her fresh and calm, smiling and attractive. So far he'd seen her draped in navy at a funeral, hysterical with fear in the elevator, without makeup and practically naked, and now blubbering like a lost three-year-old. Then he had the audacity to stand there looking so damned sexy. Her confused thoughts did little to ease the situation. "I'm sorry. It's just been one of those domino days."

Blane arched his eyebrows quizzically.

"You know," she explained with a little finger play, "one thing goes wrong, then something else, and so on and so on."

"Murphy's Law in full force, huh?" He cocked his head. "Anything I can do?"

Kenley smiled bravely into his eyes. At least she hoped that was the effect she created. What she saw there, however, was genuine concern. He exuded such warmth that it seemed to reach out across the desk and touch her and ease the pain. She suddenly had an intense longing to be held in his arms again, to have that sense of security and caring that she'd felt in the elevator. "No," she blurted out, surprised at how hard her voice sounded. The mental image of her being held protectively in Blane's arms had unnerved her. She wasn't a child. She could handle her own problems. This was just one moment of weakness. Among a growing number, a little voice taunted. "I'm just . . . that is, I'll have to work it through somehow."

Her eyes met his again and her blood tingled at what she read there. She looked away—down at the desk, at her nervous hands, anywhere but at those eyes that looked so deeply into parts of her she didn't want to share. Yet she had no secrets from him. He knew she was feeling frightened and unsure of herself. The scary thing was that she didn't know if that fact bothered or pleased her. "Is there something I can do for you? I didn't think anyone else was here this late," she said, trying desperately to steer the conversation away from herself.

"Some last-minute complications kept me in the office. Actually, I came down here on a hunch." He didn't add that he'd had a strong desire to see her again and was taking a long shot that she'd still be in. "I've been looking over the D'Evereaux file you sent over and I had a few questions."

"Oh, good. I'd be happy to answer them, and by the way, I found a few more items you should have." She reached down to pick up the papers on her desk and realized it was one of the files she'd wept over. There were tearstains on the cover. "I'm sorry. It's sort of damp."

Blane leaned toward her, taking the folder from her hand, his fingers deliberately brushing hers. "I hope this is the last time you have to cry over that house." Too late he realized the implications of his words and knew she would misinterpret them.

A light came on behind the azure eyes. "Does that mean you've found a solution?"

Blane shook his head. "No. But eyes like yours shouldn't be filled with tears. Only laughter."

Kenley looked down at her desk. "Where you're concerned, I seem to be continually in a state of distress."

"I won't take it personally," he teased.

Kenley sighed. "Forgive me, but I can't find much cause for laughter at the moment."

"Well, if I can't take the unhappiness out of your eyes, how about the hunger?"

He really was very nice. Kenley didn't have to look at him to know he was smiling. "Is it that obvious? Or did you hear my stomach growling?"

"No, mine. Why don't we go to my office and order something sent in? We can talk about D'Evereaux and you can tell me why you're sitting alone in your office crying."

"It's a sad, sad story," she warned, smiling into his eyes. "With no solution."

His voice dropped an octave, deep and seductive. "I've been told I have a strong shoulder to cry on and a good ear for listening."

"All right. Maybe I'll be able to persuade you to save D'Evereaux after your male appetite is appeased." The look in his eyes turned more intimate, and she realized how he had interpreted her innocent remark. Before she could speak, he took her chin in his hands and tilted her face upward. His dark eyes caressed her as his fingers burned against the flesh on her jaw.

"I've never known a woman who could cry her heart out and still look pretty."

Kenley pulled her eyes away from his intense gaze, her pride wounded at his remark. She'd always detested women who solved their difficulties by resorting to feminine tears. "It's a sign of weakness," she snapped.

Blane jerked her chin around, forcing her to meet his eyes. "It's a sign of character, a mark of compassion and depth of emotion. And an appetite is a healthy sign of recovery. I'm always starving after a good cry."

Kenley eyed him skeptically. "Do you cry often?"

His eyebrow arched. "What do you think?"

Kenley didn't know what to think. Blane was a continual surprise.

She picked up her purse and smiled. "I think you're Murphy's Law incarnate."

Blane chuckled loudly at that. "Oh, really?"

It was the first time he'd fully smiled since she'd met him, and the effect on her nervous system was thunderous. If the dark eyes had been compelling, the full force of his smile was downright deadly. The flashing white teeth, straight and strong, were in sharp contrast to the bronze of his skin. Kenley was totally enthralled. The smile seemed to melt inside her heart even after it had faded and his face held a serious expression once more.

"Kenley, if an apology is in order, I hope you'll accept mine."

She didn't have to ask what he was referring to. It was the kiss. "We're both adults. I wasn't aware that there was anything to apologize for."

"Good. I seem to find myself having wild impulses whenever you're around."

"Do you usually give in to impulse?" she asked as they left her office.

"Rarely. What about you? Are you impulsive?"

"Never," she replied firmly. "It's too dangerous, too costly."

"Oh? I've found that most beautiful women have a reckless streak."

Kenley set her jaw, favoring him with a stern look. "I don't want to throw a compliment back in your face, but I've never had much respect for women who used their looks to get what they wanted out of life."

He nodded as if he understood. "You feel that hard work and dedication, a few brains, make a better woman."

"Yes, I do."

"I agree."

"You do?" She was surprised. "Most men despise intelligence in a woman. It undermines their image as the omnipotent male."

"Is that a personal observation?" he asked.

"After many years of careful research."

Blane smiled. "I've found that conversation with a woman who isn't intelligent can get boring very quickly."

"I wonder," she said thoughtfully.

Blane only smiled. "Shall we discuss it further over some food?"

When they reached the Crawford Plastics suite, Blane opened the door to his office and gestured her inside. The room had a more friendly atmosphere than she remembered. Maybe it was the soft yellow glow of dusk or perhaps she was less tense than during her previous visit. Or maybe she was just tired from crying. Whatever the reason, she felt herself relax as the cozy aura of the room drifted around her like an old friend.

Blane moved to his desk and reached for the address file, flipping the cards with a flourish, his gold watch flashing against the dark hair on his wrist. "My dad was a devotee of the all-night delis. I'm sure there's bound to be one in his files. Here we are. Soilo's Deli. Are you familiar with it?"

The giggle escaped from her lips before she could stop it. "Mr. Crawford, your ignorance is showing."

"Did I butcher it?" He grimaced.

"Totally." She smiled. "The name is Soilleau, and it's pronounced *swallow,* like the bird. But yes, I'm familiar with them and they are very good."

Blane smiled, flashing his teeth, and Kenley felt that rush of appreciation she'd experienced earlier. His smile softened his strong features considerably and gave him a charming boyish appearance—one more thing to guard against.

"Anything special you'd like? Or recommend?" Blane asked.

"Soilleau's is famous for their New Orleans po-boys. I'll have a roast beef."

"Sounds good to me."

Kenley watched him as he made the call. He was perched on the edge of his desk, left hand holding the receiver loosely while the right punched out the digits. Funny how she'd never really noticed his hands before. He'd held her and touched her face, but this was the first time she'd realized how long and artistic the fingers were, how broad the palm, and how the tendons on the back flexed beneath the smattering of dark hair. She remembered the warmth of them against her neck and wondered how the strong hands would feel against her flesh.

Dark eyes found hers suddenly across the desk. She blushed but didn't look away. He held her gaze a moment then hung up the phone. Had he read her mind? Could he see what she had been imagining? "They'll be here in fifteen minutes." He stood and gestured toward the table and chairs in the far corner which were littered with books and papers. "We'd better do a bit of housecleaning before our dinner arrives."

"I'll give you a hand." Kenley followed him across the room.

Blane watched her out of the corner of his eye, admiring her graceful carriage. Tonight she looked less the business manager and more the woman, despite the fact she was wearing slacks. The light gray pants draped her hips and derriere most pleasingly. The short-sleeved white blouse buttoned up the front and gapped slightly when she moved, revealing a tempting glimpse of lace underneath. But it was her hair that he admired the most. She wore it loose and curling about her shoulders. It swayed seductively when she moved, giving him ideas and an ache in his loins.

"Why don't we pull this over in front of the window?" he said quickly. His role tonight was that of a friend, not a seducer. "I've been so busy since I arrived I haven't had a chance to enjoy any New Orleans high spots. At least I can appreciate the skyline while we eat."

"Is this your first trip to New Orleans?" she asked.

Blane shook his head. "I was here once before on business but didn't have time to do any sightseeing."

"Do you do a lot of traveling in your line of work?"

The dark eyes were guarded suddenly. "I'm on the road every couple of months."

Kenley helped him carry the round table closer to the huge panes of glass. She knew better than to push him. Maybe the casual approach would bring better results. "Maybe you'll have time to explore the city after all your work is finished," she suggested. "It's a fascinating city."

"You really love New Orleans, don't you?" he observed as he positioned a chair near the table.

"Yes, it's wonderful. I'm always inspired when I walk through the French Quarter. I wish I was a poet or a writer so I could capture the magic and hold it forever. But it's such an elusive thing. Artists continually paint it, never quite getting it right but always striving to put the essence of the city on canvas."

"Who said you're not a poet?"

"Merely an admirer."

"I'd like to see your New Orleans sometime," he said quietly. There was something else reflected in the warm brown eyes, but Kenley was unable to decipher the hidden meaning.

"I'd like to show it to you."

"I'll hold you to that. You know," he said suddenly, eyebrows rising, "I never thought to ask. Just what is a po-boy, anyhow?"

Kenley smiled. "Up north they call them submarines or hoagies."

"Ahh, good. Then I'm not going to be forced to eat some bizarre local concoction."

"Oh, no," she assured him with a smile, relaxing again. "I think even a Yankee will like po-boys. You said you had some questions about D'Evereaux?" she asked as he positioned the other chair.

Blane strode back to his desk and picked up the folder. Returning to the table, he leaned over, palms resting on the flat surface.

The angle afforded Kenley a view of his bare chest beneath the white shirt. It was covered with a mat of straight dark hair, and she caught her breath, hit with the urge to run her fingers over that well-formed surface and feel the skin beneath the black hairs. The realization was like a cold, hard slap in the face. Dear God, she must be crazy, lusting like some wanton creature after a man she knew nothing about. She had to get control of herself and this power he seemed to have over her.

There was no denying that Blane was a disturbingly magnetic man. She'd known other sexually potent men, yet none screamed it so forcefully. But, she reminded herself sternly, he was still just a man with no mystical powers other than those she had assigned to him. He was very charming, but she was impervious to such things. Alva's initial assessment of Blane came crashing back to her then. She had called him the black sheep, a con man. Could there be an ulterior motive behind his charm and attentiveness? Was his supposed interest in her welfare only a ploy, a way of charming her into dropping her battle for D'Evereaux? It wouldn't be the first time she'd been played for a fool by a man. She'd taken a course from some of the best.

"I don't have anything specific in mind, just some general questions."

Kenley snapped back to reality. "Uh, fine." Well, she had something very specific in mind—keeping this association purely business. She'd slipped, gotten caught up in his prepossessing ways and forgotten her main objective: D'Evereaux. From now on Blane Crawford was just a man. She would show him that his sly tactics were no match for her skills and determination. "Ask away."

"Is there some standard procedure in these restoration/preservation things? Some guidelines?"

Inwardly she sighed with relief. At last now she was back on solid ground. Here was a safe area, one where she was in command. "No, unfortunately there isn't. Each case is different, with its own set of problems to overcome."

"So we can't look to any governing body or ruling authority to solve our problem. What about this National Register you mentioned?"

"They don't legislate," she said with a shake of her head. "They only designate. They can help owners of historic properties obtain funds and they offer guidelines for restoration, but they have no real authority.''

Blane had paced a few feet away from the table as they talked, and Kenley had watched his every move. There was something erotic in the way his hips swayed and the way his long legs stretched before him. Savagely she jerked her thoughts back into place. She couldn't afford to be this careless.

Fortunately the delivery boy from Soilleau's arrived, giving her an opportunity to regain control.

Blane thanked the man and presented a tip, then carried the large bag of food to the table. As he opened the top, the office was filled with the aroma of warm beef and hot fries. Kenley hadn't realized how hungry she was until then. "This smells wonderful.''

Blane smiled and handed her a large sandwich, brushing his fingers against hers in the process. The contact sent little prickles of fire along her nerves and called up memories of the kiss they'd shared. He was trying to cast his spell again, and she steeled herself against it. Carefully she placed the po-boy on the table, mindful to avoid his eyes and hands when he gave her the french fries a moment later. Had he noticed her reaction? She hoped not. She didn't want him to think that his kiss had affected her in any significant way.

They ate in silence for a few moments, enjoying the delicious, albeit messy, local sandwich.

Blane nodded at the folder. "Rather a large file you've put together.''

"I tried to be thorough. I wanted your father to have all the facts.'' She gave him a piercing glare across the table. "Odd that it should have been misplaced.''

"Yes, it is. I haven't searched the files at home yet. Maybe it'll turn up there.''

Or not, Kenley mused suspiciously.

"I haven't gotten very far into that,'' he said gesturing to the file again, "but I did have one thought that I'd like to toss at you. Would it be possible to put this restoration on hold for a while? I know you said time was a factor, but aren't there some stopgap measures we could use, some way to halt deterioration, say, for a year or so? I might be in a better position to help then."

"Absolutely not. It's out of the question," Kenley said brusquely. Blane looked at her sharply, and she reined in her defenses. He was only offering a suggestion. She reminded herself she still needed to be pleasant to him. "I don't mean to be uncooperative, but in a year's time D'Evereaux will be beyond saving. This isn't a piece of machinery you can jury-rig and keep running for a while. It needs to be totally redone."

"Foiled again." Blane leaned back with a sigh, trying to figure out what had come over Kenley so suddenly. One minute she had seemed relaxed and friendly, then abruptly she had withdrawn. He wished he could detect a pattern to these sudden defensive attitudes, but so far he could find no logical reason behind it. It wasn't always D'Evereaux that brought it about; sometimes it was things he said, though the significance of his words was lost to him. It made him angry, but he wasn't sure why.

They spent the rest of the meal talking about New Orleans—the best places to eat, the must-see locations, local customs and regional differences. When the food was gone, Blane poured each of them a cup of coffee and they settled back, watching the city lighting up beneath them. "So, are you ready to tell me your sad tale? Why you were dampening my papers tonight?"

The food and coffee had lulled her into a languorous state. Blane was right. He was a good listener, and she felt inclined to confide in him. She had to remind herself that he was very likely pursuing his own objectives and had little interest in hers, but that was all right. She knew how to play the game.

"I'm not sure there's enough time tonight to explain it all," she said casually. "Mostly it's just the usual job hazards—employee problems, unpaid bills, missing furniture, botched brochures, pressure from the boss. But the biggest problem is that we suddenly find ourselves without a roof over our heads."

"What happened?"

"We lost our lease." Blane tilted his head thoughtfully, and Kenley went on to explain. "Our offices were donated by a generous benefactor, and he had to back out. We've got one week to relocate." Kenley shook her head, a wry smile on her face. "My life is in utter chaos at the moment. But—" she shrugged "—I suppose it'll pass."

Blane's eyes narrowed and his voice took on a rather sharp tone. "Chaos is a tornado ripping apart a town or a hurricane on the Gulf Coast. Chaos is what a war can do to a race of people. All you have, Kenley, is a few problems at work."

Kenley wasn't sure if he was chiding her or merely making a statement. She felt like a small girl who'd been scolded for using her mother's makeup.

Looking at him, she felt a moment of misgiving. There was a hardness about him that she'd never seen before. Underneath the polished, charming exterior was a toughness, a street-smart grit, that was startling. His eyes were cold, with a strange glint in their depths she could only describe as savage.

"I don't think—" she began, only to be interrupted.

"I'm good at solving problems," he said firmly. "How much space do you need?"

Nonplussed, she took several seconds to respond. His stern attitude was gone, replaced by open, friendly concern. "Uh, a couple of rooms. Mainly for file cabinets, the phones."

"Follow me."

He rose and walked out into the reception area and down the inner hallway, stopping at a door marked "CONFERENCE." He opened it to reveal one large room with a smaller one adjoining. "Would these do?"

Kenley's eyes widened in amazement. "Well, yes, but—"

"They're yours," he said bluntly. "My contribution to CCPS and the possible rescue of the house you love so much."

She was at a loss for words. "Oh, Blane, I couldn't possibly take this. It's a generous offer, but—"

He held up his hand, forestalling her protests. "Nonsense. My father would have liked it. You'd have accepted it from him, wouldn't you?"

"Yes, of course, but—"

"Why not from me?"

Frantically she searched for the right words. "Well, because you're not, that is, you don't . . ."

He tilted his head and met her eyes. "I'm not as dedicated to the cause?"

She felt a warmth in her cheeks. "Sort of," she admitted reluctantly.

"I'm hoping you'll change that, and having you nearby will strengthen our new pact to work together. Please?" he urged softly. "I'd like to help."

Kenley thought it over. There was no logical reason to refuse. Wrong! There were dozens of reasons, not the least of which was having Blane so close each day, having to watch him at work. The attraction was too strong already. What would happen if they worked in close proximity? It would be a constant battle. Was she up to it? Of course she was. He was only a man.

"Let me think it over," she finally said. "If I can't find anything by Friday, then I'll accept your offer."

His eyes smiled. "A last resort, huh?"

"I'm sorry. I didn't mean . . ."

He shook his head. "That's okay. I understand. Just let me know."

Kenley glanced at the rooms again. They would be ideal. But they had to be her last resort. "I'd really better be going. It's late."

Silently they returned to the office, and Kenley picked up her purse and walked to the reception area. Blane stopped at his door, leaning against the frame, his hands resting easily in his pants pockets.

She turned and looked at him, unable to totally block the effectiveness of his magnetism. She wished he wouldn't look at her that way. It blurred the edges of her determination. "Thank you for dinner."

"You're welcome."

Pulling her gaze from his compelling brown eyes, she turned and started to walk to the door, only to be halted when he called her name.

"Kenley. Just to set the record straight, there are no strings attached to my donation. Those offices will be your private property. No one will trespass unless invited." The corners of his mouth moved into a sly grin. "Feel free to scream and yell about your house. No one will stop you."

Kenley felt herself smiling delightedly back at him. This was one time she didn't object to him reading her mind. "Thank you."

Blane's smile faded, and his voice deepened when he spoke. "You shouldn't have done that," he said in a threatening cool tone.

Kenley's heart chilled. "What?"

"Smiled at me. I'm not made of stone, Kenley."

She was frozen to the spot, unable to move as he approached. He studied her a moment, hands still resting in his pockets, then lowered his head and claimed her mouth. Only their lips were touching, but the contact shattered Kenley's resolution. Her inner desires sprang to life under his kiss. Suddenly his hands were holding her face and his mouth became hot and demanding. His tongue thrust inward, filling her, draining her will even as it swelled her desire. She felt his fingers moving through her hair and cradling her skull. His lips found her temple then left a blazing trail of kisses down her throat. One hand cupped her buttocks, forcing her hips against his, and she swooned at the raging heat of his body.

A voice in the back of her mind called out to beware, to fight the feelings he could so easily arouse. Abruptly he set her away from him, breaking the spell so thoroughly she was shocked. She searched his eyes but could find no explanation in them.

He stepped back and put his hands in his pockets, not trusting himself to touch her again. "Go home, Kenley."

Her mouth opened in surprise, then set firmly, as she realized he'd been playing another one of his games. She nodded, her voice dry. "Good night."

At the door she stopped when he called her name again. "Kenley, it's late. You shouldn't go to the garage alone. When you're ready to leave, call me. I'll go with you."

Kenley couldn't believe the nerve of him. Did he think just because she'd allowed him to kiss her and had confided in him about her job that he could tell her what to do? Well, she would show him just how independent she was. Keeping her features neutral, she looked back at him. "All right."

"Promise."

She hesitated only a second before nodding her head.

Back in the safety of her own small suite, she let out a grunt of disgust. How dare he assume that she needed his protection. She'd been in that garage hundreds of time and didn't need his strong male arm tonight. Angrily she closed up for the night, locking the office door and striding down the hallway. Fortunately Blane was nowhere to be seen. It wouldn't have surprised her to find him waiting at the elevator. She jabbed the button. Let him wait all night for the call. That would teach him.

Blane didn't really expect Kenley to call. He'd seen the eyes cloud with determination. "Damn," he muttered as he went back into his office. His blood was still singing from the feel of her in his hands. He wanted to drown in the sweet, fragrant silk of her hair, wrap his arms and legs around the silken skin, and feel the sweet sheathing of her body.

Drawing a ragged breath, he set his jaw. He'd moved too fast, let his needs overcome his better judgment. He'd have to keep his own desires on a tight leash if he wanted to get closer to her. He looked out at the twinkling lights of New Orleans. Closer? Hell, if he had a brain in his head he'd lock himself up in this office and never see Kenley again. She deserved more than he could ever give her. Hadn't Yvonne and Debbi made that abundantly clear to him? Evidently not, because he couldn't shake the feelings he knew were growing for Kenley, and what was worse, he wasn't entirely sure he wanted to.

Chapter Six

In the end Kenley was forced to accept Blane's offer. Locating another suitable facility on such short notice had proved futile. Her better judgment told her it was a mistake to put herself in easy reach of his charms, but her common sense recognized the practicality of the situation. Besides, she was sure she could keep things under control. In a somewhat perverted way, the irony of the situation amused her. She would be using space in his office to try and save a house she wanted that he owned.

She had wanted to share that convoluted fact with him, but he'd been all but invisible since she'd told him she would appreciate the space in his suite of offices. He'd graciously sent over two of his employees to help them move in and even sent a live plant in the name of Crawford Plastics as an office-warming gift.

But they had been in their new location for nearly a week now and she'd had only a glimpse of Blane as he came and went through the Crawford Plastics headquarters.

Kenley told herself she wasn't disappointed, only relieved. He'd made it clear that their space would be sacrosanct and that he'd not interfere in any way. It was best. She had agreed. They both had jobs to maintain, and it was best to keep their careers strictly divided.

When Kenley returned to her office after lunch, she had trouble concentrating on her work. There'd been so many changes lately, so much upheaval in her life, that she couldn't decide what to tackle first. The walls felt as though they were closing in around her. There was a mound of work on her desk, but she had little enthusiasm for it today. What she really wanted to do was drive upriver and visit D'Evereaux. Southern Louisiana was in the midst of an unusually pleasant few days. The normal scorching heat of early September had subsided temporarily. It was a clear, balmy day, and a soft breeze drifted around the city of New Orleans. It was the kind of day to be outside enjoying fresh air and the wide-open spaces. From the back of her mind she recalled Blane's voice wondering if she ever gave in to impulse. She had told him no. But now she decided to show him that she could follow a whim now and again. Let him be the one off balance for a change. After a cryptic explanation to Alva, Kenley was out of the building and heading up I-10 in record time.

The weather was so lovely she turned off the air conditioner and opened all the windows in her small car. The fresh air swirled around her, gradually easing all the coiled-up tension of the last weeks. She allowed her mind to drift with the scenery, not focusing on any one particular thing.

By the time she arrived in Mossville, she felt calmer and more relaxed than she had in months. As she drove up the long, winding road to the plantation, she smiled. It was like traveling back in time. She could easily envision the carriages and stunning horses that had preceded her down this path a hundred years earlier.

The driveway veered to the left, affording a picturesque view of D'Evereaux at the end of the avenue of live oaks.

Her heart swelled as she took in the lovely scene. D'Evereaux stood like some tragic, fading queen, a relic from the romantic past, whose grandeur was steadily waning with the onslaught of time. Her once pristine columns were now darkened with mildew; glassless windows looked out toward the river, emptied of all hope. Others, their shutters closed tight against the ruthless Louisiana climate, were like an ugly blemish upon her beautiful facade. Vines of kudzu twined around the base of each column, the insidious tendrils spreading over the railings and across the galleries like a deadly cancer.

The once pale pink walls of the old plantation had been bleached white with the passing of time and large fragments had fallen away revealing the rough handmade bricks underneath. Marching across her battered roof were three arched dormers. But the crowning glory of the old plantation was an ornate glass belvedere that perched like a tarnished tiara on the Grand Lady's head.

Framing the vision of decaying elegance were gigantic live oaks. Gray moss, like sinister cobwebs, hung heavily from the thick limbs. Kenley refused to believe all this would have to die to make way for progress.

She parked her car near the ruins of an old carriage house and strolled leisurely toward the house. In her mind's eye, she could see it as it used to be—green lawns, flowers, the white pillars glistening in the sunlight, the scent of magnolias dancing lightly on the breeze. Reality, however, presented another picture.

The plantation was badly in need of repair and restoration, though the damage already done was well within the boundaries of salvage. It would take time and considerable amounts of money to put the decaying building back to its former position of grandeur.

Time was the greater enemy now. The years of neglect were reaching a point of no return. If the house wasn't attended to within the next few years, it would be beyond even the most wealthy of patrons and the most skillful of artisans to retrieve.

Kenley found herself walking out on what had been the expansive green lawn. It was now a tangle of weeds and broken tree limbs. As she meandered absently between the gnarled oaks whose branches hung nearly to the ground, her heart ached for the old home that seemed to be the tangible embodiment of all her romantic fantasies. She wondered, not for the first time, if she perhaps had lived a previous life as a plantation belle. But then, most young girls dreamed of the romantic antebellum days of *Gone With the Wind*. As a historian, she knew those days weren't nearly as romantic and carefree as the movies depicted, but that didn't diminish her own dreams.

She'd promised herself she wouldn't think about serious matters today, not while she was here. But as she strolled around the ruins, thoughts of Blane kept creeping into the corners of her mind.

Why did she have these confused feelings toward him? She was attracted to him and frightened by him at the same time. One minute she was thrilling to his touch, coming alive under his kiss. The next minute she was hearing warning bells. All she really had to go on were vague suspicions and a hard-earned mistrust of the unknown. Better to be safe than sorry.

There was much going on behind those brown eyes that she couldn't decipher. That arched eyebrow—was it skeptical or merely amused? He always spoke quietly, slowly. Was that because he was measuring his words, or was it simply his normal unhurried manner? Did he sincerely want to work together to save D'Evereaux or was he only seeking to prevent a battle of wills?

So many questions with no answers. His marriage—what had happened? Those two years—where had he been?

Then yesterday, more questions to add to the growing list. She'd come to work early, hoping to speak with him about D'Evereaux. Faithful Edith Pohl was gone—retired—and in her place was a lithesome blonde named Carla Nichols. When Kenley asked to see Blane, Carla had informed her that Mr. Crawford would be unavailable on Wednesdays from now on. Kenley had pressed her for more information, but Carla would only say that he would be occupied with his "other business."

So damn many questions.

Kenley stopped under the shade of one of the live oaks, reminding herself that she and Blane had only known each other a couple of weeks. Questions were inevitable and perfectly natural. Still the bells persisted softly in the back of her mind. She couldn't afford any more surprises in her relationships, even ones that were strictly business.

Vaguely she became aware of a car approaching in the distance. The sound grew louder and she realized it was coming up the road to D'Evereaux. Retracing her steps, she was halfway back to the drive when a black sports car pulled up next to hers. A man emerged, and she was startled to see Blane walking toward her. She met him on the back lawn.

"Good morning." He grinned. "Did you know you can see the driveway of D'Evereaux from my office in the plant?"

"No, I didn't. I've never been inside the plant."

"You'll have to visit. I've got a wonderful aerial view of the property."

"So what brings you to the relic?" she asked, using his own description.

"Ouch." He winced good-naturedly. "Two things. First, you."

Kenley felt her heart skip again. What did he want with her? Why did he have to look so handsome, with the breeze stirring his dark hair and the full sunlight deepening the bronze of his skin?

"Second, I thought it was time I explored the source of your passion."

For a moment Kenley thought he was still speaking personally. Perhaps he was. There was a devilish glint in his dark eyes. She decided to take the safer side of his double entendre. "I've been looking forward to giving you a tour of D'Evereaux. Where would you like to start?"

"You're the guide." He gestured for her to lead the way, and they walked slowly across the lawn. "How are the new offices working out?" he asked after a brief silence.

"Perfectly, thank you. We made the transition with very few snags. Thank you for the loan of your men to help us move."

"My pleasure."

"And the planter you sent was lovely and very thoughtful."

"I wanted you to feel welcome." He sounded sincere. "I hope the employees aren't bothering you. I didn't want you to feel as if you were imposing in any way."

"No, not at all. They've just been friendly and a bit curious." She paused, slipping her hands into the pockets of her denim dress. "Is that why you've been avoiding the office? To keep us from feeling uncomfortable?" Would he give her an honest answer?

He looked her directly in the eyes. "I told you I'd give you total privacy. I may be donating the space in my suite, but as far as I'm concerned, those offices are a world unto themselves."

"Thank you." She didn't know what else to say. Quietly they moved on. Blane seemed very friendly and accommodating today and she decided to ask him outright the things she wanted to know. Though she started with the least important. "You have a new secretary."

"Yes, Carla." He nodded. "She'll be a real asset to me."

"I tried to see you yesterday, but she said you won't be working on Wednesdays. Don't tell me you're keeping doctors' hours already and go golfing once a week."

"Do I look like a golfer?"

"You look like a great many things, but not a golfer."

His smile was slow and enigmatic. "We'll get into that later. On Wednesdays I have other matters that need looking after. It's usually a slow day at CP, so I spend the time elsewhere.''

"Your service promotion business, perhaps?" Kenley felt Blane withdraw slightly.

"Yes."

"You know, since that day in the elevator I've been wondering about your other job. Just what do you do besides save plastics plants and claustrophobic females?"

Blane took a long moment to answer. "I'm not sure you would be interested in the details. It's a very narrow field. Few people can understand the finer points. Nothing as romantic and glamorous as what you do."

"Are you successful?" she persisted.

"Reasonably."

"Ahh," Kenley drawled knowingly. "That means you make a lot of money at it."

"I make a comfortable living," he answered. "But I'm not into all this yuppie stuff. Most of the money I make goes toward more important things."

She nodded. "Translation, back into your business."

Blane turned and looked at her, his eyes filled with amusement. "All these questions about my business. Are you by any chance inquiring if I can support you in the manner to which you've been accustomed?"

"Good heavens, no!" she yelped. This was not the direction she had intended the conversation to go.

He smiled. "The answer is, probably not."

"I could care less," she stammered, trying to recover.

"I'm not in a position to purchase antique furniture and a hundred-year-old town house in the French Quarter."

"Well, to tell the truth," Kenley said slowly, "most of the antiques belong to Alva. Only a few of them are actually mine. But I take it you're not into the material side of life?"

His expression was stern when he looked at her. "I don't put more importance on things than people."

Kenley felt herself bristle. Was he trying to goad her into a fight? "Things, meaning D'Evereaux."

"It is, after all, an inanimate object. Historic or not, only a handful of people will derive any pleasure from it."

"Your opinion again."

"No. That's a fact."

Kenley put a firm hold on her anger. She wasn't going to lose control. "The fact is that you're hostile to any idea that doesn't conform to your interpretation of important. Isn't Crawford Plastics basically a thing? Are you saving it for the people of New Orleans or your family pride?"

Blane turned and smiled at her, tilting his head, his eyes warm with affection. "Always so quick to do battle whenever your house is maligned. I didn't come here to fight, Kenley."

"Then why did you come?" she asked.

"Temptation. I saw your car pull into the drive and caught a glimpse of you among the trees and—" he shrugged "—suddenly, I couldn't concentrate any longer." He stopped looking directly into her eyes. "Do you always ask so many questions?"

"I'm curious about you," Kenley admitted frankly.

He grinned, touching the tip of her nose with one finger. "Always the direct approach with you. All right, I'm thirty-nine years old, an only child. Grew up in Columbus, have degrees from Ohio State in psychology and business administration. Worked for my father, then left to start my own business. Mr. Joe Average. Right now I'm in the middle of nowhere with an extremely attractive woman at my side. Her hair is glistening in the sunlight, her eyes rival the blue sky and the dimples in her cheeks are begging to be kissed."

"Blane..."

"Hush." He whispered, stepping closer. "I've been wanting to hold you from the moment I got here." He reached out and pulled her into his arms.

Kenley told herself not to let this happen. There were things she needed to know, questions she needed answered about D'Evereaux, his job, his past. But when he looked at her with that smoldering gaze, her blood stirred and she had trouble thinking clearly. Purely a chemical reaction, but powerful, nonetheless.

He kissed her slowly, deliberately, as if gauging her response. He tasted her upper lip and pulled away. Teasingly he moved his lips over hers, then stopped again. She felt his tongue brush against her teeth, then disappear. He was tormenting her with his slowness, and she ached to taste fully of him, as before. Her arms encircled his neck, pulling his head down, seeking his mouth, making her own survey. Her fingers played with the hair on his neck, and her body arched against his. She was on fire, her knees were weak and there was a stirring deep in the center of her being that frightened and excited her at the same time. She heard a whimper and realized it was her own.

Only his arms, strong and secure, held her erect. She was lost, caught in a whirlwind of need unlike anything she'd ever experienced. Alarms were set off and she pushed away, breathless and swaying slightly from the sudden release. She moved away, one hand on her burning cheeks. "We've got to stop. It's all moving too fast, too fast."

"Yes, it is," he agreed quietly.

"There's just so much going on in my life right now, so much confusion. And in the middle of it all is this . . ." She couldn't bring herself to admit that she was attracted to him. She wasn't ready to give him that kind of power over her. "I need time to sort it out."

"I think I understand," he said calmly, releasing her. "In the meantime, why don't you give me the tour? If you're up to it." He smiled inwardly when Kenley's jaw set and her chin came up. He never tired of seeing that fire in her eyes.

"Of course I am." She walked off in the direction of the house.

He grinned and followed. He'd deliberately taunted her with his kiss, wanting to see how she would respond. Now he knew. She wanted him as much as he wanted her, though she wasn't ready to admit it yet. She had been ready to flee, but his dig at her emotional state had kept her here. That was fine. He was in no hurry. After all, he was only looking for some pleasant diversion, nothing serious.

As he followed her up onto the veranda, pushing aside the overgrown bushes, he couldn't help noticing that the undergrowth seemed much thicker on the south side of the long porch. "Looks like Mother Nature is trying to reclaim your house, Kenley."

She turned and came back to the edge of the crumbling veranda. "That's the main reason we can't wait long to start renovation—poor drainage. The house used to sit on a slight incline, and the water would all drain away toward the river. Then twenty-five years ago when the plant was built the excavation totally rerouted the natural watershed. As a result, the rain collects on this side of the house where the earth has settled. Since it doesn't drain off and takes longer to evaporate, over the years it has seriously undermined the foundation."

"Sounds like an easy problem to correct. Just put in a few trenches to drain off the excess."

A mischievous twinkle appeared in her clear blue eyes. "I intended to, but the new owner refused. He made me halt preliminary preservation work, citing the practicality of a moratorium on all work and assessments. He said it would save me time and wasted money."

Blane recalled their first meeting and his rather cold-hearted, uninformed solutions. "You don't believe in being tactful, do you?" he grumbled good-naturedly.

"Only when it's necessary," she smirked.

"Twist those screws."

Kenley smiled. "You seem able to take the heat."

Starting her tour in the center hall of the house, she pointed out various details and gave Blane a brief history of the old plantation. "There's an old man who lives near the back of the property who keeps an eye on things. His great-grandfather was caretaker here at one time."

Blane couldn't help commenting on the large assortment of furniture still in the rooms.

"Yes, it's really a wonderful stroke of lagniappe. We can use many of these pieces when the house is restored."

Blane frowned. "A stroke of what?"

Kenley laughed. "Lagniappe. *Lan-yap.* It means a little something extra."

As they walked through the rooms, the debris scattered across the floor crunched loudly beneath their feet.

Kenley explained about the dangerous conditions in the upstairs bedroom and how rain coming in through the holes in the roof had already rotted the pine floors.

"This side of the house is in excellent condition. Even the ceiling medallions and plasterwork are in perfect shape. But this is the most outstanding feature." She stopped beside the huge winding staircase. "Stand beneath it," she urged.

He did and looked upward. From this vantage point, he could see the stairs spiraling three floors above him.

"Isn't it spectacular? It's the most perfectly engineered staircase in the South. Theory has it that the treads and risers are so perfectly balanced that the entire staircase could stand alone without support of any kind."

She looked over to find Blane staring at her with a smile on his handsome face. "What are you smiling at?"

"You. Do you have any idea what a transformation takes place when you're talking about this house."

Kenley blushed. "No."

"It's magical. One minute you're this cool, determined businesswoman, and the next, an excited child on Christmas morning. Why don't you let people see this side of you more often? It's very becoming, very alluring."

His words had a sobering effect. "How much could I accomplish, being alluring?"

"More than you think."

"Use my feminine wiles to gain my objective? Now you're beginning to sound like Alva. Where would my feminist friends be today, if we still relied on fluttering eyelashes?"

"I'm not talking about coyness," he corrected, coming to her side. "Don't confuse femininity with feminine games, but don't be afraid to let people see your softer side. It won't undermine your credibility."

"What makes you so sure?"

He took a deep breath before answering. "I'm a Renaissance man. I've been through the Dark Ages and seen the light." Kenley wondered at his choice of words, but he stopped inside a huge archway, and turned to her with a question in his eyes and she was forced to go on with her tour.

"And this is the ballroom. Few homes of this period had a room set aside for that purpose. It and the staircase are what make this house unique.

"Through those glass doors at the foot of the stairs is a large conservatory. It's much newer than the rest of the house, but it was a perfect addition to the ballroom. The original owner introduced his three daughters to New Orleans society here. It must have been a magnificent sight, all those hoopskirts and the candlelight, romantic tête-à-têtes in the coolness of the conservatory."

Blane watched the glow in her eyes as she spoke. "I'd like to see you in one of those full dresses, swirling around the room with a handsome gentleman on your arm."

She laughed lightly. "Anyone in particular? General P. G. T. Beauregard, or perhaps some dashing young lieutenant?"

"I was thinking about a certain Yankee I know rather well."

"Oh, I don't know about that. He'd have to be a very important Yankee. A wealthy businessman or a planter who has moved to the South to make his fortune."

He stepped closer. "How about a hard-working man with only noble thoughts to recommend him?"

"Perhaps. If the thoughts were noble enough." She felt herself being drawn under his spell again. Blane pulled her into his arms and slowly balanced back and forth then turned into a slow impromptu dance around the room. His eyes never left hers and she felt transported, as if she had indeed returned to another era. They moved in unison, as though they'd always danced together. His eyes commanded her full attention, expectantly—as if searching for some answer in her own. But what was it he wanted to know? She had no answers to give him yet. "You waltz?" she finally blurted out.

The eyes softened and he smiled. "I was the only child of a doting mother. She wanted me to learn to do everything, including how to dance. Until now I never appreciated the ability."

"I'm very grateful to her," Kenley said softly, turning herself over to the floating sensation she felt in his arms. She wanted it to go on forever, this little fantasy. She looked into his eyes and felt that magnetic pull, as if an invisible taut wire ran between them that reverberated each time their eyes met. It was a surrealist sensation, almost mystical. But this wasn't a fantasy. This was real life and real life meant real obstacles.

"Why do you do that?" he asked when he sensed her sudden shift in mood. It had suddenly hit him that what he kept seeing in Kenley's eyes was wariness and fear. But fear of what?

"Do what?"

"Shut me out?"

"I'm not. I'm merely being cautious."

"About me? About the attraction we feel?" he guessed.

"I've been attracted to other men before. It doesn't mean anything."

"That's not an answer. What are you afraid will happen between us? Are you against some pleasant evenings, some conversation—" he touched her cheek "—a few stolen kisses?"

"Of course not. I just don't want to get caught up in something that can never go beyond this."

"Why can't it?"

"I have too many questions about you and I don't like that."

"A romantic like you, and you aren't fond of a little mystery? Especially where a man is concerned? Now that surprises me. I would have thought you were more daring."

"Not with relationships."

"Do we have a relationship?"

"No."

"Would you like to have one?"

Kenley shifted her weight, turning her eyes toward the house. How did he do this? How did he always manage to put her in a position where she had to be on the offensive when she wanted it the other way around. How was she supposed to answer that question? If she said yes, she would seem as though she was chasing him. If she said no, then she'd come off as a tease. "Would you?"

"I think so. I seem to find myself thinking about you more than I should. I know I want to be with you. I want to hold you. I know we're just getting to know each other. But you admitted you have no private life. All work and no play makes Kenley a dull little girl. We're a man and a woman who are attracted to each other. There's nothing unusual about that. Why don't you just relax, let things evolve naturally? You might be surprised at the results."

"You mean throw caution to the wind? I did that once. I dropped my guard and ignored the practicalities, and I paid dearly for the mistake. I can't risk a repeat performance."

"The prince who found another princess?" he guessed.

Kenley glared. What right did he have to ask that of her? But wasn't that what she was doing? Digging into his past. Maybe if she opened a few doors on her side he would be more willing to reciprocate. Wrapping her arms around her waist she walked to the window, the space between them a comforting barrier. "When I was in college, I lived with a guy for two years. I'd always assumed marriage was down the road, but we never talked about it then. My last year of school, Russ convinced me to drop out and go to work so he could concentrate full-time on his studies. Then after he graduated and got a good job he'd pay for my tuition and I could go back.''

Blane rubbed his forehead with his fingers. It wasn't a new story. "Let me guess. He walked out on you after graduation."

Kenley stared straight ahead, her blue eyes clouded. "A week later he married someone else. He'd been seeing her for a long time, right under my nose, and I never suspected. I thought I knew him. I sincerely believed that there was total honesty between us. No surprises." She turned back to him, eyes clear and steady. "I'll not enter another relationship blind."

"I'm sorry you were hurt. But just because one man treated you badly doesn't mean others will. Feelings and emotions have a mind of their own. They just happen. You can't summon up an attraction for someone just because he has no secrets, no hidden motives."

Her blue eyes fairly crackled. "And what about the pain and heartache? What's your theory on eliminating that?"

Blane spread his hands wide. "You don't eliminate it. It's part of the package. You can't get through life without a few good punches in the gut. How else could you appreciate the value of things, if you don't feel the disillusionment of the mistakes?"

Kenley crossed her arms over her chest and gnawed on her bottom lip angrily. "I try and learn from my mistakes. Apparently you don't or can't. Was your divorce so painless that you can't see why I'm so reluctant to let go?" The words were out before she could stop them, and she regretted them instantly. "Oh, Blane, I'm sorry," she said reaching out her hand. "I had no right to say that. Please forgive me. I get so defensive sometimes that I speak without thinking."

"Where did you hear about that?"

Guilt, like a freight train, slammed into her. Now she had to admit to him that she had snooped, pried into his past behind his back. Worse yet, that she had listened to idle gossip. "Alva heard talk in your office. If it's a secret..." she started to say.

"No, not at all. It happened a long time ago and lasted a very short time."

Kenley thought she heard a sadness in his voice. "I'm sorry. Would you like to talk about it?"

"You want to hear about my marriage?" He shrugged. "Her name was Yvonne. She assumed I'd work at Crawford Plastics for the rest of my life earning a nice fat paycheck. I hated it. When I quit to start my own business she found the sudden drop in my tax bracket unacceptable and walked out."

"Why? I don't understand?"

"Let's just say she wasn't fond of my...avocation. We divorced, and I haven't seen or heard from her since. A mutually satisfactory arrangement." His eyes were black now as he looked at her. "And yes, it was very painful."

Kenley felt ashamed of herself. She hadn't intended to force Blane to dredge up any pain. All she wanted were some answers. It wasn't supposed to be this way. It was supposed to be a nice, calm discussion. "I'm sorry. I..." She didn't know what to say to him.

Blane felt his irritation fade the moment he looked into Kenley's eyes. She wasn't being intentionally thoughtless and she hadn't meant to pry. All she wanted were some answers to some very normal questions. Only he wasn't a normal person with a normal past. And he had to protect his business. There was more at stake than just his personal attraction toward Kenley. He had other people to consider. People who had a right to some privacy. He wasn't ready to tell her everything she wanted to know. Not yet. Not until he was sure of her, of her feelings about him, about other things. If he told her the truth now, she might walk away— or worse, try to turn his mission against him as Debbi had done. If he had to give her up, then he wanted to put it off as long as possible. There might not be a future for them, but there was a present, and right now he wanted that. As much and for as long as he could have it. "Any more questions?"

"No," she said, staring at the floor.

Reaching out he enfolded her in his arms, covering her mouth with his. But this time she didn't give in to the sweet sensation, remembering how easy it would be to let her attraction get out of hand. She pulled away, smiling, yet avoiding his gaze. What would she see there? Anger, disappointment, or something she wasn't ready to deal with?

"We'd better get back. I left a desk full of work. I think I've played hooky long enough."

"You don't play hooky often, do you?" he asked as they turned their steps toward the front hall.

"No."

"No, I don't imagine you do."

Kenley glanced over at him. "What do you mean?"

"It's not efficient. Far too carefree."

"You don't think I'm carefree?" she asked.

"Do you?" he countered, eyebrow arched in challenge.

"I can be. But carefree is asking for trouble."

"Carefree gives your heart a nice glow."

"Efficient gets me further. Efficiency will save this house. It's saved others before."

Blane sighed in defeat. "Your only true passion in life."

Kenley turned and looked up at the frieze lining the ceiling. The craftsmanship, skill and artistry were all evident in the old house, despite its battered condition. "I am passionate about the plantations I save. Look at the workmanship, Blane. The attention to detail, the love put into it. Houses were reflections of their builders' emotions, their imaginations. Each one was unique, not like today where every subdivision looks just like the next. They just don't make them like this anymore. What do you see when you look at this house?"

Blane glanced around him. "I see a barn. Impossible to heat or cool, in deplorable condition, beyond repair, an eyesore. But I'll take your word for it. Anything that puts that light in your eyes has to have some value."

"Now you're patronizing."

"Never. I might not understand your love for this place, but that doesn't mean I don't respect it."

Kenley decided this was a good opportunity to bring up a discovery she'd made recently. "I found something you might be interested in."

"Oh?"

"There's a piece of property for sale just about a mile up the road from your plant. It's a little more than a hundred acres, and the price is very reasonable, considering." She watched his reaction anxiously.

"Why would I be interested in land?"

He didn't look angry so she pressed on. "Well, I thought that perhaps you could build your new plant there instead of on the D'Evereaux property."

"Out of the question," Blane said sharply.

"Well, you could have at least considered it," she barked bitterly. "You've rejected the idea without even thinking about it."

"I have thought about it. I'm familiar with the property you're referring to, and the answer is still the same. No. It would be totally impractical."

"They're only a mile apart," she said between clenched teeth.

"It would defeat the purpose of building the new facility. The whole point is to tie the old and the new together to make a more efficient and productive operation." He tried to keep the irritation from his voice but failed. "How productive could it be with half of it a mile up the road?"

Kenley's eyes snapped in anger. "I see. It's more practical to raze D'Evereaux than inconvenience anyone."

"It's gone beyond that," he explained. His patience was strained. "Everything is set up—the loans, the tradesmen. The excavation begins in a little over two weeks."

"You'll get no sympathy from me." Kenley replied stiffly.

"I told you I'd be fair, that I'd consider all the options. I have a three-month postponement clause I can use, if—and I stress if—we can find a valid reason for it."

"And just what would you call a valid reason?"

He waved his hand. "I don't know. That's your area, remember? You're the one with all the expertise in saving old houses. Look, Kenley, I'd consider the three-month extension, but we've got to find a better reason than just your love for this house."

"This is absolutely ridiculous."

"Kenley, I'm not the enemy here, remember?"

Kenley's eyes narrowed. Sparks were flying behind the icy blue orbs. "Aren't you?"

He grabbed her arm, forcing her to turn around.

"Blane, please."

"Listen to me. We were having a nice time until we started talking about the future of this damned house. Don't let it come between us now. We aren't going to solve the problem today. Let's put it aside for the time being."

"Ignoring the problem won't make it go away, Blane."

"But battling over it won't, either."

He had a point. Besides, she had been enjoying herself. It was her own fault the afternoon was ruined because she'd insisted on discussing D'Evereaux's fate. Still, the house was her primary concern right now. "I'm sorry. I just wish . . ."

"What?"

"Everything would be perfect, if it weren't for Crawford Plastics and D'Evereaux. Well, almost perfect."

"Almost?" he questioned.

But Kenley decided to let it drop. "Never mind," she said.

They made their way back to the carriage house, and suddenly Kenley stopped. Blane's car was sitting beside hers.

Her eyes widened and a smile crossed her lips, making the dimples pop out. "Is that yours?"

"Yes, of course. Why?"

"Oh, good grief." She burst out laughing, leaning against the car and shaking her head. Her laughter was infectious, and although Blane didn't understand the cause of her mirth, he couldn't help but smile. Besides, he'd never seen her so uninhibited. It was a heart-stopping sight. When Kenley laughed, she positively glowed. "What's so funny?"

"I never noticed...what kind...it's so—" Giggles interrupted her explanation.

"So what?"

"Old."

"Old? What, my car?"

Kenley nodded, grinning from ear to ear delightedly.

"I'll have you know that's a 1965 Shelby Mustang GT350!" He informed her proudly.

"1965." Her peals of laughter began anew.

"That car will beat anything new off the line." Blane couldn't for the life of him see any humor in his prized possession. "Kenley..."

"I'm sorry," she apologized, eyes still filled with amusement. "But don't you see?"

"See what?"

Kenley turned and pointed to the car. "It's old."

"So?"

She shook her head, smiling broadly. "Why do you have it?"

"Because it's a classic, and I like old cars. A Mustang isn't just a car, it's a state of mind. They don't make—"

"Make them like that anymore," she said along with him, laughing again.

Blane finally realized what was so funny. Hadn't she said almost the same thing to him not five minutes ago, regarding her feeling for the plantation? "Damn. I'm an idiot," he said, setting his jaw.

Kenley nodded, still thoroughly amused. "I've been struggling to make you understand my passion for these old houses, and you already have a passion for old cars."

"I never made the connection." Blane looked back at D'Evereaux. "Well done, Miss Farrell. You've scored a direct hit."

Kenley bit her lower lip in an attempt to halt the giggles that were swelling up again. "Maybe I won't have to struggle so hard from now on."

His eyes were warm and caressing when he replied. "You never had to struggle against me."

The giggles suddenly lodged in her throat, cutting off her air. "Oh, but I do," she said decisively. "If I didn't struggle, then I might lose myself in you and I have to avoid that at all costs." Her eyes held his, watching the questions forming in the black depths, and she turned and climbed into her car before he could ask them. She had a lot to think about before she saw him again.

Dave was stretched out on the sofa in the far corner of the plant office when Blane returned. "Boning up on your history?" he inquired.

"Crash course," Blane smiled.

"You seem to be spending a lot of time with the plantation lady. Business or pleasure?" he asked, getting to his feet and strolling to the desk.

"Both."

"Just how serious is this?"

"Who said it was?"

"I've known you a long time. I recognize the symptoms." Dave stared grimly at his friend. "You know she's looking for roots and a long-term commitment, don't you? I've seen the type before. That's not for you."

"How do you know? Maybe it is . . . now."

"Now? What do you mean now?" Dave leaned his elbows on the tabletop, his green eyes darkening. "Are you actually going to run your dad's company? Stay here and dabble in plastics the rest of your life? Throw away all we've done? The connections, the backups? Damn it, man, we've got a network better than the government and you want to give that up for Crawford Plastics?''

"No. Not give it up," he said evenly. "Maybe just move it. Get Crawford Plastics on its feet and sell out, but move our headquarters here and run the operation from New Orleans."

"Here? Now I know you're crazy. You must be having a mid-life crisis or something. Why don't you take a quick trip to the Virgin Islands with a nice dumb blonde and raise a little hell?"

"I don't want to raise hell. At least not with a dumb blonde."

"With Kenley," Dave said flatly. "I figured as much."

Blane gave his friend a warning glance. "Don't you think you should at least meet the lady before you start making judgments?"

"You're right. I'll go and introduce myself as soon as I can break away from your fascinating accounting office. But," he added, easing into a chair, "that does bring up another point. I haven't forgotten the last time your affections were involved, Blane. I remember what you went through." Dave stared at his friend. "You haven't told her yet what you do for a living, have you?"

"No. Not specifically, but I'll tell her soon. When the time is right."

"Let me give you a little warning here, pal. She'd better learn it from you. I can't keep the press at bay forever, you know, and that means sooner or later she's going to pick up a newspaper or a magazine, maybe catch the feature segment of the evening news and then you'll really be in a mess."

"I know. But there are other obstacles in the way at the moment."

"D'Evereaux," Dave said in disgust. "I'm beginning to hate that place. Almost as much as I hate Crawford Plastics."

"I'm not enjoying the job, either, but I can't just walk away."

"I know. You and your twisted sense of honor."

Blane shot Dave an icy glare.

"I didn't mean that."

He brushed the apology aside. "I can't destroy something she cares about so much without making certain there's no other solution."

Dave leaned back, sighing loudly. "Well, if there's a way to save it, I can't find it. I've been over every angle."

"So has Kenley. She suggested I move the new plant to a different location."

"See? Even she's getting desperate." Dave rose and walked to the door. "Hey Blane, about Kenley. I was serious about filling her in on what we do. The longer you put it off, the harder it'll be. On both of you."

"I know. I'll tell her at the first opportunity. Satisfied?"

There was an uncustomarily serious note in Dave's voice. "If you don't, I will. Times have changed. People don't feel the way they did when we started. There's a new understanding and tolerance for guys like us."

"I'm aware of that, Dave. But I guess old habits die hard."

Green eyes met brown levelly. "Kenley isn't Yvonne."

Blane nodded, a thoughtful frown settling on his face. No, Kenley wasn't Yvonne—or Debbi, for that matter. But Kenley's reaction to his business might be the least of his worries. He was building a nice little trap for himself with her. She demanded truth and honesty, but he'd already told her a string of half truths. How could he tell her about his job now? How could he explain his reluctance to be open and frank, when she had made it clear that was her criterion for a relationship? There was that word again. He wasn't looking for any long-term associations. But then, just what did he want with Kenley? Finding the answer to that question might take more time than he had.

Chapter Seven

The balmy weather still blessed the city Saturday morning when Kenley awoke. It had been a long, rough week, and for the first time in two months she was totally free of commitments and looking forward to spending the day being lazy and totally idle. After a quick shower, she grabbed a faded pair of khaki shorts and slipped into a cool top.

Glancing in the mirror, she couldn't help but be pleased by the drastic change in her image today. The tailored businesswoman had been replaced by someone who looked as though she was preparing to hold a car wash. Her blouse was oversized and splattered with bleach spots. The shorts were threadbare but comfortable and showed off her legs. Kenley frowned at herself. Not exactly the sleek limbs of a professional dancer. She'd always envied women with long, seemingly endless legs. Hers were just . . . legs. Not too fat, not too thin. They functioned properly and they held her body up, but there was nothing spectacular about them.

In fact, her whole figure was more rounded and curvy, reminiscent of an earlier era rather than the boyish silhouette of today. Her reflection smiled. So what? She was in such a good mood today even her figure flaws couldn't depress her. Besides, word from the fashion front hinted that the anorexic look was passé and that the more voluptuous shape was in vogue again. Models everywhere were actually gaining ten pounds. She looked heavenward and mouthed a silent "thank you."

Fairly bounding down the stairs, she fixed coffee and toast, then settled herself into a cushioned chaise lounge in the courtyard. The smell of crape myrtle wafted around her head, and a gentle breeze ruffled her hair. She felt totally alive and confident. There was even an odd sensation of anticipation, the kind she used to get before going to the amusement park or the state fair.

Closing her eyes, she leaned her head back against the cushion and let the peaceful morning lull her into a dreamlike state. As was becoming her custom, her free moments seemed to be filled rather quickly with thoughts of Blane. There was still so much to sort out about the man, not the least of which was that he was handsome, kind, thoughtful, gentle and understanding. She also had a fascination with watching him move—the way his legs and hips swiveled seductively as he walked from one room to the next, and the way his shoulders would turn when he opened a door. Kenley's giggles broke the quiet of the small courtyard. Good grief, she was behaving like a teenager again.

Sipping her coffee, she smiled as the music from her radio played softly in the background. She was only half listening when the music segued into a weather report of the storm in the Gulf. The tropical wave had become a tropical storm, and it was hovering out in the Gulf, gaining strength and speed. It looked as though Louisiana's luck had run out. They were going to get their first hurricane of the season.

While she was pondering the hazards of life on the Gulf Coast, the buzzer at her front gate sounded. Who could be here on Saturday morning? Alva was out of town and there were few others who would stop by her home without calling first. She glanced at her scruffy attire. Even her hair was in a wild state, pulled back haphazardly with a clip. She looked a mess. The buzzer sounded again and she peeked cautiously around the corner trying to catch a glimpse of her unexpected caller. "Blane!"

"Good morning," he called, his deep voice rumbling slightly down the outside hallway that separated her building from the one next door.

Kenley quickly hurried to the gate, unable to keep from smiling as she opened it. Despite her disheveled state, she was ridiculously glad to see him. "Hello. You're out and about early."

Blane leaned against the ornate cast-iron bars and tilted his head toward her, his eyes caressing her in a way that made her blood warm. "I'm on business."

"Sounds serious."

"It might be."

"Then by all means, come in."

He followed her to the courtyard, watching the sway of her hips as she went before him and thinking how her casual clothes and tousled hair made her look younger and disarmingly childlike. She was the most lovely and adorable thing he'd ever seen. And it was getting damned difficult to maintain a safe detachment.

"Sit down. I'll get you something to drink," she said cheerfully.

"Sorry, no time."

"Oh?" She nearly choked on her disappointment.

"I want to hire you."

His statement puzzled her, but she couldn't read anything in the dark eyes. "Me?"

Blane rested his elbows on the arms of the chair, casually intertwining his long fingers. "You offered to show me New

Orleans and I'm here to take you up on the offer—if you're not too busy."

Her heart soared. "No, not at all." She was shocked at how eager she sounded and told herself to calm down. No need to let him think she was overly pleased by his request. "I'd be delighted to show you the city. But you don't have to pay me."

"No, I insist." His eyes twinkled. "Payment is called for."

Kenley cocked her head suspiciously. "Just what sort of payment do you have in mind?"

"Tsk, tsk, Miss Farrell." He wagged a finger at her. "Such bawdy thoughts this early in the morning. Here's my proposition. I'll assume all financial responsibilities for the day—food, transportation, tickets, as well as any souvenirs, etcetera. All you have to do is point out local attractions, provide pertinent historical facts and, in general, introduce me to The City That Care Forgot."

"Oh, I see. It's kind of like a date?"

"Something like that." He smiled.

She didn't know if it was the smile or the tone of his voice that won her over. It could even have been the way he looked. The navy slacks he wore accentuated the muscles in his long legs, and the white summer sweater with the red windowpane design was a most arresting contrast to his dark hair and tanned complexion. He looked crisp and cool—and downright gorgeous. She felt like a rumpled swamp rat in comparison.

"All right. But New Orleans is a big city. We can't possibly see it all in one day."

"Okay, then we'll start with the French Quarter."

Kenley laughed. "Even that's a rather tall order, but I think I can give you a good view of it in a day. Let me run and change. I'll be down in a few minutes. Help yourself to coffee or whatever. It's all in the kitchen."

Blane waved her away. "I'll find what I need."

Kenley scurried up the stairs and began riffling through her closet. She felt bright and sunny and deliciously happy at the prospect of spending the day in the Quarter with Blane. Her hand reached out and grabbed an aqua sundress with a hot pink belt that seemed to match her mood. She slipped her feet into a pair of cool sandals, ignoring the warning voice in her head that told her to wear something more sensible to walk the streets of New Orleans. She wanted to look attractive and pretty today, and she couldn't pull that off while wearing chunky sneakers.

She touched up her lashes and added some blush to her cheeks, but her face was so aglow with happiness that even she had to admit makeup would be gilding the lily. After running a brush through her hair, she started to pull it back with a clip again then decided to let it hang freely around her shoulders. It was more becoming that way, and she wanted to look very feminine for Blane today. The little warning bell inside her head began to ring once more, but she shut it off firmly.

Blane had contented himself with waiting in the courtyard, enjoying the privacy of the colorful hideaway. He was entertaining thoughts about getting Kenley alone here in the moonlight with soft music playing in the background when he saw her coming toward him through the dining room. Her eyes lit up when she looked at him and he wondered what it would be like to see that look every day of his life. How would it feel to be the source of that glow in her eyes? He took her shoulders in his hands and smiled down at her. "I was afraid you'd be busy today or turn me down because I didn't call first."

"I'm glad you came," she admitted without hesitation.

She was so lovely he couldn't resist the temptation to bend down and kiss the tip of her nose. "Ready?"

Out on the sidewalk, Blane started toward his car.

"Oh, you don't need that," she told him. "All the things I want you to see are within walking distance."

"Fine." He reached out his hand and she slipped hers into it. It was warm and secure, and she felt strangely at home by his side.

They strolled up Barracks Street toward the old U.S. mint, then wandered leisurely through the expansive French Market. As they walked around the historic old district, Kenley pointed out interesting examples of architecture and famous eateries, told stories about earlier inhabitants and explained a little about how the Vieux Carré had changed over the past two hundred years. They ended up at Washington Artillery Park across from Jackson Square, gazing out at the muddy water of the Mississippi and watching the ships making their way upriver toward Baton Rouge.

The sound of a soulful trumpet drifted over the air, and Blane watched as a scrawny old man stood on the wooden walkway atop the levee, pouring his heart into a battered instrument. "Who is he?" he asked quietly.

"Nobody. Famous, that is. Just a man who likes to play his horn by the river."

Puzzled, Blane asked, "You mean he wasn't hired by someone to lend atmosphere?"

"No." Kenley smiled. "He plays because he wants to. If the crowd likes his song, they'll toss a little something into his hat. That's his only payment—that and the satisfaction he gets from sharing his music with anyone who cares to listen."

Blane couldn't quite grasp the new idea. "Interesting. Is he a beggar? I mean, is this a job for him?"

"Maybe." She shrugged. "Maybe not. The French Quarter has hundreds of people who entertain just for the fun of it. He might be down on his luck and looking for a few dollars to buy food, or he might easily be a successful businessman who likes to unwind on the weekends by blowing his horn. You just never know."

As they listened, the music was interrupted by the whop-whop of a helicopter, and Kenley glanced at it briefly. They were a common sight here in oil country, so she dismissed it and looked back at Blane. His head was tilted back, and he followed the course of the chopper with his eyes. He looked down, then stared beyond her into the distance.

Kenley felt a chill touch her heart as she looked into his eyes. There was a strange sadness in the brown depths, and something else—a knowledge, a wisdom that she'd seen before in other eyes but couldn't place. Then she knew. It was the look of an old man, one who has lived a long life, seen all the good and the bad, and come to understand them as only the very old can.

Kenley was alarmed at the discovery. Why would a young, healthy man like Blane have that look in his eyes?

She was suddenly overwhelmed with a desire to take him in her arms and comfort him, though comfort him against what she hadn't the faintest idea. He seemed so alone at this moment. Suddenly his eyes met hers and she felt embarrassed, as if she'd intruded into some private corner of him. But then he grinned, the look vanished, and his eyes were once again warm and friendly.

"Is there any place around here to get a cup of coffee? I could use some." He was startled to hear Kenley burst into laughter, her dimples flashing. "What's so funny?"

Kenley shook her head, her lips still curved in an amused grin. "It's easy to see you're a foreigner."

"Why?"

"Because if you were a native, you'd know there's only one place to get coffee in New Orleans—the Café du Monde."

After Kenley introduced Blane to *café au lait* and *beignets*, they continued on with their tour. The sad look never reappeared in Blane's eyes. In fact, he was charming and at ease the rest of the day. They visited the usual tourist traps, listened to jazz, walked down bawdy Bourbon Street and ended a perfectly enjoyable day with a carriage ride through the old streets.

New Orleans took on a new life after dark. The historical, carefree atmosphere was replaced by a more raucous one. Still, it was one of the most romantic cities in the world, and she sighed softly in blissful contentment.

Blane took her hand, enclosing it in his larger one until hers was a small fist in his palm. "Did you have a nice time today?"

"Oh, yes, perfect. Thank you."

He opened his fist and brought her fingers to his lips, kissing them tenderly. They rode in silence, enjoying the sights and sounds, letting the gentle sway of the carriage relax them. Kenley wondered about her feelings for Blane at the moment. She felt so comfortable at his side, so complete, but she was afraid to examine the feeling too closely, for fear it would shatter the beautiful illusion. Instead she turned her eyes on the old city as it drifted lazily past.

"I've lived here for five years, and I never get tired of this place," she said softly.

"It could grow on you," he replied, gently caressing the back of her hand with his thumb. "Many things about New Orleans are starting to grow on me."

Kenley looked into his eyes, and even in the dark she could read the message there. Her body responded instantly, as if there was some bond between them. She was grateful when the buggy stopped and she could tear her eyes from his. "Oh, how sweet," she said softly when she realized that they were parked in front of her own house. "He's brought us home."

"I don't think either of us could have made the trip on foot." Blane helped her down, thanked the driver and gave the horse a friendly pat.

Kenley unlocked the gate and stopped at the French door leading to the living room. "Won't you come in? I can fix you a drink or something to eat."

"Do you want me to come in?"

"I'm not ready for the day to end," she admitted softly.

"An evasive answer, but I'll take it as a yes."

Inside he stopped her before she could get too far, taking her arm and gently pulling her around to his chest. He whispered into her ear, "You have the most delicious curves."

She smiled, leaning her hand against his chest briefly then looking up at him. "If you ask me, there are far too many curves."

But Blane shook his head. "You're perfect."

Kenley looked askance.

"Really! Do you have any idea how uncomfortable it is making love to a skinny woman? Everywhere you touch is hard and bony."

"I really wouldn't know."

"I do know you're the most interesting and the most exciting tour guide I've ever had. I *won't* recommend you to my friends, though. I want to keep you all to myself. I'd like to hire you again soon. There's much more I'd like to learn about . . . New Orleans."

"Any time." Kenley allowed herself to be drawn into the warm depths of his brown eyes. "I like showing you around."

"And I'd like to show you just how you affect me." His lips found hers, his tongue invading her mouth hungrily.

The invasion was met with eager surrender and a matching hunger of her own. Her need for him seemed to grow stronger each time she was in his arms. Foolishly she'd hoped to build up an immunity to his touch, but he seemed to be breaking down her resistance instead. She was succumbing to it like an insidious disease. Sooner or later she'd have to give in. She ached for him, felt her control melting away under the taste of him, but from somewhere deep inside she felt the brake being pulled. Blane felt it, too, and drew away, looking down at her with a sadness in his eyes.

"What are you afraid of, Kenley?" he asked softly, his voice caressing and gentle. "Did Russ leave such deep scars that you can resist what's happening between us? He must have been a stupid fool. Didn't he realize what a precious, fragile thing he had?"

"Me? Fragile?" She shook her head. "Hardly."

"Oh, my sweet Kenley," he said, tilting her chin upward with his fingers. "You try so hard to be tough and self-sufficient. Haven't you learned that it's okay to let someone else be strong once in a while?"

"I don't know how," she whispered, surprised at her own candor. "I'm not sure that I can."

"Then maybe it's something I can help you learn."

"Maybe. One thing I do know," she told him, looking deep into his eyes. "You make me happy. I don't understand it, but it's true."

"Don't try to understand it. Just enjoy it." He kissed her forehead. "I'd better go. You may have great strength of will, but I don't. If I stay here much longer... I'll see you Monday." He turned and walked to the door, looking back briefly to smile and wink. Then he was gone and Kenley felt such a wave of misery it nearly buckled her knees.

She shouldn't have sent him away. She should have let things take their natural course. No, she'd done the right thing. It was still too soon to be thinking about a more intimate relationship with Blane. She knew him better now, knew he was kind and decent. But it was what she didn't know that worried her. Several times she'd tried to draw him out, to find some answers, but he cleverly changed the subject. Why had he looked so old today, so worn? Was the estrangement from his father still so painful? He didn't seem so scarred when he talked about him. In fact, she had detected affection in his voice. So what was it she had seen in his eyes? If she had to make a list of the points for and against him, the plus column would be the longer. But it was the minus column that was important to her.

Kenley was very selective in her male companions. She chose them for their minds, their creativity and intellect and mutual interest and a shared point of view toward life. That they be physically attractive, had never been high on her list of important qualities. A relationship based solely on outward appearance led only to disaster, like her sister's four dismal marriages. As long as the man was handsome and willing to take care of her, Lena didn't have to stand on her own two feet and take charge of her life.

Since her unfortunate college experience, Kenley had always controlled her romances. She was the leader, and the men followed the rules and moved at her pace. More often than not, she terminated the affair before it progressed to the bedroom. But she had a feeling Blane Crawford would be in full control of any relationship he was involved in. He would be very demanding, accepting nothing less than complete devotion, loyalty and love. There was nothing halfway about him, which meant he probably wouldn't accept a woman with a life of her own and goals other than his comfort and pleasure, and that broke all her rules. He was everything she vowed to avoid—handsome, charming and mysterious. A triple threat.

Yes, sending Blane away had definitely been the right choice. Still aching and trembling from the magic of his touch, her body belied her decision. Why did common sense always seem to be at war with one's emotions? Why was the emotional quotient so erratic and blind to the practical aspects of life?

Kenley battled the questions for hours in her head. She'd gone directly to bed after Blane left, but sleep had been elusive.

She told herself repeatedly that she'd done the right thing in sending Blane away. But if it was right, why did she ache so? Why did every nerve in her body call out for him? It had been a perfect day, the most beautiful she could ever remember. It could have culminated in an even more beautiful, intimate way if she had allowed it. Her attraction to Blane had mounted with each moment they were together. Even the simplest things took on a sensuous tone when he was involved. The breeze had stirred his thick, dark hair as they'd stood at Artillery Park, softening his features and giving a younger plane to his square jaw. She had wanted to reach out and smooth back the strands over his ears, but she hadn't, afraid of the consequences if her guard should drop.

The realization was a shock. Was she so afraid of love, of Blane, that she threw up barriers automatically?

God, she hoped not. Surely she was more in tune with her feelings than that.

Kenley stared at the ceiling for hours, trying to sort through her maze of emotions. What was it she really wanted?

That was easy. She wanted to lean on Blane, to turn all her problems over to him. Let someone else struggle, let someone else take care of her, for a change, and provide a safe haven from the endless decisions and loneliness.

Her conscience reared its head, but this time she turned away. Job satisfaction and equal opportunity didn't carry over into all aspects of life. Sometimes a woman needed more—someone to share with, to depend on.

"Fool," she said aloud. Had she forgotten the hard lesson she'd learned early in life? That you can't depend on anyone but yourself? Especially not a man.

She had vowed not to end up like her mother, living as merely an extension of her husband's personality. Without him she had virtually ceased to exist, an empty shell bereft of purpose and direction.

As a result, Kenley had been forced to take charge of their small household when her father left. Barely fifteen, she lacked the necessary skills and knowledge, but somehow had found the strength to become the decision maker. At least her father had helped them financially, his one decent act after running out. But the emotional responsibility had fallen on her young shoulders. Her mother had spent her married life oblivious to bills, banking, insurance and all the other annoying details of everyday life. She'd concerned herself only with her children and the world of housework, depending upon her husband for everything else, content in her role as dutiful wife and mother. Then one day the husband was gone, and she was totally unprepared to go on alone. She had fallen apart, unable to cope with even the simplest of tasks.

Kenley's younger sister had also turned to her for advice and support. Whenever Lena had a problem, their mother would always send her to Kenley. "She'll know what to do. She'll be able to handle it." Subsequently, when Kenley left home, Lena had transferred her dependence to one husband after another. But like their father, each had eventually proved to be unreliable, and Kenley had sworn that she would never turn her life over to a man. She had vowed to become self-sufficient, totally responsible for every aspect of her life.

Until Blane Crawford had appeared, she'd succeeded beautifully.

But he had thrust himself into her world, and suddenly all her convictions, her mandates about the course her life should take, were scattered like so much rice on the wind. He had penetrated her mind and her heart despite her attempts to prevent him.

She couldn't think about Blane in any context without her true feelings taking hold. The events of the day played again in her mind, and somewhere during her memories she finally fell asleep.

Chapter Eight

The sandy-haired man walked into the new offices of CCPS and stopped at the table in the center where an attractive young woman stood. "The plantation lady, I presume," he said cheerfully.

Kenley smiled and nodded. "I guess you could call me that."

"Good morning. I'm Dave Kesler."

"Yes, I know. I've seen you around, and your boss has spoken of you often."

He looked delighted. "Good old Blane singing my praises again, huh? But just to set the record straight, he's not my boss."

"Oh? Sorry. I just assumed that."

He shrugged off the mistake. "No problem. I have to remind him of the fact frequently myself. He loves to command people. An old and very bad habit of his."

"So, just what is your position, Mr. Kesler?" she inquired. She wouldn't have been surprised if he'd said court jester. There was something whimsical about him.

"Reclining, mostly." His eyebrows did a Groucho Marx imitation, and Kenley couldn't help but laugh. "Technically we're associates. That means I'm more than an employee but less than a partner. More like partners in crime. I handle the numbers game."

"That sounds shady."

"Boring is more like it. I'd love to delve into some creative bookkeeping, but unfortunately for me I was cursed with an honest soul." He looked positively angelic, and Kenley found she liked this amusing friend of Blane's.

"I'm sure Blane must be delighted with that trait. What else does your job entail?"

"When I'm not doing his mathematical computations and advising him on various investments, I act as his conscience."

"Does he need one?"

"Frequently." Dave glanced around the cluttered office. "So what do you do here?"

"We rescue historic structures from oblivion."

His expression was deadpan. "Why?"

"To preserve the past so we can better understand the future," she explained in lofty tones.

Dave's green eyes rolled ceilingward. "Oh, then you'd probably *love* the Victorian cookie jar we're living in now."

"You mean The Shackleford House?"

"If you mean old man Crawford's house, yeah. It's like living in a back room of the Smithsonian. All that antique furniture and that fancy woodwork and old carpets and old rugs and old dishes and old windows and old commode... well, you get the picture."

Kenley laughed. "Yes, I think I do."

"You see, I'm a chrome-and-glass man myself. You know—modern, clean lines, mirrors."

She nodded in understanding. "You favor the minimal school of decorating."

Dave frowned. "If that means the uncluttered look, yep, that's me."

"Well, then you'll hardly appreciate what I do here, Mr. Kesler."

"Dave. Call me Dave."

"All right, Dave. You can call me Kenley."

"Actually I do appreciate it." It was the first serious expression he'd worn since arriving. "I may not want to live in a museum, but I do understand that there's great value in saving parts of our past. In fact, that's the reason I stopped by. One of them, anyway. I wanted to meet you and let you know if there's anything I can do, just give a yell. Don't know if I'll be much help, but I'll give it my best shot."

"That's very thoughtful of you. Thank you." She smiled. "And the other reason?"

"Oh, this." He held out a small package to her. "It was delivered to my office by mistake. It looked important."

Kenley knew immediately what the package contained. "Oh, the journal. I've been waiting for this. It might be full of new information about D'Evereaux. It was written during the construction of the plantation by Alcee Rondeau. The Rondeau family lived near Garyville about three miles farther north. Their third daughter, Alcee, kept a journal most of her life. Her father, James, built D'Evereaux for his second daughter, Millicent who married one of the Le-Blancs from New Orleans. A friend of mind at Louisiana State found it in an old storage room at the library. It might give us just the ammunition we need to save D'Evereaux." She stopped when she saw the smile on Dave's face. "Sorry. I tend to get carried away when I'm talking about D'Evereaux."

There was a twinkle in his green eyes. "I can understand now why Blane is so anxious to help you. In fact, I understand a lot of things better now. Like why he comes in singing all the time. It's disgusting."

"I would think you'd like him being in a good mood."

"I got nothing against a good mood. But Blane couldn't carry a tune in a duffel bag if his life depended on it."

Kenley laughed lightly. "I'll remember never to ask him to sing for me."

"Smart lady." He cocked a finger at her, then looked at her in an odd way.

She had the impression that he was checking her out, evaluating her for some reason. For Blane? But the moment passed. Perhaps she was merely imagining things. "Since you're the money man for Crawford Plastics, maybe I should be talking to you instead of Blane. How does it look from your angle? Saving D'Evereaux, that is."

Dave shook his head. "I wish you hadn't asked. Frankly, at this point we're at a standoff. It's one or the other, but not both. I've still got a few options to look over, though. How about you?"

Kenley tapped the desktop idly with her fingertips. "As much as I hate to admit it, I'm at a standstill, as well. I've got some calls in to other preservation groups to see if they have any suggestions, but . . ." She shrugged. "I won't give up easily. There has to be a way out of this deadlock."

"Well, don't worry. I've seen Blane slide out of tighter spots than this one. They don't call him the Artful Dodger for nothing."

"What?" She could see Dave immediately regretted his words.

"Aw, it's just a nickname from the Dark Ages. Forget it. Look, I'd better be getting back. Won't get a thing done, if I gossip with the neighbors all day. Nice meeting you, Miss Far . . . uh, Kenley. I'll put in a good word for you with my associate."

With a wink, Dave sauntered out, leaving Kenley with a strange tightness in her stomach. Artful Dodger? What sort of a nickname was that? The Artful Dodger was a thief, a pickpocket. How did Blane get a name like that?

* * *

Alva set her fists on her hips and frowned at her friend. "I suppose you're going to stay and dig through that old journal until daylight?"

"No, just long enough to scan the first couple of sections. I must say, Miss Alcee Rondeau had atrocious handwriting. I can barely make out some of these words."

"Hmm," Alva grunted unhappily. "Well, next time tell her to use a laser printer so you can decipher it more easily."

Kenley smirked. "Cute."

"Why don't you take that thing home with you?"

"I will. I just want to verify some of the dates she mentions against the records we have here. I promise I won't stay too late."

"Good. You got no business hanging around an empty office building to all hours." She turned and walked to her desk, covering her typewriter and the computer. "I think Mr. Crawford is still in his office," she said pointedly, glancing in Kenley's direction. Her friend was concentrating on the old book. "I saw a light under his door," she added, a little more loudly this time.

Kenley dragged her attention away from the faded pages of the diary. "What did you say?"

Alva clicked her tongue. "I never saw anyone who could get so deep into anything as you do. I said, Mr. Crawford is working late."

"Oh, fine. Thank you," she answered and went back to her book, barely hearing Alva say good-night.

Kenley lost track of time as she delved into Miss Rondeau's fascinating life, though it was a struggle to read the words on the brittle yellow pages. Not only was Alcee Rondeau's handwriting poor, but the passage of time had faded it to the point where it was barely visible on some lines. She had to strain to read almost every word. Suddenly a name popped up, grabbing her attention. She read it again, her eyes afraid to believe what she was reading.

Father has engaged Mr. Raymond Parker of Ohio to design and build Millicent's house. Mr. Parker was reluctant to travel so far from home without the comfort and solace of his dear wife and numerous children. Papa has offered him a sizable stipend and the use of sister Elise's home for him and his family until the house is completed. Mrs. Kemper of The Shadows was most put out as she had attempted on several occasions to engage Mr. Parker, who has steadfastly refused to ply his trade in an area of the country that he terms "The Devil's Washroom."

Kenley sat back in her chair, a smile lighting her face. Raymond Parker had built D'Evereaux? All the information on D'Evereaux so far had suggested that Charles Dakin of New Orleans had been the designer and architect of the plantation. Kenley's mind thrilled with the new bit of knowledge. This could change everything. If Parker had built the home, then that meant it was the only one of its kind in the Deep South since he had always confined his work to the eastern seaboard. Closing the book, she grinned, feeling like a giddy child. She wanted to dance around the room and shout for joy. If this was true, then she might be able to save D'Evereaux by the simple fact that the house was a rare example of Parker's work. It at least opened up new avenues of negotiation. She could run up to Baton Rouge and contact the Louisiana legislature, if necessary.

This news was too glorious to keep to herself. She had to tell someone about it or she'd burst. Vaguely she recalled Alva mentioned Blane was working late, but it was after eight, too late for him to still be here. Darn. She really wanted to tell him about her discovery. Funny how he was the first one she thought of in regard to the house. From his point of view the news would hardly be welcome, yet she longed to share it with him. Despite their opposing positions, she'd found him very easy to talk to. That was something she'd never found with Russ—or any one else for that matter.

Not really expecting to find him, Kenley was delighted to see the light still shining under his door. When he didn't answer after several knocks, she quietly opened the door and peeked in. He wasn't anywhere to be found, and her enthusiasm dimmed considerably. Disappointed, she started to leave when a faint sound reached her ears, metallic, as if someone was using machinery. She placed the sound, then— the weight machine in the small room adjoining his office. Blane had installed it shortly after taking over. Alva had mentioned it the other day.

Her excitement swelled again, blocking out everything else. Briskly she walked toward the room. The door was ajar and she pulled it open, eager to tell Blane about her wonderful discovery. Her smile grew brighter when she saw him, but it froze on her face and she stopped short.

He was sitting astride the machine, slowly pushing the thick bar up over his head then lowering it. He wore only jogging shorts and socks; his chest was bare. From her position, Kenley could see each muscle in his back ripple as he forced the lever upward. His shoulders seemed even more broad now, the biceps glistening with a film of sweat, evidence of his exertion.

Her gaze traveled down toward his thighs and calves, and she was unable to take her eyes from the flexing and tightening of his powerful legs.

Her earlier discovery was forgotten. This new one was infinitely more exciting. She had never doubted his masculinity—it permeated everything he did—but this was a raw, primitive side of Blane that she'd never seen. It left her mouth dry and her blood heated to red-hot in her veins. A part of her knew she should leave, but another part of her wanted desperately to stay and watch the fascinating movements of his body as he worked on this seductive machine.

"Oh, Kenley. I didn't hear you come in."

She jumped at the sound of his voice. She hadn't realized he'd seen her. Grabbing a towel, he draped it around his neck and walked toward her. She licked her lips, spellbound by the inviting mat of dark hair that spread across his chest and narrowed as it disappeared into the waistband of his gray shorts.

"What are you doing here so late?"

"Uh, I was reading." It was impossible to get her lascivious thoughts under control. "A journal," she added awkwardly. He was standing only inches away, and she could smell the faint odor of perspiration and that heady, tangy aroma she'd come to associate with him. His maleness surrounded her, and her eyes seemed riveted on his chest as it rose and fell rhythmically.

He smiled a slow, knowing smile, with that hint of amusement he always had. He was reading her thoughts again—an easy task this time. Her interest was blatantly obvious.

"Did you want something?"

Oh yes, she most definitely did. The knowledge was like a pitcher of cold water thrown at her face. How long had it been since she'd wanted a man this desperately, desperately enough to throw caution to the wind? "No," she replied, quickly taking a step backward. "No. I just found something I'd been looking for." *You!* her mind screamed. "An unexpected surprise." You, in only socks and shorts. So much for cerebral attraction. Good old animal magnetism wins again. "It can keep. I didn't realize..." Blane moved closer, and she took another step backward. "Don't let me interrupt." Why was she holding back? Everything she'd ever wanted was standing in front of her.

Before she could move again, Blane reached out and fingered the fabric of her sleeve near the wrist. "You're never an interruption," he said softly. Kenley could feel the heat of his fingers through her blouse as they rested on her arm. The contact set her heart pounding. She made one last feeble attempt to move away, but his hands held her wrists, pulling her close.

"You can't ignore it anymore, sweet Kenley. I won't let you. It was meant to happen. It's been coming since that first day in the cemetery."

"No," she whispered, but she could feel her determination being lost in the depths of those wonderful dark eyes that seemed to reach into her very soul and warm her from deep inside.

"Don't fight it," he breathed into her ear. His hands moved slowly up her arms, across her shoulders, to the side of her neck. The sensation weakened her knees. Gently his hands cradled her face, his thumbs brushing lightly against her cheeks.

"Must I persuade you?" He bent his head, touching his lips to hers. The kisses were soft, testing, as if giving her time to adjust.

Kenley struggled vainly to keep some measure of control. But his nearness, the gentle kisses, the hardness of his chest damp and hot against hers, broke through her barriers and set free a flood of emotions that overwhelmed her. All her inhibitions vanished. There was only Blane and the delicious sensation his touch created. With a moan she slipped her arms around his neck, pressing herself against him.

Arms like steel wrapped around her, lifting her up against him. The gentle kisses were now hot and scalding, as he devoured her mouth like a starving man.

She didn't resist. Her hands greedily explored the muscles on his back. Her body was on fire, consumed with a need far greater than his kisses could assuage.

His tongue plundered her mouth and she whimpered, her body melting into his, molding to every hard, muscular slope. His lips left hers to taste the area behind her ear, the side of her neck, then upward to her temples and eyelids. His hands were entangled in her hair.

"Let me love you, sweet Kenley," he breathed softly. His words were like an invocation in her ear, and she buried her face in his neck in silent assent. His hands stroked her hair, slipping beneath the chestnut strands to caress her neck. She could feel his heart beating wildly against her.

The steel arms eased their hold, and she looked up into his eyes. The lids were hooded, and behind the long lashes she could see the boiling fever of his desire. Gently he turned her toward the other room, the fingers of his free hand touching her chin, keeping her eyes locked in his.

He stopped in front of the wide windows, the reflected light from the city below casting seductive shadows over his hard muscled body. She reached out and rested her palms against his chest, reveling in the feel of the smooth, dark hair. Her hands slid downward to his sides, then he tilted her face upward for a brief, searing kiss.

His fingers touched the buttons on her blouse, releasing each one as his mouth explored her neck and jaw and nibbled at her earlobe.

Kenley was helpless under his skillful touch. He slipped the silk from her shoulders and tensed with delicious anticipation, her skin turning to fire when his lips touched her. They trailed across her shoulders and collarbone, lingering on the pulsating hollow of her throat.

Her hand, idle during his undressing, slid up the hard contours of his chest and around his neck, encircling it as she sought his lips. His tongue danced teasingly over her teeth as his hands released the zipper on her full skirt. He stepped back, allowing it to fall to the floor. His mouth curled in an appreciative smile, the dark eyes like incandescent coals.

Slowly he tugged at her half-slip, sending it to the carpet. Then he fastened his thumbs in the band of her hose and peeled them and her panties away. As he knelt in front of her, she rested her hands lightly on his shoulders to maintain balance. She felt so intoxicated, so doused with his magic, it seemed as if she could float away on the heat of it.

Stepping out of the hosiery and feeling his hands sliding up her legs, she trembled, inflamed by his sensuous undressing.

His palms scorched her skin as they moved over her hips and sides and around her back. She was incapable of movement, of response, as he removed the lace bra. Something in the back of her mind told her she should be uncomfortable standing naked in front of him, but she didn't. She felt only flushed and alive.

His eyes devoured her greedily, then he enfolded her in his arms again, his body fairly sizzling against her. Her breasts crushed against him, the dark hairs tickling her nipples.

"Oh, God, you're so incredible," he whispered. "Do you know how much I've wanted this?" His hands cupped her bottom, forcing her hips against the center of his desire, and she cried out with the force of her need. "Kenley, you're so incredible, everything I ever wanted," he said softly against her hair.

The words drifted to her through a delicate mist. He moved away, leaving her suddenly cold, and she opened her eyes to see him tossing pillows from the small love seat onto the floor. Then quickly removing his shorts and socks, he stood before her, the magnificent male, glorious and powerful in the night light. He stretched out over the pillows and held out his hand.

She went to him willingly, happily, and with no reservations. He enfolded her in his arms, engulfing her with his torrid passion.

His hot palm followed the curve of her hip around to her stomach and up her rib cage. Then the hand closed over the swell of her breast, igniting new levels of desire. He massaged the soft mound, his fingers urging the rosy tip to hardness. Kenley writhed in his arms, moving with the delicious pulsating rhythm of her body.

Lips, scalding hot, covered her aching nipple, taunting it further with slow, torturous suction. She whimpered, seething with exquisite agony. His tongue encircled, teased and sucked until she thought she would suffocate from the sensation. Then he turned his attention to the other breast, repeating the sweet torment. His hands glided over her glowing flesh, gently exploring and petting.

She was adrift on a sea of rolling sensations, a world made only of his lips, his tongue and those wondrous hands, gentle and hot.

Under his touch she felt glorious, like a rare, exquisite prize, worshiped and loved.

His finger gently skimmed her hips, venturing lower, parting her thighs, and she cried out when he found the center of her being. She was lost, consumed with an urgency as old as time.

He covered her then, his hard, sweltering body arching over her.

As he presented himself to her, she opened up, eager and desperate for fulfillment. He probed slowly, infuriatingly, until she begged softly in his ear. Her words broke his restraint, and he thrust deeply, filling her, sending her exploding into a blazing dimension of desire. They rode the fiery waves together, ablaze with the glory of their joining.

Slowly the white-hot passion cooled. Kenley basked in the wondrous afterglow. He still held her close, protected and cherished in his arms. She became aware of his soft breath on her forehead and the sound of his heart beating beneath her ear. Her fingers smoothed the dark mat of hair that sloped over his chest, then dug underneath to feel the warmth of his skin. She looked up into his eyes and felt her heart sing with joy. He smiled, one finger leisurely tracing the outline of her jaw.

His voice was deep and slightly husky when he spoke. "I'm sorry about the floor. I wanted our first time to be special, memorable." He brushed the hair from her cheek.

His concern touched her heart. "It was special," she assured him softly. "Very special."

His eyes caressed her, sending a warm glow over her heart.

Slowly he rolled onto his back, pulling her on top of him. Kenley reveled in the sensation, gazing down at him with renewed passion.

"You are so lovely," he whispered.

She smiled, her fingers lazily exploring his face, the lines on his forehead, the soft, fine hair near his temple and the coarse gray ones that rested at his ear. She touched the small mole on his left cheek, then the lips that had taken her to a world she'd never known. "I never expected this to happen tonight."

"Me, either. Why did you come here?" he asked.

It was a struggle to remember. "Uh, I found a book ... a diary. It's not important now."

She looked into his eyes, seeing the fire smoldering again, and her heart leaped in response. Strong hands encircled her waist, pushing her up his chest until her breasts were over his mouth. He captured one, licking and teasing. The sensation was electric. It sent her hurtling on rocket flames. Her body was ablaze. She rose higher, higher, then felt herself being pulled down, impaled upon the hot, hard maleness of him, rotating, turning, until the flames burst in the sky and flickered, leaving her weak and sated on his chest.

They lingered that way quietly, contentedly, for a long, long time.

Kenley had no idea what time it was when she left Blane's office. He saw her to her car, held her, kissed her, and she drove home in a beautiful daze, her thoughts drifting on the lingering wonder and magic of his lovemaking.

Lovemaking had never been so wonderful for her. Her previous sexual experiences had been uneventful, at best. She'd always felt more like a spectator than a participant. Russ had been impatient, his own immediate satisfaction paramount in his mind. Her needs were an afterthought.

The other relationship in her life, the one she had actually allowed to progress to the bedroom, had been equally unexciting—pure physical release, no tenderness, no sharing. She had never understood the world's preoccupation with sex.

Now she was forced to question if she'd been with the right men. Or perhaps she had not cared enough for the others. Love in Blane's hands was turbulent, wild and searing, yet so very, very tender. He had been sensitive to her needs and her fears, and his gentle persuasion had been to please her and satisfy her desire, not his own. He had held her like a precious, delicate treasure, yet they had made love on the floor. She, who had always avoided anything the least bit offbeat, had made love to a man on the floor of his office in front of a window that overlooked all of New Orleans. In his hands, all her restraint had vanished. She had thrilled to his touch, responded wantonly to his kiss, and he had opened up a new world to her. She had tasted the forbidden fruit and been left with an insatiable appetite.

The power he had over her now was terrifying. How had she strayed so far from her course? Her behavior had been reckless and irresponsible. What had happened to her strength of will and determination? She had boasted to Alva about wanting a predictable man. But she had tempted the Fates with her pompous dictates and they had laughed, giving her the very thing she feared most—a man of mystery.

But against the magic of his touch she was helpless. She had leaped into the fire, oblivious to the consequences. Yet even as she riled against it, her body ached for fulfillment again. She felt a rush of joy each time she thought of him standing before her, tanned, strong and glorious in his manhood. Whenever she closed her eyes, she could feel his hands gliding over her flesh, his lips teasing her mouth, his tongue stroking her nipples. She could still taste him, feel him throbbing deep inside her. Reckless or not, she was glad it had happened.

Chapter Nine

The National Weather Center had dubbed it Dwight, and it was working itself up to becoming the first killer hurricane of the season. Normally by late September hurricane season was slowing down. Few tropical storms formed when the air started to cool. But Dwight was a determined fellow. Born as a large tropical wave in the lower Gulf, he had swelled to storm strength rapidly and had been elevated to full hurricane status six days ago. Since then he'd played games with the meteorologists, stalling out in the Gulf, drifting first to the east, then the west, changing directions with every gust of wind, all the while gaining strength in the center. Gulf Coast communities held their collective breath waiting to see which of them would bear the brunt of Dwight's wrath. Because of its precarious position, New Orleans was particularly watchful.

Finally word arrived. Dwight was pushing at the mouth of the Mississippi River. Estimated winds were 175 miles per hour, the strongest hurricane in over a decade. He'd chosen New Orleans for his target and was bearing down upon the Bayou City at fifteen miles per hour.

The weather conditions in southern Louisiana were of little concern to Blane Crawford. The rain was a minor annoyance and only added to his already gray mood. He hadn't intended to make love to Kenley the previous night, only to coax from her an admission of her feelings toward him. But she had responded so sweetly, so willingly to his kiss that he'd lost control. She felt so glorious in his arms. He was like a man parched, arid, and she was a cool, clear, rippling stream that he drank from greedily, trying to satisfy his insatiable thirst.

He gave her everything he had, poured his heart and soul into his hands and his lips, frightened at how easily he'd lost himself to her. He'd opened up parts of himself he'd never known before. The realization scared the hell out of him. Kenley had touched something deep inside, something so private, so secret he wasn't sure he understood it himself. He'd never allowed himself the luxury of total abandonment with a woman. He'd always kept a little corner locked away, a protective shield around his soul. He'd seen too much, been through too much to allow anyone to penetrate his stronghold. It was the only thing of value he had left after the Dark Ages.

Yet Kenley had slipped beneath his barrier, shattering it to oblivion. He felt vulnerable, exposed. He didn't like the sensation, at all, but damned if he knew how to correct it.

That trap he'd laid was closing in tighter every day. She wanted truthfulness and honesty, and he was too battle-scarred to offer that blindly. He should have walked away when he had the chance. His only hope now was to try and erect a new wall around his emotions and keep his distance from Kenley until he could settle the D'Evereaux situation. Once he was back to his own line of work he'd be too busy to think about a pair of sky-blue eyes and a set of adorable dimples. It was best. There was no future for them. And it was too late now for a simple casual relationship.

His lower jaw worked in frustration as he fastened his seat belt and forced his full attention on the drive ahead of him.

It was almost a relief when Dwight finally chose his target. The long days of wondering whether the storm would hit the beaches of Alabama and Mississippi or the delta and bayous of Louisiana had taken their toll on the Gulf states' inhabitants.

Kenley sent everyone home early after the announcement was made. Some streets were already flooded. Residents of New Orleans never took hurricane warnings lightly. They remembered Camille, Audra and Betsy. Kenley was the last to leave the CCPS offices. Dwight was due to hit the city late this afternoon, but she wanted plenty of time. There was a lot to do.

She was on her way out when she decided to stop by Blane's office and see if he needed any help preparing for the storm. He was, after all, a Yankee, and unfamiliar with the necessary precautions needed to weather Dwight. Kenley smiled inwardly. It was a nice excuse, but it couldn't hide the fact that she was anxious to see Blane. When she approached his outer office, she was surprised to find the new secretary, Carla, still there. "Shouldn't you be going home?" she asked.

"That's just where I'm headed," Carla assured her, reaching for her purse. "I meant to be out of here earlier, but things keep coming up. It's amazing how many people will work until the last minute," she commented, locking her desk. "Can I help you with something?"

"Yes. Is Blane still here?"

"No. He hasn't been in all morning. But Mr. Kesler is here, if you'd like to see him. Go on in," she urged. "I know he's not doing anything."

"All right, thanks." She pushed open the door and scanned the room, her eyes coming to rest upon Dave Kesler. He was slumped down in a chair with one foot propped up on a low table—and he was holding a human leg in his hand! She froze.

Dave looked up sheepishly, waving the appendage in the air. "Hi. I . . . uh, I dropped my leg."

Kenley could only stare at the sight of him holding his own calf and foot.

"I'm really sorry about this," he said as he sat up and began hastily attaching his prosthesis. "I don't like to spring this on people. It's sort of a shock for them under the best of circumstances, but finding me like this . . ." His voice trailed off.

"I, uh, wanted to see Blane," she stammered. She'd never suspected that Dave had a wooden leg.

"Sorry. He's not here. Anything I can do for you?" He stood and straightened his pants leg over the artificial limb and walked toward her. His gait was smooth and fluid.

"How did you . . . I mean . . ." Her face reddened. She couldn't believe she'd said that. It was gauche, totally insensitive.

Dave chuckled softly. "Don't be embarrassed. Few people know about my leg. I lost it in Nam."

"You were there?"

"Two tours, First Cav. I brought home two Purple Hearts, but I left one of my legs behind."

"I'm sorry."

"Don't be. I do just fine with Pete." Kenley looked puzzled, and he tapped his lower leg and smiled. "You know, as in Peg Leg, etcetera."

"Oh."

"So what did you want to see the big guy about?"

Dave's casual attitude went a long way toward regaining her composure. "Mainly to see if he, that is, you needed any help getting ready for Dwight." She glanced at the heavily taped windows. "But I see you're all set here."

"Yeah, the maintenance guys did that this morning."

"You'd better be getting home, too," Kenley warned.

"Just how bad is this thing gonna get, anyhow?"

"From the reports we're getting, it could be worse than Camille in '69." Dave looked blank. "Several hundred people died. You really don't know what you're in for here, do you? Haven't you been listening to the radio?"

He shrugged. "Those weather guys always exaggerate."

Kenley shook her head. "Haven't you gotten anything prepared?"

"Like what?"

She sighed in exasperation. "Okay, first you need to get to the store. Stock up on canned goods, bottled water and batteries. Candles, too. We may be without power and water for quite a while. Go home, fill up the tubs with water, board up windows or tape them, and bring in all small objects from outside."

Rubbing the back of his neck, he grimaced. "I didn't realize it would get so bad. I thought the folks here were just being overly cautious."

"You can never afford to take a hurricane lightly, Dave. Never."

"Uh, look, Kenley, I think I should tell you something. Blane went up to D'Evereaux this morning. And as far as I know, he's still there."

Kenley caught her breath at the implications. "He went up there in this storm? For heaven's sake, why?"

"I honestly don't know. We were talking about the renovations and about the dozers coming in a few weeks, and he suddenly gets this wild hair. He changes his clothes, says he's going out to D'Evereaux to check out some way to solve everybody's problems." Dave tugged at his ear and looked at Kenley guiltily. "He's also told me to keep all this under my hat."

Kenley was already way ahead of Dave. "Did he say when he was coming back?"

"No. I just assumed he'd be home when I got there tonight."

"Well, call him. See if he's back. Please."

Dave picked up the phone and dialed, but no one was at Shackleford House to answer. "Look, let's not panic," he said calmly. "He left a good while ago and he's got plenty of time. When's this hurricane due to hit here?"

"Around four this afternoon."

"Then there's no problem." Dave smiled confidently. "He's probably on his way back right now. Look, you go on home. Get yourself situated for this storm, and as soon as Blane returns I'll have him call you."

"Dave, you don't understand," Kenley persisted.

"Yeah, I do. And I know if you're not home safe and sound Blane will chew me out with a vengeance. He'll be fine," Dave said, steering her toward the door. "He's a resourceful guy. Trust me. I've known him a long time."

"I don't know." She hesitated. "You promise to call?"

"Scout's honor."

Kenley frowned. "Were you ever a Boy Scout?"

"No, but Blane was."

She smiled sardonically. "I'll just bet he was." Dave was probably right. She was jumping to conclusions again. Blane knew about Dwight and he'd be well on his way back to New Orleans by now. "Okay, but you promised to call."

The rain beat down relentlessly, drenching everything in sight and swelling the rivers and bayous to overflowing. Water accumulated rapidly in the delta. Blane was amazed. There was no place for the overflow to drain in these already saturated lowlands. Innocent roadside ditches suddenly became small rivers, spilling over the roads and creating obstructions in mere minutes. Blane felt great relief when he spotted the green historic marker announcing D'Evereaux. Fighting the rain and the slick road surfaces had made him tired. His muscles were cramped and his back was starting to ache. He pulled into the road leading to the old house, finding it very slow going. The water met in the middle in more than one place, and it was impossible to know just how deep it stood. Finally the tree-lined drive of

D'Evereaux appeared and he turned in, stopping his car near the first of the numerous outbuildings. Peering through the rain he could make out D'Evereaux looking like a tattered gray ghost in the storm.

Was one old house worth all the mental energy he was expending? And what about the financial risk he had assumed? Dave had been less than enthusiastic about his decision to take advantage of the three-month extension on the loans. They were on a tight budget, every day counted. There was a very real possibility that he could lose everything by delaying.

Oddly enough, it was Dave's complaints that had spawned this trip to Mossville.

"Geez, if it was up to me, I'd call in the dozers tonight, have them flatten the damn thing and be done with it. No house, no problem. Then we could just move right on back to where we belong."

It was the mention of the dozers that had brought Blane out to D'Evereaux in the rain. It was the perfect opportunity to find out if his idea was feasible.

A sudden forceful gust of wind rocked the little car. Maybe he should have waited to make his inspection, but it was too late now.

He remembered Dave's warning about the storm and flipped on the radio. It didn't take long to get an update. There was only one topic of discussion on the airwaves now. Dwight had already reached New Orleans. "Great." It had hit sooner than he'd expected. Well, he'd wanted to examine this idea under the right conditions. He hadn't exactly wanted a hurricane, but it would definitely give him the information he needed.

Blane steered the car up to the large barn near the south side of the house, for some protection from the wind. He wasn't anxious to get out into the downpour, but he'd come this far. Reaching in the back, he pulled out his poncho and struggled into it. No use putting it off. The weather would only get worse.

Head bent low, he trudged past the outbuildings and toward the back of D'Evereaux. He started his survey on the south side, walking out beyond the house and into the fallow land that bordered Crawford Plastics. The water flowed rapidly by in small but ever-growing streams. He glanced in several directions, then moved on, the sound of his wet boots squishing in the saturated earth.

Returning to the old house a while later, he started around its pillared porches to the front. Near the southeast corner he suddenly found himself in knee-deep water. With a muttered oath, he turned and went in the opposite direction. The rain came in cold sheets, and the wind gusts grew stronger by the minute. Distant thunder rumbled loudly across the land. Near the front veranda, Blane took a brief respite from the downpour by huddling in the shelter of the thick pillars. Frowning, he looked into the gray rain. It wasn't going to let up, and he certainly couldn't get any wetter than he already was. What the hell. He lowered his head and stepped into the deluge once more, this time directing his survey to the acreage on the north side of the old house.

Nearly an hour later he turned his feet in the direction of his car. He was cold, wet, hungry and tired, and like a fool he'd stayed here much too long. If he didn't head back to New Orleans now, he'd be right in the middle of the hurricane.

Halfway to the driveway Blane stopped, unable to believe his eyes. His car, along with the barn and several small outbuildings, was standing in three feet of water! Two thoughts flashed immediately through his mind. The first was that he wouldn't make it back to New Orleans, the second that his precious car was now a muddied mass of steel and soaking wet foam rubber. He didn't know which made him feel worse—being stranded in the boondocks at a fallen down old house, or seeing his prized possession ruined while he stood by helplessly.

It was obvious that he couldn't seek refuge in the car. That left the old plantation. He turned and peered through the rain at the huge ghost. The water was quickly making a claim on the house. From where he stood, it looked as though D'Evereaux would soon be an island unto itself. The entire first floor would quickly be underwater at this rate. Suddenly he thought of Kenley and her love for this old plantation. He glanced back at his Mustang, feeling a new empathy with her.

For a moment he considered wading out to the car to retrieve his flashlight and a blanket, but he remembered that they were both on the floor of the backseat, which meant neither one of them would be of any use now. So much for being prepared. At least the old house was drier and relatively safe from the storm. Turning, he trudged back along the path toward the conservatory and the dubious comfort of the deserted plantation.

The lines at Schwegmann's were long and the aisles crowded as Kenley stocked up on provisions. She hardly noticed the long wait, however, for her thoughts were preoccupied with Blane. Was he back yet? Had he run into any trouble? What if he had been blown off the road or caught in a flash flood? Her memory recalled all the horror stories she'd heard about people underestimating the force of a storm such as Dwight.

Kenley had already decided long before she pulled up at her town house that she had to know about Blane at any cost and had mentally made a list of the things they would need. Her first objective after she reached the warmth of her kitchen was to pick up the phone and call Dave. No one answered at the office, so she tried the house.

A wave of relief filled her when Dave's voice answered the phone. But the message wasn't a good one. Blane hadn't returned to New Orleans. That left only one thing for her to do.

Quickly changing her clothes and stuffing a few things into a nylon sport bag, Kenley went downstairs and started collecting the items she knew they'd need. Dwight was moving slowly. It would be six o'clock or so before the full force of the storm reached Mossville—plenty of time to get out of New Orleans. The reports over the radio grew more grisly by the minute, and she finally turned it off. But the silence only gave birth to equally disturbing scenes in her mind of D'Evereaux being blown away in the storm and Blane lying dead among the ruins.

After one last survey of her supplies, she pulled on boots and a heavy raincoat and braved the weather. The wind was already blowing wildly. Thunder and lightning rumbled and flashed. She fought her way back and forth to her car, loading the various bundles in the backseat.

Getting onto the freeway was no problem; moving after she was there was another story. Traffic on I-10 was always a tangle, even on weekends, but now with everyone trying to get home or out of town, it was nearly at a standstill.

The rain was coming down in sheets and she had to keep the wipers on fast, though even that didn't help completely. The thump-thump of the blades seemed to echo the thoughts in her head. Fool-ish, fool-ish. It *was* foolish, driving all the way to Mossville in this storm. She wasn't even certain that Blane was there. He could have gone to the plant or some other place entirely. She asked herself for the hundredth time why she was doing this. It was ridiculous, insane, completely reckless. But each time she asked the question, she came up with the same answer. She couldn't bear to leave Blane alone in this storm without food or water. More to the point, she would go crazy wondering if he was all right, if he was safe and protected from Dwight. The winds, floods and spin-off storms were too uncertain to take chances with. Add to that his inexperience with hurricanes. How many people unfamiliar with the killer storms had lost their lives because they'd failed to take the necessary precautions or hadn't understood the dangers involved?

Sending up a silent prayer for his safety, she gripped the wheel tighter and pressed on through the driving rain.

Chapter Ten

The traffic crawled through Orleans Parish and Metairie, easing somewhat near Kenner and the airport. When she pulled off I-10 in LaPlace it was raining so hard it was nearly impossible to see where she was going. Kenley guided the little car slowly along narrow highways, straining to locate the old back road that would take her to D'Evereaux. She knew from experience that the main route to the plantation would have long since been inundated. The only way in now was via the old field driveway that came up behind the carriage house.

A sigh of relief escaped her when she saw the turnoff. Her journey was almost over. She steered onto the crumbling old road, but the rain had been falling for some time and even this alternate route was covered with water in several sections. It slowed her progress even more. Silently she prayed she wouldn't get stuck in any of the potholes or low-lying areas.

Finally the outline of the carriage house loomed in sight, and she felt much of the tension ease from her neck and shoulders. As she guided the small car forward, she caught sight of Blane's Mustang parked on the other side of D'Evereaux near the barn. Her relief at finding him here meshed quickly with alarm. Was he inside? Had he been trapped? Swept away with the current? A sudden vision of her life without Blane flooded her mind, and in that instant she realized just how deeply her feelings for him reached. Somewhere she'd stepped over her imaginary line of restraint and was dangerously close to falling in love with him. Why else would she have braved the dangers of Dwight to be with Blane. It was more than just his safety or well-being; her heart was involved now. She had foolishly succumbed to her physical longings, and in doing so had given him power over that one area of her life. It had been a reckless thing to do, done in a moment of weakness. Memories swamped her mind and she relived the glorious sensations she'd experienced in his arms. She was asking to be hurt. But despite the loud voice of common sense that taunted her, she didn't regret it. She was glad it had happened. She knew now what she'd been missing, what to look for in the future. But not with Blane. She had to put a stop to this relationship before it went any further. She had to be sensible. It was imperative she regain control of the situation while she was still able. Contrary to the popular adage, once was more than enough. If she slept with him again she wouldn't be able to stop, ever. But with a little willpower and determination she could curb her emotions and redirect her feelings.

A gust of wind shook the car, and Kenley pulled her thoughts back to the matters at hand. Her main objective now was to keep Blane from seeing how much she cared. If he knew the true state of her feelings he might press the advantage and expect commitments she wasn't ready to make. She couldn't let that happen. No matter how much she cared. For now, she would keep her feelings for Blane to herself, at least until she could sort it through and examine the practical side of her emotions.

The Mustang caught her eye again, and she was filled with sympathy. Blane must be heartbroken. He loved that car, and now it was being ruined by three feet of muddy water.

Easing off the brake, she continued along the eroded carriageway. Her goal was the arched cypress doors of the conservatory near the rear of the house, but the ground was saturated and her small car was nearly mired in the mud twice before coming to a stop a few feet from her target. She honked the horn, long and loud, hoping to alert Blane. When he didn't appear, she gathered up as much as she could carry and opened the car door. The wind slammed into her and she was forced to bend double as she dashed for the house. Stumbling inside, she dumped the heavy bags on the floor, shaking the excess water off her hands.

"What the—"

Kenley looked up to see Blane standing across the room on the steps that led into the main house. His hands were on his hips and there was a fierce scowl on his face.

"What in hell do you think you're doing?" he demanded.

"I'm bringing you supplies so you can wait out the storm."

He marched toward her, his eyes black with anger. "You little idiot! Don't you know you could have been killed coming out here in that storm?"

His jaw was held in a line of steel as he glared down at her. For a moment Kenley felt a flicker of fear. Blane would be a formidable enemy. His anger seemed to come from deep, deep within. As usual when around Blane, though, her own fighting instincts kicked in. She looked him in the eyes unwaveringly. "Unlike you, this is not my first hurricane. I knew precisely what I was doing."

"And do you want to tell me just what that was?" He pointed a finger at her. "Huh? Did it involve risking your neck just to bring me a damn lantern? You could have been blown off the road, washed into the river. Didn't you think of that?"

"Yes," she barked. "I also thought about a damn Yankee who was so stupid that he comes out here in the middle of the worst hurricane in ten years totally unprepared. I couldn't believe it when Dave told me you'd gone to D'Evereaux."

Blane dropped his arm, taking a deep breath. "Dave told you. Well, I'll deal with him later. Right now I want to shake that head of yours right off its shoulders." He grabbed her and did shake her—once. "You pigheaded little fool. I would have been fine. I've been through storms like this before. It sure as hell wasn't worth risking your life over."

"I thought it was," Kenley said defiantly.

Blane's eyes softened, the anger faded. "Oh, sweet Kenley," he whispered, pulling her into his arms. "I'm sorry. But when I saw you standing there dripping wet and realized what you'd done, you scared me stiff. I don't want anything to happen to you. And I don't want you risking your life for me."

Kenley felt his warmth surrounding her, unable to withstand the way it made everything seem right and wonderful. "And I don't want anything to happen to you. Why do you think I came out here? I couldn't have stayed in New Orleans not knowing if you were safe."

Blane kissed the top of her head. "Well, I must admit, I wasn't looking forward to being here alone. And I can't think of any better company than you." He gently eased her away from him, looking her in the eye. "But promise me you'll never do that again."

"Gladly. Driving in that rain was no picnic."

"Come on," he said with a smile, "let's get this stuff inside. You must be exhausted."

"I am. It took forever to get out of town."

"Where do you want to bivouac?"

"Oh, wait, there's more in the car."

"Kenley..."

She disappeared out the door, returning a few minutes later with two bulging plastic trash bags, smiling happily. She held them up for Blane to see. "Blankets. We should be set for the duration now."

Blane was frowning again. "You are the most pigheaded woman I've ever met."

"I'm not pigheaded. I'm persistent," she corrected.

"Stubborn."

"Tenacious."

"Perverse."

"Determined!"

His frown slid quickly into a grin, then a chuckle. Kenley joined in. For the first time she considered how nice being stranded in D'Evereaux with Blane might be. She looked into his eyes and felt a surge of affection mixed with profound relief. He was all right, safe, sound and very attractive. His jeans were damp and clung to the muscles in his legs like a second skin. His shirt was open at the throat, and she could see the dark hair on his chest. He had a habit of standing with his weight on one hip, giving a seductive list to his body. It put a smile on Kenley's face. He seemed completely unaware of the message he conveyed.

"Thank you for coming to my rescue, but isn't this backward? Shouldn't the knight rescue the lady?"

"You know what they say—turnabout is fair play and all that. Besides, this is the nineties. It's perfectly acceptable for women to ask men on dates, call them on the phone, and if need be, rescue them from their own stupidity." Dimples flashed in her cheeks.

He grimaced. "Thank you."

Kenley picked up the bags and started across the room toward the main part of the house. "Come on. We'd better get settled in before we lose what little light there is."

"Where to?" Blane called, gathering up the rest of the supplies.

"Upstairs. The nursery, I think. It's on the protected corner of the house and has only two small windows."

"I thought you said the second floor was unsafe," he asked as they started to climb the spiral staircase. He was momentarily distracted by the enticing view of Kenley from the back.

"The only room that's really unsafe is that front bedroom. That's where the roof leaks, and the floor was rotted badly. But the rest of the upstairs is sound as a dollar. Besides, the nursery has the only fireplace that works, and we'll need a fire before the night is over."

"How do you know the fireplace works? You bring all your male friends here during storms?"

Kenley didn't even glance back at him. "Hardly. I know because I have researched this house thoroughly."

"Why am I not surprised?" Blane replied sarcastically.

At the top of the second floor, they turned right and entered the small nursery. Kenley set her bundles down and gestured for Blane to do the same. "Just put those there for now. We'll unpack in a minute." She walked toward the fireplace, then made a sweeping glance of the room. "Clean out the debris from the fireplace and find something to use as a grate. A couple of old bricks would work fine. We'll need firewood. There should be plenty of usable wood around. Oh, unpack the radio—I think it's in that satchel over there—and tune in to the weather so we can keep track of Dwight. I brought a sleeping bag, some blankets and pillows. And there's canned goods and bottled water in the other bag. And there should be plenty of..." She looked up at Blane, who was leaning against the door frame with an amused, tolerant smile on his face. Kenley felt a surge of remorse. She sighed and leaned back against the wall. "I'm being very bossy, aren't I?"

Blane chuckled softly. "That's okay. I think my male ego can take orders from a woman without serious damage."

"I'm sorry. I guess I'm just used to being in charge."

"Don't be. After all, you're the expert on houses and hurricanes." He walked to the window and tested its strength, then stopped in front of the fireplace to examine it. "You were right about this. It should draw well. We'll need a lot of wood, though. That's a big fireplace." He rose and walked to her side. "How about I go collect something to burn while you unpack? Or would that offend your feminist sensibilities, handling food and household items like that?"

Kenley gave him a haughty smirk. "No, not at all. My ego is capable of taking orders, too. Even if it is from a man."

"Oh, good. Isn't equality wonderful?" he teased.

After Blane left, Kenley marveled at his attitude. His male ego didn't seem the least bit threatened by her directions. It was rare to find a man so secure in himself, in his maleness, that he could truly treat a woman as an equal. She smiled to herself. Just another point in his favor to add to her plus list.

The supplies were almost unpacked when Blane returned, and he smiled at the large assortment of items. "Looks like you thought of everything."

Kenley acknowledged his remark with a curt nod of her head. "In addition to being pigheaded, I'm also very efficient, remember?"

"As a matter of fact I do, so the next efficient thing for you to do is to come help me carry up more wood."

She followed him downstairs to the center hall. Her heart ached when she passed the dining room and saw that the water was slowly seeping in, spreading across the floor like a brown monster. At this rate, the entire first level would be flooded before long. She closed her eyes to the sight and turned away. D'Evereaux would have to wait. The prime concern now was to find enough wood to last through the night.

When Kenley returned to the nursery, Blane was already there. He'd stacked the assortment of crates, lathe boards and broken furniture in the corner and was examining the window to the left of the fireplace. "I don't suppose you brought a hammer and nails or some duct tape with you?" he asked.

"No."

"Well, I guess we'll have to trust to luck." He shrugged. "I was going to secure the windows. The shutters on the other one are solid enough, but this side is missing." He glanced over his shoulder. "I hope you brought matches. I don't smoke."

Kenley looked over at Blane with a quizzical expression. "You don't smoke, don't drink. Don't you have any vices?"

"A few," he replied with a twinkle in his eye.

"Then it must be women or gambling."

Blane looked surprised. "Aren't they the same thing?"

"In some circles. Okay, so you like to gamble. Let me guess—horses, cards or roulette?"

His answer was noncommittal. "I've taken a few chances in my life."

Kenley nodded knowingly. "Like coming out here with a hurricane at the front door. Why did you come here today?"

He shrugged in response, crossing his arms over his chest. "I wanted to look over the land, check out a few things."

"In the rain?"

"What better time? I know nothing about this piece of property, except that it has a house in the middle of it. I wanted to see where the water stands, how it drains, where it needs to be built up."

For the new plant, no doubt, Kenley speculated. It was always his first concern. "Here," she said, tossing him a disposable lighter. "You know, we could use some furniture."

He snorted good-naturedly. "And some electricity and a stove and a refrigerator and maybe a TV, one of those battery-operated kind." Blane watched as the flames took hold on the dry wood, licking higher and higher until the fire came fully to life.

"I'm serious. And I know where there's an old sofa. Come help me bring it in here."

She led him to a front bedroom. "There it is." She pointed to the tattered red sofa tucked away in a far corner. "Think we can move it?"

"Piece of cake."

Together they carried the old sofa into the nursery and placed it in front of the crackling fire. "There." Kenley stood back and admired the effect. "That's better. We could use a table or two, though."

"I think I saw a couple downstairs."

"Good. I'll clean up this sofa a bit. Isn't it a lovely old piece? I'll bet it was beautiful when it was new."

Blane had stopped at the door and turned to watch Kenley as she fussed over the faded and scratched piece of furniture. He marveled against the two sides of this woman. One was the efficient organizer, the career woman, a crusader for the past; the other was an excited little girl, soft, vulnerable, with a romantic heart. It was a fascinating combination that he would never grow tired of. He could get used to having her around. Life with her would never be dull, only unpredictable. The direction of his thoughts jolted him back to reality. How had his feelings gotten so far out of hand? All he wanted was a nice little affair, some pleasant companionship to help pass the long months ahead while rebuilding CP. Yet somewhere along the way he'd started having thoughts and ideas that rarely entered his mind. At least, not for a very long time. But whenever he was with Kenley he felt the pull of domesticity. The idea should have terrified him, but for some reason it didn't.

Kenley noticed his scrutiny. "Something wrong?"

He smiled slowly, with great affection. "No. Not a thing."

"While you're downstairs, I'm going to run up to the attic and see what else I can find. I'm almost certain there's more furniture in that north room."

"Be careful," he said before starting down.

The staircase spiraled upward to the attic, where large dormers allowed the last few rays of daylight to seep through. Still she had to strain to see in the dim light. She checked the south room first, but failed to find anything worth carrying back to the nursery. The room across the hall, however, was nearly overflowing with discarded belongings. The owners, having no further use for these things, had left them behind, but Kenley harbored the hope that some of the pieces could be restored and put on display when D'Evereaux was opened to the public. Her only concern now, though, was comfort during the storm. Slowly she made her way amid the odds and ends—a few broken chairs, some picture frames and a wicker rocker with the seat missing. Easing past the narrow stairway that led upward to the belvedere, she briefly entertained the idea of watching Dwight from the roof of D'Evereaux. As frightening as a storm could be, there was a certain fascination in watching nature's fury unleashed.

Moving forward, she spotted her objective. Standing in the far corner, piled with books and boxes, was a plain wooden bed complete with mattress. Smiling happily, she wound her way through the clutter and began clearing off the boxes. The mattress was stained but still in one piece. At least it would be better than sleeping on the hard floor. Roughing it had never been high on her list of fun things to do.

Quickly Kenley returned to the nursery to seek Blane's help in moving the old bed. When she stepped inside, she saw that the little room had been transformed. The fire burned cheerfully in the grate, the frayed sofa sat snugly in front of the marble fireplace, and two tables positioned nearby held food and the lantern.

Outside the wind raged, but here in one corner of D'Evereaux was a safe haven, a cocoon of warmth and light impervious to the harsh rain and the rampant fury of the hurricane. It was a cozy world unto itself, where she and Blane could hide from the outside and all the problems that lay between them. She could pretend for the night that they were the only two people on earth. A small voice warned she was flirting with danger, but she silenced it quickly. What could it hurt? Reality would come crashing back in soon enough.

"Find anything useful up in the attic?" Blane asked as he came up behind her.

"Yes." She turned and smiled. "There's an old mattress in that west section we can use, if you think you can drag it down here."

"Sure. Anything I can do to keep the boss happy," he said with a smirk.

A few minutes later, Blane struggled through the door with the shabby mattress, maneuvering it to the far wall. A cloud of dust rose as it hit the floor.

"Well, it might not be clean, but it's dry and soft," she noted with a smile.

"I don't know about you, but all that activity gave me an appetite. What all did you bring in your food sack?"

Kenley grinned and strolled over to the nylon satchel. "The very best in hurricane-survival cuisine. Lunch meat, chips, cookies, fruit, juice and coffee."

"Coffee? With its own battery-operated pot, I suppose."

Kenley held up the jar. "Instant. We can heat water on the fire."

They worked together over the meal, then settled on the sofa to eat.

Blane stared at the frayed fabric and frowned. "What is this thing made of? It's hard as a rock."

"Horsehair," she explained through a bite of ham. "Stuffed with Spanish moss."

"Remind me never to buy one of these."

The wind howled through the old house, whistling in the cracks and screaming like a banshee between the crevices. Outside it sent the rain pounding against the galleries while ripping limbs from the trees and hurling small objects through the air like deadly missiles.

Kenley watched the window, but she didn't have to see outside to visualize what was taking place. "I think Dwight has come to call."

"Yes and he'll be here all night from what I heard. Think we'll be able to get out tomorrow?" he asked.

"Maybe. We're likely to be flooded in here for another day, depending on how fast the water drains."

A loud crack like the sound of a powerful bullet split the air, and Kenley jumped.

"You okay?"

"As well as can be expected, considering we're stranded in the middle of a hurricane," she said brusquely. Drawing her feet up under her, she settled more comfortably in the corner of the sofa, her fingers toying with the remnants of her sandwich.

Blane studied her covertly, noting the way her eyes darted toward the window and her teeth gnawed on her lower lip, and felt that protective urge coming on again. "Talk to me," he said firmly.

"Just like in the elevator?" she asked with a rueful grin.

"It worked pretty well, didn't it?"

He was right, but what was she supposed to talk about? Saving D'Evereaux? This hardly seemed the time. "I could use a drink," she muttered softly, placing her paper plate on the floor.

"It wouldn't help. Only make you more jittery."

"You must think I'm a real jellyfish," she said with a shake of her head. "I'm afraid of elevators, afraid of storms." Afraid of you, she almost added. "And I cry like a baby at the drop of a hat."

"No, I don't think that at all. I think you're human, with the same fears and concerns that everyone has." He glanced at her out of the corner of his eyes. "Despite the tough take-charge image you work so hard to project."

"You don't think I'm tough?"

"Sure, but not indestructible. No matter what you might believe."

"You don't know me well enough to say that," she corrected defensively, knowing it wasn't true. He knew almost everything about her.

"Don't I? I know your deep dark secret, and I know how passionate you are. I'd say I'm off to a good start."

"Start for what?"

"Whatever it is that's happening between us. You aren't going to deny that something *is* happening, are you?"

"No," she admitted, looking into the fire. "But I'm not going to give in to it, either. This sudden...interest we feel is moving too quickly. I think maybe we'd better slow down, step back."

"Are you afraid of what might develop?" he asked after a long pause.

"Yes."

Blane smiled and nodded. "It is a bit overwhelming. But maybe we're not coming at this from the right angle. Maybe all it means is that we've both found what we've been looking for," he offered gently.

Kenley looked at him sharply. "You mean like Kismet and that love-at-first-sight nonsense? No, that's a fantasy. It only happens in the movies and books."

"You don't believe in fantasy?"

"No," she said positively. "I gave up fairy tales as a child."

"That's a shame. I just rediscovered them." He stared off into the distance as he spoke. "For a long time I didn't believe in anything. Thought life was a huge joke played on the human race. Then I found a new direction and a measure of contentment. A life that was solid, secure and satisfying." His eyes touched hers. "But when I met you, I realized the color was missing from my neat little world. The excitement, the fantasy was lacking." Blane reached out and ran the back of his hand across her cheek. "And I find you very exciting."

She wanted to pull away, but it was impossible. The look in his eyes held her prisoner. "The kind of excitement you're referring to isn't what a solid relationship is built upon. Real affection for one another takes time to grow and deepen."

"Really? I feel like I've known you since that moment in the cemetery."

Kenley recalled the piercing assessment she'd felt that day and quivered. "We're not even compatible," she whispered, fighting the growing awareness his very nearness created. Her body was remembering things her head told her to forget.

An amused grin touched Blane's lips. "Oh. I beg to differ with you. I'd say we were exceptionally compatible."

His reference to the previous night gave her the strength to move away and block out the memories. "You mean love conquers all?" she scoffed with a tight smile. "The only thing love conquers is common sense. Maybe if people took a more practical look at their relationships before they got too involved there would be fewer divorces." She hadn't intentionally meant to bring up Blane's marriage, but her words were no sooner spoken than she felt him withdraw. She also knew her next thought was wrong, but she couldn't prevent herself from wondering yet again what his ex was like. Was she tall and dark, short and blond, ultra-feminine or wholesomely athletic? And was Blane attracted to her because she reminded him of his wife or because she was a direct opposite?

"Maybe you're right," he said, rising and walking to the small table. Now was as good a time as any to tell Kenley some of the things she wanted to know. "I should have known it wouldn't work. We were totally wrong for each other. Yvonne was very much her own person, sure of herself and what she wanted. But there was a serenity about her, a regal quality. I suppose that's what drew me to her in the first place."

Swallowing the lump in her throat, Kenley tried to ignore the way Blane's voice roughened when he spoke about his wife. "You must have loved her very much."

"No," he replied bluntly. "I didn't. I chose her for all the wrong reasons. But she was so untouched, so clean and civilized. A direct opposite from the life I'd been leading, the places I'd been and the things I'd seen for the previous two years. I guess I wanted someone as far removed from that as I could get. Looking back on it, her leaving was the best thing that could have happened to me. But at the time—" he shrugged slightly, rubbing his forehead. "What hurt the most was the way she just cut me out of her life without any regrets, any second thoughts. Just a simple change of name and address. With no more consideration than she'd give to changing her shoes." He turned and met her eyes. "So you see, I'm not so good at judging people myself."

Was that a warning he was giving her or a confession? And why did she always feel uncomfortable when he finally answered her questions? She had a right to know, didn't she?

The storm winds increased, bashing against the house, intruding into their small haven and Kenley closed her eyes, mentally scolding herself for being so weak-willed with both Blane and Dwight. Opening her eyes she focused on Blane as he hunkered down and stirred the wood in the fire, then stood and rested one arm on the mantel. Finally he broke the long, heavy silence that had fallen between them.

"Kenley, about last night."

She knew this was coming. It had to be discussed. But now that the moment had arrived, she found she wasn't ready to face it. Especially in light of her new feelings for Blane. If his comment about misjudging people was meant as a warning, then she fully intended to follow his advice. It was just a matter of her head getting control over her heart. "What about it?" she said with as much nonchalance as she could dredge up.

"What are we going to do about it?"

"Nothing," she replied quickly. "We are both adults, with adult needs and desires. It happened, but it needn't happen again." It was a struggle to keep her tone level and measured. She didn't want him to see that just thinking about last night sent pinpoints of longing dancing through her veins.

"Are you saying you don't want it to happen or that it shouldn't?"

Kenley looked away. "Both," she said firmly, amazed at how difficult it was to say that and willing herself to be stronger.

"I see." Blane felt as though he'd just been kicked in the gut. For some reason he didn't understand, Kenley's indifferent attitude toward their night together made him feel cheated. He'd never considered himself the world's greatest lover, but he'd always tried to be gentle and considerate and give as much attention to his partner's needs as his own. For Kenley to treat their lovemaking so casually hurt like hell. Had he imagined the responses he'd felt in her? Had he been so caught up in his own discoveries that he'd completely failed to understand her feelings?

Part of his mind reminded him that this was just what he'd wanted. No strings, no entanglements. He should be glad she was so sensible about the whole incident. After all, he had wanted to rebuild his protective barrier, but now that he was on the verge of putting it back up he found he didn't want it anymore. He didn't want this relationship with Kenley to end or even stagnate. But he didn't know where he wanted it to go, either. "Are you saying that last night meant nothing to you?"

"Of course it meant something. I don't give myself to just anyone. But I don't think it would be wise for it to continue." She was determined to be logical about this. "We're business associates. We're on the opposite sides of a difficult situation. The conflicts are stressful enough without the complications of any kind of personal involvement."

"So you're going to completely ignore this attraction between us. Pretend it doesn't exist?" he demanded, one hand on his hip.

"It exists," she admitted reluctantly. "But that's no reason to behave irresponsibly. You might like to take chances, but I don't."

"What are you taking a chance on, Kenley?"

She hadn't wanted to get into this, but since he was forcing the issue, she might as well open all the gates. "You," she shot back at him. "You're a mystery to me. You drop into my life like some character out of a bad movie, work your way into my... affections, and I don't know anything about you, except the bits and pieces I hear in the office. No one ever heard of you before Seth died. You have some sort of business you won't talk about, you refuse to work on Wednesdays, but no one knows why, and for two years of your life you disappeared from the face of the earth. It doesn't give me a feeling of security, all these questions, and I get a new one every day. I don't like surprises, Blane."

Blane ran a hand through his hair in frustration. "You can't know everything about a person instantly. No one can. You said so yourself. Part of the delight in getting to know someone are discoveries you make along the way."

"That depends on whether the discoveries turn out to be merely charming facets of their personality or serious character disorders."

"What are you talking about?"

"I'm trying to be practical about this. I don't dive into unknown waters without checking the depth first."

Blane cocked his head, a deep crease appearing between his brows. "How can you be this practical about emotions? Especially those between a man and a woman? It's not something you analyze and dissect, to find out how and why it works. You have to lead with your heart, experience it, let it sustain you as it grows. It's the only thing in life that really matters, and you can't just explain it away like an illness."

"I'm not trying to explain it away, I just want some reassurances. I want to know what's ahead."

"That's not possible. No one knows that."

"You can have a pretty good idea," she persisted. "If you're totally honest with one another."

"Okay, fine." He relented. "Plan ahead, keep your eyes open, but don't close them to possibilities you might not have seen. Life doesn't offer any money-back guarantees. All it promises is opportunity. It's up to us to take advantage of it or throw it away. Don't throw away what's happening between us, Kenley."

"Opportunity to be hurt again?" She shook her head. "It's safer to put your trust in something solid and substantial, something that time can't destroy."

Blane set his jaw. He knew where this was leading, and he didn't like it one bit. "Like D'Evereaux."

"Yes. Like D'Evereaux," Kenley said between clenched teeth. "People change. Relationships crumble. But this house has withstood time, weather and progress, and it'll be here long after we're gone."

"This house is just a lifeless pile of brick and wood," he said, jamming his hands into the back pockets of his jeans. "This hurricane could wipe it off the map. A couple of bulldozers could level it in a day. You said yourself it was ready to fall apart if something wasn't done soon. When that happens, it'll be gone forever. What sort of dependability is that?"

She turned her back, refusing to answer.

"People are the only things in life that are worth caring about. Making a commitment to another human being, extending a hand to help someone else, giving back instead of taking. Those are the only things that make sense in the world. Believe me, I learned the hard way. But cutting off your emotions and putting your faith in an object—" he shook his head "—that's no way to exist."

"All D'Evereaux needs is some money and skilled craftsmen to save it," she persisted. "Don't you see, that's something I can fix. It's predictable. It's a logical problem with a logical solution. But relationships and people, they aren't so predictable. They're too full of surprises and unforeseen complications."

"I never said relationships aren't difficult. They don't just happen, they have to be worked at, guarded constantly. Yes, it's work, but the rewards are more than worth it." Silently she shook her head, putting a severe strain on Blane's patience. "Kenley, you're trying to control something that can't be controlled. No one can do that. Not even someone as determined as you."

"You just don't understand."

Blane rested his hands on his hips and looked at the floor a few seconds, as if measuring his next words. "What I see is that you're throwing up roadblocks against problems that don't exist."

She refused to admit he'd hit a nerve. She did jump to conclusions, but it was better than being blind-sided. Still his lack of understanding hurt, and she responded defensively. "Fine. Then remove some of the roadblocks. Answer my questions, so I don't feel like I'm standing at the edge of a washed-out bridge with someone's hands in the middle of my back ready to push!"

"Ask away," he replied, his hands making a sweeping gesture. "What is it you want to know, Kenley?"

His compliance threw her off guard momentarily and she said the first thing that entered her mind. "Where were you for those two years?"

Blane sighed softly, knowing it was pointless to hold out on her any longer. He'd just have to get it out, and hope she understood. Though in her present frame of mind he seriously doubted that. "I was in the army."

It was a possibility she'd never considered, and she wondered why it hadn't occurred to her before. But why was he so secretive about it? "Is that where you met Dave?"

Now it was Blane's turn to be off guard. "How did you know Dave was a veteran?"

"When I went to find you this afternoon, he was in your office and he had...that is, I saw him without his...artificial leg."

He took a deep breath and shook his head. It was all going to come out now. He just wished it could have happened differently. "We didn't serve together. We met in a hospital stateside."

"You were wounded?" Kenley asked. Her mind immediately conjured up a rash of horrible images. But Blane quickly dismissed them.

"Nothing serious. It happened near the end of my second tour in Nam."

"Vietnam?" Kenley felt a rush of relief. He'd been in the army those missing years. It all made sense. It was perfectly logical. The relief was replaced quickly by a feeling of profound sympathy. Blane had been there, gone through that awful war. Her heart went out to him and her eyes made a quick assessment, as if she'd never really understood him before. She had to force herself to concentrate on what he was saying, catching only the end of his sentence.

"Dad was furious when I deserted."

Kenley was shocked. "From the army?"

"Not from it, to it. I worked at CP all through high school and hated it. I was young, a freshman in college, and I had no idea what I wanted to do with my life. So I joined the army. Vietnam was winding down, but it was still pretty hairy over there. I had a perfect excuse to stay out of it, being an only son, but I wanted to go."

He moved back to the sofa and sat down. "When I got back I went to work at CP again, but by that time I had a pretty good idea of what I wanted to do. Dad didn't exactly embrace the idea so I knew I'd get no help from him. Not exactly a new problem for me then. Vietnam vets were considered little better than the scum of the earth. I was used to it."

Kenley was still sorting through all that Blane had told her. It explained so many things. His odd remarks, which had sounded so ominous before, took on a whole new meaning. His comments about not believing in anything and about life being a huge joke made total sense now, as did his irritation at her continued use of the word "chaos." To her, just a word. To Blane, something horribly real. He'd referred to himself as a Renaissance man emerged from the Dark Ages. She knew now he'd been to hell and returned much older and wiser. She'd seen the look in his eyes, even recognized it, but had been too self-absorbed to understand its meaning.

Her heart tightened in regret as more clues paraded through her mind—the helicopter in the French Quarter, his frequent use of military terms, his overwhelming concern for people. He was one of the forgotten soldiers, the men who had lost so much and been ignored and shunned by their own country. Men who were part of a war that had nearly divided the country beyond repair. "You were one of them," she breathed softly. Blane suddenly turned his back and she searched frantically for something appropriate to say. "I'm sorry." It seemed so inadequate, so unbelievably shallow.

Blane's deep voice broke into her thoughts. "Anything else you want to know? My favorite brand of coffee? My social security number? How I like my eggs in the morning? My favorite color? Do I sleep in the nude?" He didn't like having to justify himself to her. But what he liked even less was Kenley's reaction to his being a veteran. It was hard to mistake her sudden withdrawal. The problem was that he couldn't decide if she was disgusted or merely surprised. Abruptly he stood and walked across the room, leaning against the door frame, staring out into the broad hallway.

To Kenley, Blane's sudden irritation indicated she was hitting a nerve and maybe getting too close to things he was still hiding. Part of her wanted to believe that he'd told her everything, but her scars were too deep and had been carried too long.

Disappointment coiled in his stomach at finding himself back in the same old position. It didn't seem to matter what type of woman he fell for, she couldn't accept him as he was. He'd felt Kenley's scrutiny after he told her he was in Nam. She'd looked him over inch by inch as if he was somehow different, warped. He'd seen variations of it before. Like Yvonne's scornful glare when he turned his back on a secure financial future, and that calculating glint in Debbi's eyes when she saw a unique opportunity to advance her career. And what would Kenley's expressive face reveal when she knew the full truth? Would she try to use him to save this damned house?

No, he wouldn't accept that. Whether it was his gut instinct speaking to him or merely wishful thinking, he knew Kenley was made of stronger stuff than that. He was sure of it. He was equally sure that he couldn't come clean now. Not until he had time to tell her the full story and gauge her response. He wanted her to trust him, but with her past experience he couldn't blame her for being overly cautious. He wanted to think that given the right time and place he could make her understand. He wanted to believe that Kenley was different. He'd known passion and caring before, but never the kind of intimacy and fulfillment he experienced with Kenley. But what did she feel? Was she denying the attraction because of her experience with Russ or because she didn't care and didn't know how to tell him? Kenley was obsessed with the truth. If he pushed her, she might tell him something he didn't want to hear, but he had to know, good or bad, because he was already too deep into this to pull back voluntarily.

Turning, he walked back into the small room and seated himself on the sofa, forearms resting on his knees as he gauged his words. "Why did you come here today?" he asked quietly.

His voice was low and seductive, and she avoided his eyes. "I told you. To rescue you, remember?"

"Why did you want to rescue me?"

"That's a silly question. You were stranded in a hurricane."

"Why?" he persisted. It was almost a command.

Kenley rose from the sofa and stood by the fire, her back to him. She wasn't ready to answer his question. "Because I care about you and I didn't want anything to happen to you. It's dangerous out here all alone."

Blane came and stood behind her. His nearness sent tingles of awareness along her spine. Closing her eyes, she felt her body respond instinctively, remembering the feel of his hands upon her skin. She wished he would move away. With him so near, her brain refused to function properly.

"Care about me? What's that supposed to mean, Kenley?" He turned her around forcing her to look at him.

"Just what it implies. You're important to me."

"How important?"

"Blane, please." She tried to move away, but he refused to let her go.

"Tell me."

Why was he pushing her on this? "What do you want me to say?"

"That you feel the same way I do. That you feel something more than affection for me. Is that so much to ask?"

"Yes!"

"Why?"

"Because I can't allow you to get control of me. I can't allow you to take over my life. If I give in to you, and I could do very easily, then I'd have to give up my identity. I'd lose who I am."

"I don't want to control you. I want to spend time with you, get to know you better and see if what we feel is more than mere infatuation."

"I can't."

"What are you afraid of? I'm not Russ. I'm not out to use you or hurt you? Can't you trust me that far?"

"I've been told that before. Trust me, Kenley—I know what's best, Kenley." Her eyes filled with moisture and she shook her head, stepping away from him. "That's how it begins. I start trusting, then little by little I lose who I am and start becoming someone you want. And before I realize it, I'm caught, unable to think or breathe without help, just like..." Her voice was raspy and she looked away trying to calm herself.

"I understand that Russ wounded you deeply, but you've got such a death grip on your emotions you aren't even living anymore. Sooner or later you're going to have to let someone else into your heart, Kenley, or else this fear you have will strangle you."

"Maybe after we have this problem with D'Evereaux and CP all worked out, then we can talk about some sort of personal arrangement...."

"Damn. Can't you commit to anything other than this house?" His chest felt as though it was going to explode. He'd been wrong. She wasn't any different from anyone else.

"Is that what this is about, commitment? Yes, I'm committed to D'Evereaux. I understand it. I know it won't rip my heart out and leave it bleeding on the floor. Can you give me the same assurance?" she shouted.

"You're blowing this thing way out of proportion. You're overreacting."

"Am I? Tell that to a woman who'd been married for seventeen years, who'd spent her life devoted to her husband and children to the exclusion of everything else, who depended on her husband to the extent she had no mind of her own. She couldn't balance a checkbook, couldn't drive, didn't have an opinion that wasn't his first. Then one day he doesn't come home. She gets a phone call from Arizona. Seems he has another family out there, a wife and three sons, and he'd decided he prefers them to the two daughters he left in Virginia." Kenley struggled to keep the tears from falling. "He didn't even say goodbye."

Blane felt sick. Twice in her life she'd been deserted without warning. No wonder she was so afraid of trusting her emotions to someone else. "Oh, Ken," he said softly.

"Do you know what my mother did? She started to shrivel up and die. She had no idea where to start taking control of her life. I had to take over. Fifteen years old, and I had to be the head of the house. She never understood why he left, what she'd done wrong, how she'd failed him. But I knew. I knew exactly what she'd done wrong." Her eyes were brimming with tears, and her chest heaved with painful emotions.

"Ken, I'm sorry. But those were different times. You're not like your mother. You're strong, capable, intelligent. I don't want to change any of that. It's one of the things that attracted me to you. Your job is part of what makes you special."

Tears began to slide down her cheeks. "Oh, God, Blane, she couldn't even read the water bill."

Blane's heart ached for her. So much responsibility so young. The disillusionment had scarred her deeply. He reached out to hold her, to soothe away some of the hurt, but she pushed him away.

"No. Just leave me alone. Please. I swore I'd never be like her, never give up who I am for a man. I made a mistake once. I won't do that again. Not even for you!"

The nursery that had once felt so warm and safe now seemed to be closing in, becoming suffocating and cramped. She turned and hurried from the room, ignoring Blane's shout, praying he would just leave her alone.

The wind seemed much louder and closer here in the hallway, but Kenley was only partially aware of the hurricane now. She just wanted to find a place to think and hide from Blane. She had to put some distance between them, so she could sort everything out.

At the bottom of the stairs she automatically entered the conservatory. The large, nearly all-glass addition to D'Evereaux had always been her favorite room.

Kenley stepped through the door and burst into tears. The lovely old room was already sitting in a foot of water. It seemed the final insult. She sat down on the steps and cried. Nothing made sense. There was no order to her life, no control, only chaos and disaster in every direction, and Blane was at the heart of it. He seemed to have the script. He knew the ending to this story and precisely how they would arrive there. She, on the other hand, was left to stumble blindly along, ad-libbing at each encounter. But even though her feelings for him seemed to grow stronger each moment, she couldn't let it override her own need to be self-sufficient. She couldn't allow herself to become immersed in this intense attraction and lose sight of who she was. How could she compromise without giving up the control she'd fought so hard to gain? The howling wind seemed to be an echo of her own tormented soul.

Chapter Eleven

Blane called after Kenley and followed her to the door, but stopped when he realized it was futile to try and reason with her now. They both needed time to cool down. Walking back to the fireplace, he rubbed his forehead in thought. He'd been a fool. No wonder Kenley was so afraid to give in to her feelings. She'd been betrayed twice in her life. His reluctance to confide in her only added to her fears. He understood a great deal more now, why she put such a premium on truth and openness and why she wanted a partner who was predictable, with no secrets. She'd been betrayed by all the men in her life, and from her standpoint, he was just one more big question mark that could only lead to pain. She wanted to trust him, but she'd been burned too many times in her life and he couldn't blame her for being scared to give in to her emotions too quickly. If he'd only known about her father, he would have handled the whole thing differently. They both had been frightened to open up all the way, to look too closely at what they were feeling because of their pasts.

Walking back into the nursery he stood at the mantel, his tongue worrying his bottom teeth, his forehead creased in concern. Something even deeper had motivated Kenley's outburst. The pain he'd seen in her eyes went beyond a fear of commitment, beyond Russ and possibly even her father's rejection. There were several solutions to their problems, but she wouldn't accept any of them. Why? He'd learned to trust his gut in these matters and it had rarely let him down. It was telling him now that Kenley wasn't being totally honest about her feelings. She was still putting up roadblocks.

A fierce gust of wind bashed the house, followed by the crash of yet another tree falling under the strength of the storm. Suddenly Blane didn't like the idea of Kenley being alone in the house somewhere. In her state of mind, there was no telling where she would wander. Despite her belief that the old house could withstand the force of Dwight, Blane wasn't nearly as certain. He'd feel much better with her sitting safely beside him in the nursery.

He was halfway down the stairs when he heard what sounded like an explosion followed by Kenley's scream. He bounded to the first floor, taking in the situation at a glance. A huge limb from one of the old oak trees had been propelled through the glass wall of the conservatory. Wood and glass were everywhere, the splintered fragments of both being blown about like matchsticks in the resulting whirlwind. Frantically he searched for Kenley, praying she had not gone into the room. His heart stopped for long seconds when he saw her huddled against the wall along the steps. He yanked open the door, the force of the wind and the rain pinning him in mid-stride momentarily. Bending low, he fought his way the short distance to Kenley. Thank God she'd not been farther into the room. When he reached her side, he took her shoulders in his hands and tried to speak to her, but the wind stole his voice the instant he opened his mouth. Pulling her close, he turned her face to his chest for protection and began to half drag and half carry her up the stairs to the relative safety of the gallery.

Once inside the main house, he released his hold only long enough to force the door shut against the storm. Then he scooped her up and hurried upstairs. From what he could see with a cursory inspection, she wasn't hurt. But she was crying and murmuring softly into his chest.

"It stings. It stings. I saw it coming."

"Hush. I know," he said as he topped the stairs. "You'll be okay."

In the safety of the little room, he placed her gently on the sofa and quickly retrieved blankets to wrap her in. His face was lined with worry and concern. "Are you all right? Do you hurt anywhere?"

Kenley shook her head and wiped her eyes. "No. I don't think so. It just stings. I saw it coming and I couldn't get out of the way. It was so fast."

There were tiny cuts on her hands and cheek, and he opened up the first-aid kit. He felt his heart rate slow and return to normal, though his fingers still shook as he tended her superficial wounds. When he'd seen her in that room, he'd thought his world had ended. To lose her now, when there was so much he wanted to share with her, would have been Fate's cruelest twist.

Reality was foggy for a while, but now she could feel herself slowly calming down under Blane's gentle ministrations. But when she closed her eyes, she saw again that horrifying moment when the conservatory had exploded around her.

It was cold and wet, and the wind's momentum pinned her to the wall with a force she couldn't overcome. She felt frozen forever in this wind tunnel of stinging rain. Suddenly there were strong hands on her shoulders, pulling her away, turning her into the hard, warm safety of his chest. Then she was out of the wind and the rain, and the noise disappeared briefly, leaving her feeling alone and cold. She opened her eyes and recognized the gallery. It was quiet here...and dry. Then the hands returned and she closed her eyes again, feeling herself being lifted up against Blane's chest. As he carried her up the stairs, she began to regain her senses, but the glass and splintered wood had left their marks. "It stings. It stings," she heard herself saying. "I saw it coming."

The memory sent a shudder through her, followed by a wave of relief that she was safe again. She opened her eyes when Blane's voice filtered through to her. "Are you all right?"

His thumb was gently stroking her cheek, his eyes boring into hers as he continued. "When I saw you in that room, I..."

Suddenly he looked away and rose from the sofa, but Kenley thought she saw a glistening in his dark eyes. Tears? Her heart contracted.

"You need to get out of those wet clothes," he said after tossing another log on the fire. "Did you bring extra?"

Kenley nodded. "In that red bag."

Blane brought the bag to her, sitting on the edge of the sofa. She unwrapped the blankets and kicked off her shoes.

"Here, put this on," he said, handing her the oversized white shirt she had packed.

"There should be some jeans and underwear in there, too."

Blane rummaged around then shook his head. "Sorry. Shoes, socks and a shirt."

"But I know I packed them. I washed yesterday and stacked everything on top of the...drier," she finished with a groan. "Which is where they're still sitting." In her haste to pack, she'd never gotten back to the laundry room to get them.

Blane reached out and fingered the fabric of her shirt. "It looks sturdy enough to preserve your modesty." His dark eyes twinkled with mischief. "Go on. Get changed. I'll heat some water." As he crossed the room, he looked back at her and grinned devilishly. "I promise not to peek."

Kenley moved to the corner near the bed and pulled off her clothes, keeping her back toward Blane. She was soaked through, so even the lacy underthings had to go. The shirt felt wonderfully warm and comfortable, though she hadn't realized until now how high the sides were cut or how thin the fabric was. It made her painfully aware of the fact that she was completely naked under the white shirt, bringing back vivid memories of the night before in Blane's office, memories she ached to repeat but knew were out of the question for now.

Picking up her socks, she walked back to the sofa. Blane turned to look at her as she approached, his dark eyes traveling the length of her body and back. The blood in her veins sparked.

"Very flattering."

Kenley tried to ignore what his eyes were doing to her. "Shouldn't you change, too? You're soaked."

"I've been wet before."

"Don't be silly. Neither one of us needs to get sick from this little adventure."

"Ah, yes. We must be practical." He grinned the grin that always seemed to have a meaning different from his words.

As he began to unbutton his shirt, Kenley realized the repercussions of her innocent instructions. She watched as he draped his shirt on the woodpile, then bent down to poke at the fire.

The firelight flickered over him as he worked, the shadows accentuating the muscles in his back and arms. She remembered how those muscles felt under her fingers, the way his body felt against hers, the hands, strong and gentle as they held her, touched her and carried her to...

"You all right?"

Kenley blinked and jerked away from the direction her thoughts had been traveling. "Yes. Fine," she replied quickly. "I guess I'm still a little dazed."

"Sit down," he said softly, taking the socks from her hands. "Give me your foot." He joined her on the sofa.

"I can do it."

Slowly he shook his head, reaching out to take her left foot in his hand and resting it against his thigh. He slipped the sock over her toes, his strong fingers encircling her ankle. The contact sent waves of desire along Kenley's spine. He took her other foot then, and she tried to ignore the feel of his warm hands against her skin.

His gentleness penetrated her barriers again. It would be so easy to love him. If only there weren't so many obstacles still in the way. She often wondered why she struggled so hard against him. He had the power to break through her toughest defenses with just a word, a touch, sometimes with only a look. It was a frightening power. "That's fine. Thanks," she said, jerking her feet free from his stimulating contact. "I'll be okay now." She could feel Blane's eyes studying her, analyzing her reactions. If only she could read him as easily as he could read her. At the moment he seemed to be expecting something from her. "I'm sorry for the way I acted earlier. I shouldn't have run off that way."

"No, you shouldn't have," he said bluntly.

Kenley looked over at him. He was probing her with his eyes again. She shifted uncomfortably, making sure the shirt was properly arranged. "You were right," she admitted reluctantly. "I did overreact."

"Yes. You did."

"I guess it was just stress." Why did she feel compelled to explain herself to him? "I've been under a lot of pressure lately. All the problems with D'Evereaux, and sorting out my feelings for you, and now being stranded in a hurricane... It's perfectly understandable."

"Reliving the past is never easy. For anyone."

Damn. He was doing it again. Cutting like a surgeon through all the garbage and getting right to the heart of the matter. Her defenses were too weakened to carry her through this one. She closed her eyes and rested her head on the back of the sofa. The tears sprang from out of no-where, surprising even her. "My house. My beautiful house. How much more can it take? There's a foot of water in the conservatory, and now the windows are all gone, and the first floor is turning into a damn bayou. The trees are being ripped apart. And there's nothing I can do to stop it. I have to sit here and watch it die. I feel so helpless." Kenley fully expected Blane to come and comfort her as he always did.

Instead he rose and stood by the fireplace, one hand gripping the mantel, the other resting on his hip as he struggled to control the wave of anger inside him. "For God's sake, Kenley, be honest with yourself," he shouted. "This isn't about D'Evereaux, or your dad, or even our feelings for one another."

Kenley was jolted out of her tears by his verbal attack, and she stared at him wide-eyed.

He came and sat beside her, taking her face between the palms of his hands. "What's really bothering you? Tell me. Let me help."

Kenley felt the tears forming anew. There was no defense against Blane when he was being kind. "I don't know. Everything's so confused. Nothing makes sense anymore." All the agonies seemed to fuse together in her chest and swell up into her throat. A sob escaped then burst into a fit of crying that shook her to the core. Blane held her until she'd cried it out.

When the sobbing eased she blew her nose, wiped her eyes and sat back, turning her gaze toward the ceiling. "What's wrong with me? I used to be so confident, so adaptable. I could handle any twist and turn that came along. And I never cry. Never! Now I turn into a puddle for no reason. I hate it. Crying is such a stupid, useless thing to do."

"No, it's not useless. It's healthy," Blane countered. "It's a way of working past all the emotional baggage we carry around and need to unload from time to time. It's part of growing up."

"I'm thirty-two years old. Isn't it a little late for me to be growing up?"

"Everyone grows at a different rate."

"You were probably born grown-up," she observed sourly.

"No." He chuckled. "I'm still working on it."

"Why is life so complicated? Why do I feel so confused about everything?"

"You can't get what you want until you know what it is. What is it you want out of life, Kenley?"

"Exactly what I have," she said firmly. "My work. I'm very happy with my life. I'm successful. I've got a wonderful job, good salary. I have good friends and a nice home. I've got everything any woman would want."

"Do you?"

"Yes. What more is there?"

"You tell me." He brushed the still damp hair away from her face and looked into her eyes. "You know, you're not the only one who hears rumors. I've heard several about you since you moved into my office."

"What sort of rumors?"

He shrugged. "That you're not yourself. That you seem unhappy, dissatisfied. That maybe you're disappointed with your job or your life."

A new ache filled her heart. The truth hurt. Still she shook her head in denial, squeezing her eyes shut.

"Kenley, don't hide. Tell me what you really want."

Even as she struggled against it, she felt the barriers crumble. "I want to quit. To run away. I'm tired of it, of me. Everyone says I'm wonderful, clever and strong. I can handle anything. 'Isn't she remarkable?' But I'm not. I feel like a fraud. I have exactly what I set out to get, but it doesn't make me happy. There's no satisfaction anymore. I have this empty spot, this hole inside that I can't fill."

Blane took her hand, listening intently as she talked.

"I find myself dreaming about things I never thought I would."

"Like what?"

"Like a husband, home, even children. Someone to help share the burden. But then I feel so guilty and afraid."

"Those are perfectly natural desires. Why should you feel guilty?"

"Because it took years of hard work and sacrifice to provide women with the opportunities they have today. My mother had no career choice. But I did. And I contributed my time and effort toward ERA. I marched, I petitioned, I did whatever I could. I believe in their cause, and I've lived my life that way. To throw that all over now to be a wife and mother would be betraying the women's movement. It would be devaluing all the hard work that put us where we are."

There was a hint of amusement in Blane's eyes. "I hardly think one woman's defection would alter the course of women's rights either way. But don't you think you've chosen a very narrow interpretation of the ideas behind the movement? I don't claim to be an expert on the subject, but the way I see it, women's lib isn't a fixed doctrine, some dogmatic religion that allows only one interpretation. They were fighting for the right of each woman to decide the best life-style for herself. They're not saying everyone has to have a career, just the opportunity and flexibility to choose. We all have to adjust to the times and circumstances."

Kenley brushed her hair out of her eyes. "How can this be happening to me? I always had a clear picture of my life. Such a concise plan."

"No one can really plan how his life will go. You can make a road map, but you can't foresee the detours and the potholes."

Her blue eyes looked questioningly at his brown ones. "Are you a detour or a pothole?"

His smile warmed her. "Right now I'm only a mile marker."

Kenley sighed raggedly. "When did it all change? Where did I fall out of step?"

"It's a gradual thing. What we want out of life when we're twenty may not seem very important at thirty, and vice versa."

"I feel so helpless. I've lost control of every part of my life, and I don't know how to get it back."

Dark eyes pierced hers. "Why do you need control?"

Kenley was momentarily nonplussed by his question. She'd never asked herself why control seemed so vital. "Because if I lose control, then everything will fall into chaos."

Blane frowned. "That word again. Okay, let's do some hypothesizing here. Worst case scenario."

"What do you mean?" she asked as she dabbed at her eyes.

"Let's say you've lost control. What happens?"

"I could lose D'Evereaux."

"There are other plantations that need saving, aren't there?"

"Yes, but this one is special."

"You told me they're all special in their way."

Kenley mulled that over. "Well, then I could lose my job."

"You're not qualified to do other things?"

"Yes, of course I am, but—"

Blane was relentless. "What else?"

"I could lose my town house."

"I saw a For Sale sign on the building next to yours the last time I was there."

"You have all the answers, don't you?" she said in irritation.

"But that's the point, don't you see? Short of losing your life, there's nothing that can happen that's so bad you can't recover. The key to life is flexibility, being able to roll with the punches. It has nothing to do with control."

Kenley considered what he'd said. He was right. She could get other jobs or houses, but the one thing she couldn't replace was Blane. It hit her like a blinding flash. He was all that mattered. She looked into his eyes. "I could lose you."

He smiled and touched his fingers to her chin. "Not a chance," he whispered then pulled her into his arms, his lips closing possessively over hers, claiming her heart.

Kenley felt the fears and confusion beginning to fade, to slide slowly back into their proper places. When their lips parted, she reached up and traced the outline of his lower lip with her fingertips. "You're so wise. How do you make things seem so logical and simple?"

"How do you make them so complicated?"

Kenley sighed. "Practice, practice, practice."

Blane gave her a skeptical glance. "I thought that was how you got to Carnegie Hall. Come on. You've got to be tired. I'm going to put you to bed for the night."

Kenley didn't resist. She was thoroughly drained and exhausted. The bed looked too inviting. She allowed Blane to tuck her in, then followed him with her eyes as he walked back to the fireplace. The wind seemed to be louder, a constant pervasive sound, like a freight train with no end. She tried to ignore it and concentrate on the things she and Blane had discussed, but she was very tired and drifted off to sleep quickly.

From across the room, Blane watched her tenderly. Even in sleep she was the most adorable thing he'd ever seen. Yet his forehead creased in thought as he gazed at her. Nothing had really been settled between them. They'd each aired some very intense emotions but had reached no solution. Was it any wonder she was afraid of getting emotionally involved with a man, even on a casual level? He ached for her and wished that he could put her fears to rest and remove the scars that had been inflicted on her emotions. But he carried more than a few scars himself, and he knew it took time and a lot of patience to cover them over permanently. He'd have to get everything out in the open soon, make sure she felt he was being totally honest. He'd been relieved when she hadn't pressed him about his business. She was still adjusting to him being a veteran. Now wasn't the time to tell her. He wanted a quiet place and time to explain and clear up any misconceptions she might have. He remembered her reaction when he said he'd been in Vietnam and felt his gut tighten. "You're one of them." Would she understand? Could he make her accept it? Still he clung to the hope that once he told her she would back him up one hundred percent. His eyes strayed back to Kenley's sleeping form. Her arm was draped over the edge of the mattress looking soft, pink and glowing in the candlelight. His fingers twitched as they remembered the silken feel of her skin under his hands. A loud boom shook the old house and Kenley sat up with a jolt, her blue eyes wide with fright.

Blane quickly moved to her, stooping down to urge her back to sleep. "It's nothing. Probably another tree. Lie down."

Kenley took his hand and looked into his eyes. "Stay with me."

There was a need for comfort in her plea, and Blane steeled himself. Was he strong enough? Could he stay close, with only a thin piece of fabric between them, and not demand more? He'd just have to test his willpower. "Scared of the bogeyman?"

Dimples flashed. "Yes. The Hurricane Dwight kind."

Blane eased onto the mattress and Kenley scooted over, keeping her back to him. She snuggled closer until she rested against his chest. His blood was on fire, but he forced himself to hold her as if she were a scared child instead of the woman he desired with a power that matched the raging hurricane. He did allow himself the pleasure of nuzzling her hair, which feathered around his chin. She smelled sweet, fresh. The lingering fragrance of her favorite perfume clung to the white shirt. His heart beat against her back, and he closed his eyes, remembering the feel of her beneath his hands and the way her body had fit so perfectly against his.

All she had wanted was his comfort, nothing more, yet being so close she realized she wouldn't be content with only that. She'd never understood addiction. Never understood what drove people to endanger themselves, that titanic need for something that was so blatantly wrong. Yet here she was craving his touch with an intensity that frightened her. He'd begun opening up to her tonight, telling her about his marriage, and his missing years in Vietnam. She'd been wrong to be so suspicious of him. Wrong to try to fight against him. Perhaps he was right. She should just release the stranglehold on her fears and see what was ahead for them. She felt him shift against her and melted inside. She was getting in over her head, but she didn't think it mattered any more. He was a slow poison that had gradually built up in her system until she was unable to find an antidote. "Blane," she whispered.

"Hush. We've talked enough for one night. We aren't going to settle anything in the next few hours. Just close your eyes and sleep. We'll find a way to work things out. We'll go slow, take our time. Whatever you want to do. I can be very patient when I'm waiting for something of value."

"I just wanted to tell you that I really do care for you. Very much."

A rush of searing heat filled his veins, and as he felt her press her body closer, the restraint he had tried so hard to maintain snapped. His hand moved across her abdomen and slowly down her hip and thigh, sliding under the thin shirt. She felt delicious, cool and smooth. His hand traveled upward along her side, coming to rest on the sweet mound of flesh. He heard her moan softly, and she arched against his hand, nipples erect and anxious. His lips found the nape of her neck and trailed kisses around to her jaw and behind her ear. He was lost in the smell and the feel of her. She filled each of his senses to overflowing. His hand roamed eagerly over her soft curves, petting, exploring every inch of warm flesh.

She turned in his arms and he crushed her close, his lips traveling down the long throat to her shoulders. He was starving, greedy; he wanted to taste every inch of her. Her hands were pinned against her sides, trapped but not idle. A jolt of white-hot fire pierced his mind as her hand inched across his belly and downward, her finger gently teasing the tip of his passion. He groaned and buried his face in her hair. She grew bolder, encircling him with her small, cool hand, driving him wild with ecstasy. Urgently he slid her up his chest. His mouth closed over one rosy tip, sucking slowly, gently, savoring the sweet taste of her. She offered him everything with total abandonment, and he was too consumed with desire to think of anything but his great need. His fingers found her moist center, and she arched in his hands, head thrown back, writhing as he took his time loving her. He was lost, on fire, insane with need for her.

Holding her close, he rolled onto his stomach and drank in the sight of her beneath him, supporting himself on his elbows. Her eyes were misty blue, her face glowing from his touch. Soft arms encircled his neck. Her dimpled mouth teased his throat and chest, and his heart thundered violently in his ears. He heard her call his name softly as she undulated against him invitingly, opening for his pleasure, and he plunged full-force, sheathing himself in the sweetness of her silken body. She gave unquestioningly, and he devoured her gift and asked for more. He thrust again, riding the wave of his passions like a man who has nothing to lose, and still she gave until he burst from the sea more totally sated than ever before.

Cradling her in his arms, he kissed her gently, then they drifted off to sleep as the storm wreaked havoc around them.

Chapter Twelve

It was the stark utter silence that woke Kenley, the sudden absence of roaring wind and driving rain. She was still cradled in Blane's arms; still felt the glow of their lovemaking. She had given herself totally to him, wanting to give to him the way he had given to her that first time.

His lovemaking had seemed more fierce this time, his passion intense, almost driven. She had opened all of herself, and he had filled her so completely she was almost afraid of the new sensation.

There were still questions, still obstacles, still things that frightened her, but in his arms nothing else seemed important. Common sense vanished. As she watched him sleep, the dark eyes opened and she smiled.

"Dwight gone?" he asked when he realized the room was silent.

Kenley shook her head. "Just the eye passing over."

"I'd better check the fire."

Rolling off the mattress, he picked up his jeans, sliding them over long legs. Kenley slipped her arms into her shirt, not bothering to fasten the buttons.

"I think we need more wood. You stay put, and I'll be right back." He walked to the bed and tousled her hair, then pulled her to her feet, her body full against his. "Do you have any idea what you do to me?"

Kenley pressed closer, the feel of his hard chest against her partially exposed skin arousing her desires again. "I'm beginning to." Her hand slid down his side and strayed across his stomach toward the front of his jeans.

He caught it deftly and smiled into her eyes. "Hold that thought." With a devilish grin, he swatted her bottom as he turned and left the room.

Kenley wrapped her arms around herself, drifting in the heady sensation she was experiencing. None of it made sense, none of it was practical or logical or rational, but for some strange reason she didn't care. She wished the hurricane would go on forever and that she and Blane could stay here in this cozy little love nest and never have to deal with the rest of the world and its petty problems.

Blane had been gone only a few minutes when the wind started to kick up again. It came as suddenly as it had stopped, as if some giant switch had been thrown. On the heels of the wind came a thunderous crash that reverberated through every section of D'Evereaux. Kenley was infused with fear. "Blane?" Her mind filled with a barrage of horrible scenes of him hurt or dying. Nothing could happen to him now. Fear blocked out all rational thought, and she screamed his name and started toward the door, only to find him there ahead of her. "Oh, Blane," she said with a heartfelt sigh of relief, "I thought something horrible had happened to you. I didn't know where you were and I was so scared. What was that noise? Are you all right? What was it? Are you hurt?"

Hastily he dropped the pile of wood on the floor and reached out. His arms encircled her, solid and serene. "I'm

LEAD WITH YOUR HEART   213

fine. I didn't do an in-depth survey, but it looks like you lost part of the roof on the south side."

"But are you okay?" she asked, dismissing his report. "You weren't in there when it happened?"

He shook his head. "No."

"I was so frightened. I don't want to lose you."

"Are you sure?"

"Yes. But you'll have to help me. There's still so much to think about, to learn. I've never been good at dealing with changes."

He smiled knowingly. "Well, I've found that change is usually for the better. Don't be afraid of it. Or of me."

"I'll try." Her arms snaked up around his neck and entwined in the dark curls below his ears.

His hands slipped under the shirt and moved up her sides and across her back. Then their mutual need burst to life again. This time there was an equal sharing, a perfect balance from one to the other. Oblivious to everything else, they merged their bodies, emotions and hearts. Outside Dwight returned.

Dwight had expended his wrath during the night, making way for the bright, clear sky and blinding sunshine that followed in his wake. Blane and Kenley had surveyed the aftermath of the hurricane from the belvedere atop the roof of D'Evereaux and later watched the receding water from the upper balcony. Blane marveled at how quickly water came and went in the bayous.

Within the walls of the plantation, time had ceased to exist. It all felt so natural, so comfortable, as if they had been together for decades rather than days. They'd created a fantasy world of joy, love and discovery, and had lingered in the small nursery until late in the afternoon, reluctant for it to end.

But soon the real world demanded they return. They packed Kenley's small car and started home, leaving Blane's mud-caked classic to await a towing service.

Overall, however, the aftermath of Dwight's visit had been far below expectations. Aside from lowland flooding, countless fallen trees and the inevitable cleanup, the city of New Orleans had emerged relatively unscathed.

The days after Dwight seemed to be encased in a golden glow. Kenley smiled to herself at the thought. It sounded so trite, but it was true. Everything seemed brighter, warmer, more exhilarating than it had before. Her thoughts were constantly on Blane; her heart seemed to throb his name with every beat.

They saw as much of each other as possible, but storm damage and power outages at the plant kept him in Mossville for long hours. It was ironic how the steel structure of Crawford Plastics had fared little better than the 150-year-old antebellum home she and Blane had sought refuge in.

Each time Kenley was with Blane she could feel her inner fears fading, her reservations losing their strength under his gentle, loving attention. Even the demands of job and life seemed to take on new purpose now. She was getting reacquainted with things she'd lost—trust and a belief in dreams.

As she looked back over the weeks since Blane had come to New Orleans, one thread ran solidly through the picture. Every time she had been scared, depressed or alone, he had sensed her need and helped her through. She was even beginning to believe that she had found someone she could truly depend on.

Dave leaned across the desk, staring his friend in the eyes. His mouth was set in a firm line. "I hope you know what you're doing. It sounds like a hell of a gamble to me."

"Maybe. But I started the wheels in motion when I took the three-month delay on the construction."

"I think you should tell Kenley about this." Blane's stern expression clearly said no and Dave shook his head in disgreement. "She may hate it. She might have some hang-up about destroying the historical significance of the plantation."

"Not till I'm sure it'll work. I've still got to meet with Duprey about dismantling the place. It'll depend on his inpection."

"Isn't this sorta underhanded?" Dave asked, still not convinced.

"Not if it works."

"And if it doesn't?"

Blane didn't want to think about it. He ignored the question. "How're the real-estate people coming?"

"Great, just great," Dave drawled sarcastically. "You've got offers coming in already. Oh, and they have some land lined up for you to look at Thursday morning."

"Good."

"Look, Blane, be careful, huh? This thing could backire on you, explode right in your face."

Blane rubbed his forehead, unwilling to admit his own reservations. "I will. If Duprey tells me what I want to hear, hen it'll all go down as planned."

"Nice and neat, huh? You get what you want, and Kenley gets what she wants. Why do I have the feeling this isn't going to be as easy as it sounds?"

"You're a born skeptic."

"Yer damn right. I just hope all these balls you're juggling don't land on your head."

After Dave left, Blane thought about his warning. Timing would be crucial, along with a heavy dose of understanding from Kenley. It was a risky project. He'd realized hat from its inception, but he felt sure she'd approve of his decision. There really was no other solution.

Thursday morning seemed to drag by. Kenley was anxiously anticipating her date with Blane that evening. He had made reservations at Commander's Palace, one of her favorite romantic restaurants. But mostly she was looking

forward to their after-dinner plans. Blane had told her he
wanted to talk, to tell her about some decisions he'd made
and to clear up any lingering doubts in her mind.

Despite their frequent times together, they'd had no se
rious conversations. It was as if they both feared that tack
ling the problems now might spoil the magic spell they were
living under.

But tonight was the night. Kenley could feel it. Tonight
they would go to Shackleford House and sweep away all the
small cobwebs in the corners of her mind. She still had so
many questions about his work, his past and that odd nick
name. But the questions had been downgraded from ugly
suspicions to mere curiosity. The important thing was being
with Blane, feeling the sense of belonging and security that
could only be found in his embrace. Because she realized
now why he had made her feel so unnerved, so scared, that
first day at the cemetery. She must have sensed from the
start that he would somehow change her life and force her
to reevaluate everything she believed in. With Blane she felt
warm, secure and happy—and more like a woman than she
ever had before. And now she knew why. She loved him. It
was useless to deny it any longer. But even as the discovery
warmed her, it frightened her, too. Tonight she would tell
him and he would end all the questions and erase all her
fears.

Glancing at the clock, she grimaced. It wasn't even noon
yet. She still had to get through lunch and the whole after
noon. It seemed like ages since she'd felt his arms around
her, though in reality it had been just last night. Today he
was in Mossville, out of touch, and not due back in town
until late afternoon. He had told her he'd be at the town
house around seven o'clock. That was eight hours away!

Maybe if she took an early lunch it would make the day
seem shorter. With a smile, she caved in to her illogical rea
soning and picked up her purse. Too bad Alva was out at
The Cottage all day. She always made time pass quickly with
her sharp wit and constant grumbling.

As she walked through the main reception area, Kenley noticed that Carla was gone. She was usually a permanent fixture in the outer office—first to arrive in the morning and last to leave at night. Kenley often wondered when she ate lunch, or even if she ate.

She was still wondering, when she pushed open the glass door to the corridor and caught sight of Carla standing at the elevator. There was a man with her. It was...Blane. What was he doing back in New Orleans? He was supposed to be at the plant all day. Kenley pushed the door wider and stepped partially into the corridor. The conversation drifted back to her and she stopped, riveted to the spot.

"If it weren't for Wednesdays, Blane, I don't think I could survive," Carla said, looking up at him.

His put his arm around her shoulders and gave her a quick hug. "That's the idea, Carla. It helps to have someone who understands. Someone who's shared the same feelings and experiences."

Carla sighed. "My husband doesn't understand at all."

Blane nodded sympathetically. "But I do. Don't ever forget that."

"How can I? It's because of you I'm here." She pulled his face close for a quick kiss.

Kenley felt as if the ground had suddenly been pulled from beneath her. Her stomach contracted and there was a loud ringing in her ears. Part of her tried to turn away, but her mind was besieged with shock. She was turned to stone, unable to move or take her eyes from the couple in front of her.

Blane pushed the elevator call button again. "Now when we get to D'Evereaux," he was saying, "I want you to keep a record of everything. The dozers might already be there, but I don't think that'll interfere with the demolition guy."

Carla chuckled. "Oh, Blane..."

He shrugged. "The minute we get his decision, we can roll on this. It's got to go down fast, or I'm going to be in a lot of trouble."

The elevator arrived and he held it open. "You're likely to be in trouble either way," Carla said as Blane followed her into the car "If Kenley finds out..."

The doors closed, leaving Kenley reeling from the impact of what she'd witnessed. Dazed, she backed into the reception area and blindly moved toward her office. An icy hand clutched her heart. She felt as though she'd had all the wind knocked out of her lungs. Could it be true? Blane and Carla? She struggled to comprehend. Her heart wanted to deny what she'd seen and heard. But it played in her mind's eye like a recurring nightmare—the embrace, the kiss, Carla professing her need for him, Blane telling her how well he understood her.

Her stomach twisted in pain. Had Blane been seeing Carla all along? He must have. Carla said she was here because of him. Maybe he'd brought her from up north. Suddenly she remembered his comment about making love to skinny women. Carla was thin, model-thin. Kenley felt weak and ill. How neat, how tidy. Keep the lover nearby, a married lover whom he spent every Wednesday with.

Kenley put her face in her hands. She longed to cry, to scream, to ease some of the suffocating pain that raged through her, but she was strangely numb. "Please don't let it be true," she whispered. "Not Blane. Not now."

My husband doesn't understand me.

I do.

It's because of you I'm here.

The pain finally welled up in her throat. *"No!"* Savagely she took her arm and swiped the top of her desk clean. Papers and folders scattered everywhere. It didn't alleviate the anguish.

The scene replayed again and again, only this time she saw the end, too. Heard the words *dozers, demolition* and *D'Evereaux.* A new emotion overtook her. "Oh, my God." The implications were too horrifying. Her mind recoiled, unable to believe Blane would destroy D'Evereaux behind her back.

But he'd said there was something of grave importance he wanted to talk to her about tonight. Some decisions he'd made that would solve all their problems. Could he have meant this? Surely not. He couldn't possibly think that destroying the house was a solution. It would ruin everything.

Kenley didn't stop to analyze further. There was only one way to find out. She grabbed her car keys and headed out. They only had a half-hour head start on her at the most. She could still catch them.

The shock and numbness were fading, replaced by fear and anger. She'd been set up like a naive child. He'd suckered her in with vague promises to save D'Evereaux, then when she refused to relent, he'd tried new tactics; make love to her, win her over body-and-soul and then do as he damn well pleased, hoping she'd be too besotted with love to care.

How could she have been so gullible?

She asked herself that question a hundred times on the way to the plantation. But another question seemed to form in the back of her mind, too. What if she was wrong? What if there was an explanation for the things Carla had said? She'd been mistaken about those years he was in Vietnam. She'd conjured up all sorts of explanations, none of which had come close to the truth. Maybe this had an equally simple explanation.

She wanted desperately to believe it was a mistake. Her heart ached. Surely Blane wasn't so underhanded that he'd sneak out and demolish D'Evereaux behind her back. She had to prove to herself that he and Carla were going to D'Evereaux for some other purpose. She had to believe in him. If she couldn't, then she couldn't believe in anything ever again.

All she had to go on were her instinct and intuition, and her track record in both areas spoke for itself. The scars of her past had been with her a lifetime and had only recently started to heal. The thin layer of trust and belief that had formed could easily be torn apart.

She clung to the hope that the house would be deserted, that her faith in Blane was justified and that it was all some sort of horrible mistake. She was sick with worry and fear about what she would find when she reached the house. A small voice pleaded, "Please don't let him be here."

But her hope was crushed when she rounded the bend in the road. Between the trees, she could clearly see Blane standing on the treads of a bulldozer, gesturing toward the plantation. Carla stood nearby.

Disappointment, cold and bitter, filled her soul, and in that instant something precious splintered and died.

In its place came the old, familiar feelings of anger and determination. The cynicism she'd recently put to rest returned in force. White-hot anger surged through her, and she took it out on the small car as she roared up the drive and jerked to a halt. Slamming out of the car, she walked toward Blane, anger surrounding her like armor. He jumped down off the treads when he saw her coming. From the expression on his face, it was clear he hadn't expected to see her.

"Kenley, what are you doing here?" he asked.

"You never intended to save D'Evereaux, did you?" Her voice was hard and sharp.

In a flash he realized how it must look to her. The bulldozers were painfully incriminating. "No, you don't understand. This isn't what you think."

"You didn't think I'd find out about this, did you?" Blane held up a hand to forestall her, but she plunged ahead. "You seduce me into your bed, then you come out here and level D'Evereaux behind my back."

"No, they're not here to tear it down."

"No more lies, Blane. I've had more than enough of them. Don't think you and your little playmate—" she jerked her head toward Carla "—can get away with this."

"Kenley, listen to me." He grabbed her arm, but she yanked it free.

"Don't touch me. Don't ever touch me again. I'm going to fight you with everything I have. I can't stop you, but I can make your life hell if you go through with this."

"Would you just listen?"

"I made that mistake once. Not again." She turned and walked off.

Blane went after her, grasping her arm and spinning her around to face him. "You're not leaving here until I explain."

Kenley's eyes were blue steel. "You couldn't possibly explain this away."

"Those dozers are here to fix the drainage, not to tear down the house."

"You're a very accomplished liar. Quick with the excuses."

"Kenley, believe me—"

"Believe you? I did. I trusted you. I lov—" No, she wouldn't say that to him. Not now. "But it was all a game to you."

"Excuse me, Mr. Crawford," a stocky middle-aged man called as he walked toward the battling couple. "I don't see any real problem here. We can start taking it apart right away. I'll have my men and equipment out here day after tomorrow."

Kenley felt like she was going to black out. She took advantage of Blane's momentary distraction to pull free.

"That's fine. Kenley, wait!"

Kenley had reached her car before he could get free of Duprey and go to her. "Kenley, wait."

"Tell it to your girlfriend."

The car roared off in a spray of mud and gravel.

Blane stood helplessly behind and watched her car disappear in the trees. He had to straighten this out. She'd caught him in the middle of some dangerously misleading circumstances, with a platoon of heavy equipment and a man who talked about taking her house apart. What else was she supposed to think? He had to go after her and explain, even if he had to beat her door down. His gut twisted at what he'd done to her. He'd seen her feelings for him dying right in front of his eyes. It wasn't supposed to happen this way. It was supposed to make things right, not wrong.

He turned and ran his hands through his hair, a knot of fear growing by leaps and bounds in his stomach. God, he didn't want to lose her.

Carla joined him, putting a hand gently on his forearm. "Blane, I'm so sorry. Do you think you can straighten it out?"

"I don't know. She was irrational. Maybe when she calms down. I don't know. I'm afraid I may not be able to fix this one."

"I can talk to her if you'd like."

"No. I'll do it. You and Dave were right. I shouldn't have kept this from her. I just couldn't face the disappointment in her eyes if it fell through. Now it might be too late for anything."

Chapter Thirteen

Kenley barely remembered the ride home. When she reached her town house, she went straight to her room and fell across the bed. The shock, anger and hurt had given way to profound heartache, a pain so intense that it seemed to be destroying every nerve in her body. The betrayal went deeper than any she'd ever known, and she gripped the cover on her bed with her fists, twisting it violently. Slowly the tears began to fall, and once she'd given in there was no force on earth that could stop them. Her body was racked with sobs. Tears scalded her face and choked her. She could hardly breathe, but even the tears couldn't provide solace for her aching heart. Kenley was exhausted both physically and mentally, but there seemed to be no escape from the endless torment. There was no one to blame but herself. She deserved to suffer like this. She'd broken her own hard-and-fast rule, lost sight of her direction and purpose, and fallen prey to the charms and persuasive touch of an untrustworthy man.

No matter how attractive, no matter how sincere he seemed or how firmly he professed his devotion, there was always that one unknown secret that could change everything.

She'd tried to be cautious, to keep her feet on the ground and a sharp eye on the way ahead. But Blane had been a skillful lover. He'd known how to penetrate her defenses. *Trust me. Believe in me.* Those words had sounded alarms, but she'd turned them off, unable to withstand the steady onslaught of his magnetism.

Even now her body responded to the memory of him. The touch of his hand, the warmth of his lips. She hated herself for being so weak, hated the way her physical desire could so easily override her intellect.

What was wrong with her? Why did she always believe them? She had adored her father, worshiped him. Yet he had preferred sons to daughters. Russ had led a secret double life and managed to keep his treachery from her. Seth Crawford hadn't been the dear, sweet man she'd thought, either. He had promised her so many things, led her to believe that he would give her D'Evereaux. Like father, like son. If Seth had followed through on his promise, none of this would have happened.

Blane was the cruelest mistake of all. She'd given everything she had to him, her most precious gifts, and he had callously tossed them aside.

Kenley sat up on her bed and caught sight of her reflection in the mirror. Her hair was tangled and damp, her eyes were bloodshot, her cheeks swollen and streaked with tears. Suddenly she was furious with herself. He wasn't worth this, and she'd wallowed in these recriminations long enough. From now on, it was strictly a crusade to save D'Evereaux. She'd deal with him as she would any other opponent, and she knew exactly where to start.

Alva was first on her list. Kenley called and instructed her to collect all the paperwork and bring it to the town house, saying she'd be unable to go back to the little office in Blane's suite. From now on she'd do her work at home.

Alva had been full of questions, but Kenley ignored them. She'd grieved and licked her wounds long enough. Now it was time for action. D'Evereaux was her main objective. She had to forget Blane and the way he'd made her feel. Forget the eyes that touched her soul, the hands that held her so gently, the way she still craved the feel of him inside her.

"Damn him!" Her anger flared anew. Determinedly she went to her desk and picked up the phone. She had just finished her call when Alva arrived.

"You wanna tell me why you're working here instead of at the office?" she groused.

"Better atmosphere," Kenley answered curtly. "I just talked to Cal Schlein and explained about Alcee Rondeau's diary."

"You mean that D'Evereaux was probably built by Ray Parker?"

"Right. The diary is our only proof now, but I think it's enough to get us a temporary restraining order on the grounds that the property is a rare example of Parker's work and therefore historically significant. It'll give me something viable to fight with now."

Alva frowned at her young friend. "You're going to get a restraining order against Blane?"

Kenley ignored the amazed look on the older woman's face. "Yes. I told Cal the house was already being dismantled, and he said he could probably get Judge Mancuso to issue the order within the hour."

"You can't be serious."

"I can cite precedents, if you like. Magnolia Mound—citizen intervention halted demolition in the middle of the night." She reached for a folder and continued. "Cal said he'd call the mayor, if need be, and see if he'll set up a committee to study the problem. I may have to go up to Baton Rouge, too, and stir up a few people. At any rate, we should be able to put a halt to the demolition and give Mr. Crawford something to think about.''

"What happened between you two? Yesterday you were higher than a kite, and today you're saying things like this.''

"I woke up. You know the old song, 'The Party's Over.'''

"Does this have anything to do with those bulldozers?''

Kenley whirled around. "You knew about that and you didn't tell me?''

"I only heard talk this morning.''

"I should have suspected treachery from the start.''

"Treachery? He was trying to help.''

"By leveling D'Evereaux?'' Kenley was incredulous.

"No. He was going to build up the ground around the foundation and keep the rain from standing on that south side.''

Kenley remembered Blane trying to tell her about the drainage but held her ground. "It's a cover story. He was talking to a demolition expert who was very anxious to take the place apart.''

"I didn't hear about that, but I can't imagine Mr. Crawford being involved in anything shady,'' Alva stated emphatically.

"Can't you? No, I suppose not. We were both blinded by his good looks and charm.''

"I'm too old to be charmed, kiddo,'' Alva said quietly. "I'm also too old to be fooled. He's a good man, and I think your feelings for him go deeper than you're willing to admit. But for some reason you're using this house as a shield to keep Blane out of your life.''

"What do you really know about him, Alva? Nothing. Bits and pieces that don't add up and a truckload of questions.''

Alva nodded thoughtfully. "Well, there were those two years...''

"Vietnam. He was in Vietnam,'' Kenley answered quickly.

"Oh? Well, that explains the look in his eyes some-times."

"What look?"

"Haunted, sad. As if he'd seen something he couldn't forget."

Kenley's lip curled in disgust. "He was haunted by his old love."

"What?"

She started to reply, then remembered she was talking to the town crier. "Let's drop it. I don't want to talk about it. It's over. I learned my lesson. From now on, all that matters is D'Evereaux."

Alva frowned. "I don't like this. You've become ob-sessed with that place."

"Don't be ridiculous."

"When Seth bought it, you were only very interested in preservation. But when Blane appeared on the scene, you made it a crusade. I've never seen you like this before. I don't like it."

Kenley ignored her.

"You've made it a test. One he can't possibly pass be-cause you keep changing the rules. Save the house or else you can't have me. I don't think you really want it saved, because then you'd have to make a commitment. But if he destroys it, then you're free. He becomes the enemy. You don't have to deal with him, because he's just another guy who didn't cut the mustard."

"Don't be so dramatic. I made a mistake, that's all. I misjudged him," she said, gritting her teeth against her friend's piercing assessment.

"You've got that right," Alva agreed firmly. "You've lost track of what's really important, kiddo. You're putting your love for that house above your feelings for Blane."

"What I feel or don't feel for Mr. Crawford has nothing to do with it. It won't change a thing."

Alva came and stood at Kenley's side. "Do you really want to save D'Evereaux at the expense of a man who obviously adores you? Would you be content to walk through empty rooms when you could have had Blane?''

''There are too many questions.''

''And whose fault is that?'' Alva accused. ''Okay, so maybe he goofed. He should have handled it differently, but he made a mistake. We all do from time to time, even white knights on handsome steeds.''

Kenley toyed with the papers on the small desk, refusing to answer Alva's insightful comments.

''Remove the obstacles, Kenley, before it's too late. For once in your life, trust your heart.''

''I trust the facts. I trust what I saw and heard,'' she said softly.

Alva put her hand on Kenley's shoulder, squeezing it gently. ''Don't believe everything you hear, and only half of what you see.''

''Just bring my work here from now on. I won't be going back to the office. We'll move as soon as I locate a suitable place.''

''Think it over for a day.''

''No.''

Kenley felt worse after Alva left, restless and strangely guilty. Alva had always talked to her like an errant daughter, only this time her words hit an uncomfortable chord.

Don't believe everything you hear. Kenley went over it again. She'd heard Carla's affection for Blane and his for her. Heard the talk about D'Evereaux and the demolition man, heard Carla's laughter and taunting, ''If Kenley finds out...''

Only half of what you see. She'd seen Blane and Carla together, seen them embrace, seen the dozer on the property and the stocky man who wanted to tear the house down.

And what about his business? She still knew nothing about it except that he referred to it as an ''organization'' and himself as a ''promoter.'' It couldn't be legitimate. If it were, why was he evasive about it?

Even Dave had commented that Blane needed a conscience, that they were "partners in crime." Had he been trying to warn her that day, hinting that she was out of her depth? Blane himself admitted that he sometimes took chances, though he wouldn't admit to any particular vice. Obviously it was women.

And the nickname. Artful Dodger. The implications there were endless. He probably got it from dodging husbands.

No, Alva was wrong this time. Her eyes and ears hadn't deceived her. She just hadn't seen the truth soon enough. She was merely an amusing diversion, someone to fill up idle hours. She was his Thursday, as Carla was his Wednesday. Any way she looked at it, it still came up wrong.

With everything set in motion, there was nothing more she could do now, so she curled up on the rattan sofa in her studio to wait. Exhaustion finally claimed her and she drifted into an uneasy sleep, waking shortly before six o'clock when her friend, attorney Cal Schlein, called to report that Judge Mancuso had granted the restraining order and that it had been delivered to Blane's office about an hour before. He also told her he'd put in some calls of his own to several influential people, and he seemed very optimistic. Kenley couldn't help but wonder how Blane had reacted to the order. He was probably furious.

She didn't have long to wonder. Blane was at her door ten minutes later, and she told herself she was glad he'd come so quickly. The sooner this was over, the better. She'd promised him a fight, and he was going to get one. Pushing the release button on her gate, she lifted her chin. He couldn't beat her this time. She had the upper hand. But when he loomed before her, dark and menacing, she had cause to question her position.

His eyes were dark as anthracite as he waved the paper in her face. "What the hell are you trying to do?" When he'd finally been able to break away from D'Evereaux, the long ride from Mossville had given him plenty of opportunity to run through several stages of emotions. First anger at himself, then regret, then resentment at Kenley for doubting him without even giving him the courtesy of an explanation. Then when he'd returned to his office and found the restraining order, his temper had exploded.

"Preserve a landmark," she replied evenly.

"I've had calls from the mayor, the editor of the *Picayune*. Damn it, even the lieutenant governor called to put in his two cents' worth. Why did you have to make this a legal battle, Kenley? I expected better from you."

"I can give as well as I get."

"You're slitting your own throat with this, only you're too pigheaded to see that." His voice was hard and sounded ragged and scratchy.

"No, you're wrong! I believed your lies once. But not again. You may have destroyed my house, but you won't destroy me!"

"It's *my* house! I can destroy it any time I damn well please. I don't need your approval. But it just so happens, I was trying to save your damn house!" he shouted, frustrated with the helplessness of the situation.

"By 'taking it apart,' as your friend so quaintly put it?"

"By rerouting the drainage. That's why the dozers were there."

"I don't want to hear this." She turned away, closing her mind to him.

"You will hear it. I was going to tell you about my plans for D'Evereaux tonight."

"How?" She whirled on him. "'Oh, I leveled your house today, dear, and by the way, you and I are finished?"

Blane's dark eyes widened, his anger dissipating at her train of thought. "You and I? We're not over. I love you." Hell of a time to discover that. But it was true, he realized. Probably had been for some time. No woman had ever taken hold of his mind and heart so completely before. He stretched out a hand toward her, but she pulled away, blue eyes tarnished with pain and hurt.

Kenley recoiled at his declaration. He was being deliberately cruel. How could he say that to her now, after...
He reached out to her but she cowered from his touch, focusing instead on the anger born of his betrayal.

Blane was taken aback. He'd been prepared for fury, but what he'd found was anguish. For the first time since he'd arrived, he looked at her closely. Her eyes were red and swollen, and she appeared totally forsaken. He'd come to the town house prepared to shake some sense into Kenley, but he realized now how brutally he'd wounded her. He ached to hold and comfort her, tell her it was going to be all right. "Don't hide behind that house, Kenley. This isn't about D'Evereaux, and you know it. It's about you and me—"

"Me and how many others?"

"What kind of crack is that?"

"Don't play dumb. You do it badly. I know about Wednesdays, Blane. Your little secret is out."

Blane's heart sank. Dave had warned him this might happen. He should have told her sooner. He'd wanted to at D'Evereaux, but she had reacted so poorly to his being a veteran that he'd wanted time to probe her feelings more closely before revealing anything.

Unfortunately, he couldn't decide if she was angry about his profession or just that he'd kept it from her. If she objected to his business, then there was little hope for them. He wouldn't give up his mission. "I was going to tell you tonight."

"Tell me? How modern of you and how thoughtful to wait until after you had seduced me."

"I was hoping I could make you understand. A lot of people have reacted badly to the idea."

Kenley couldn't believe her ears. "Badly?" she said with all the sarcasm she could find. "Why should I react badly to your little weekly diversion?"

"Diversion? Is that what you call what I do?"

"You have a better word? Though next time you want to keep a secret, I wouldn't choose a public place to display affection. The wrong people might see you."

Blane's forehead creased, and he shook his head in confusion. "What are you talking about?"

"It's no use, Blane. You don't have to lie anymore."

His mind raced through the day's events. It was obvious Kenley wasn't talking about his work. But what, then? Who had he been affectionate with lately? The only one he'd even talked to was Carla. Carla! Had Kenley seen them at the elevator? Frantically he tried to recall what was said, what Kenley might have seen or heard. "You're wrong, Kenley. You misunderstood."

"Yes, I did. I misunderstood it all."

"Will you listen just once?" He held her shoulders, but she refused to look at him. "You saw me with Carla this morning, didn't you?" She didn't speak, but he could read the answer in her face. "Carla is a friend. Nothing more. She needed to talk. She was in Nam, a nurse. Do you understand?"

He sounded so sincere, so innocent, but she'd been deceived before by his silken tongue. "You'd better go."

"Kenley, please. Don't do this to us."

"There is no us." Finally she looked directly at him.

Blane's frustration was threatening to explode. "You're the most obstinate, narrow-minded, suspicious..." Suddenly he let her go.

Kenley felt a jolt deep inside. She thought she saw a sadness, a pain in his dark eyes, but she turned her back.

He knew it was pointless to try and work this out now. Maybe in a day or so she'd be calmer and he could try again. He walked to the door and turned back to her. "I never meant to hurt you."

"Get out!"

Without another word, Blane turned and walked out.

Chapter Fourteen

The days all ran together now, each one like the one before—slow, uneventful, devoid of excitement or satisfaction. Kenley ate, but didn't taste the food; slept, but didn't rest. She moved through her daily tasks with little desire. Even her crusade for D'Evereaux held little comfort.

The argument with Blane had taken all her anger and resentment, even her will to fight back, and left her feeling old and empty.

Alva reported that some of what Blane had professed was true. The dozers had indeed excavated the property around D'Evereaux. As for the house itself, it was very systematically being dismantled. The restraining order had been revoked, and Kenley couldn't find out why. Cal was looking into it.

Word had drifted back through the grapevine that Carla was a very happily married woman with two children, and her job as Blane's secretary and friend was their only connection. Kenley wanted to believe it, but realized that even married women had affairs, and what woman could resist the potent sexuality of Blane Crawford? She certainly hadn't!

What Kenley felt now wasn't shock or horror but an emptiness, a hollow, dead feeling. Before she'd been filled with strong emotions—anger, hatred, fury and pain. Now she only felt alone.

Kenley automatically pressed the release on her front gate when it buzzed late Wednesday morning, assuming it was Alva with more work. Instead she found Dave Kesler at her door. "Come to twist the knife?" she said coldly.

Dave looked her over closely. "Looks like you're doing a pretty good job of that yourself."

"What do you want? If you're here on behalf of your boss, you can turn around and leave. I don't know how you got around the restraining order, but I'll find another way to stop Blane and Crawford Plastics and your other organization." The last word was heavily laced with sarcasm.

Dave chuckled softly. "You make it sound illegal."

Kenley favored him with a knowing stare.

His green eyes widened. "Is that what you think?"

A soft snort of derision escaped her. "Blane has some sort of vague 'business' that no one talks about, and when you do it's referred to as the organization. He calls himself a promoter and slinks off every Wednesday to devote himself to—" she hesitated "—whomever or whatever."

Dave scratched his neck and grimaced. "I guess it might look that way."

Kenley sighed in disgust. "I'm sure it's perfectly natural to a man with a nickname like Artful Dodger."

Dave's chuckle turned into a full-fledged guffaw. "Geez, Blane said you had an imagination, but you're one for the books."

"Glad you can find some humor in this situation."

Dave shook his head and came to her side. "Artful Dodger was his nickname in Nam. He was a chopper pilot, and he got the name because he could dodge ground fire like a damned magician.''

Kenley didn't know what to say. Even when he wasn't around, Blane was able to puncture her indignation. ''Oh.''

Dave leaned against the desk, crossing his arms over his chest. ''Mind if I tell you that you look like hell?''

''Thank you,'' she drawled coolly.

''Blane looks even worse.'' He watched her reaction closely, smiling when he found what he was looking for. ''Come on. I think it's time Uncle Dave interfered.''

''Come where?''

''On a little ride. I want to show you something.''

''Sorry. I've got things to do,'' she refused.

''Nothing that can't wait, I'm sure.'' He watched the hesitation in her eyes. ''Besides, I've got all the answers you're looking for. But I won't give them to you unless you come with me.''

They were on their way out of the Quarter before Dave picked up the conversation. ''You know, for two intelligent people, you both are behaving like a couple of jerks.''

''How kind of you to point that out.''

''All part of the service.'' He grinned smugly.

Kenley was getting impatient and beginning to regret coming with Dave on their mystery tour. ''Where are we going? I've got a ton of work waiting on my desk.''

''Isn't that a coincidence. That's just where we're going, to work.'' He smiled and ignored Kenley's unspoken question. ''Seriously, I've never seen Blane like this. He's hurting bad.''

Kenley felt an unwelcome surge of concern but ignored it. ''He brought it on himself.''

''Yeah, I guess he did.''

''You agree with me?'' Her surprise was evident.

''I agree that Blane should have consulted with you about his plans for D'Evereaux. But don't be too quick to pat yourself on the back. Don't forget, you're the one who assumed Blane and Carla were having a little fling.''

Kenley turned away, refusing to continue this conversation. It was going nowhere.

Dave wasn't so easily discouraged. "He just wanted to surprise you."

"Well, he succeeded. Brilliantly."

"Judgment calls are tricky. Coaches have to make them all the time. When a big game is on the line, sometimes he has to take risks. If he tries a daring play and wins the game, he's a genius and they pat him on the back for being a brilliant strategist. But if his long shot bombs, then he's a stupid idiot who should be fired."

Kenley turned and frowned, her eyes clouded with confusion. "Is that analogy supposed to mean something to me?"

"If Blane's plan had come off the way he wanted it to, you'd be overflowing with gratitude. He'd be the big hero. But instead, he's the bad guy—just because things got mixed up."

Dave pulled into the parking lot of a small brick building. The discreetly placed sign on the front read Veterans' Aid Center.

"What are we doing here?"

"This is where we spend Wednesdays," he said blithely as he turned off the engine. His eyes twinkled as he sat back and waited for her reaction.

Kenley's mind flashed through all the things she'd read about soldiers who had served in Vietnam—the emotional problems, the flashbacks. Was Blane still having problems from his war experiences? Was that why he was here? Was he afraid to tell her?

Dave read the concern on her face before she could mask it. "Scared?"

"No," she said firmly. Whatever it was, she could handle it.

"Good. I have one request before we go in. Blane will probably be mad as hell that I brought you here, but ignore it. Sometimes he doesn't know what's good for him. But I want you to try to keep an open mind about this. Don't judge him too harshly before you know all the facts.''

''I don't understand.''

Dave grinned gleefully. ''I know. That's why you're here. I just don't want you jumping to any more wrong conclusions.''

Kenley started to defend herself, but decided to keep quiet. Perhaps she had been wrong about Carla. But D'Evereaux was another matter.

She followed Dave into the building, consumed with curiosity and a healthy dose of fear. Dave spoke briefly with a man in the lobby, then guided her down a hallway, stopping at a door emblazoned with Blane's name. Kenley's curiosity grew.

When they stood in the center of the quiet office, she turned to Dave and asked, ''I don't understand. What is this about?''

''This is Blane's business. The Veterans' Aid Centers. He started them shortly after he left Crawford Plastics. It wasn't easy in the beginning. Most everyone wanted to forget the guys in that war, not help them. But eventually people woke up and things improved. We've got centers all over the country now, all independently owned and operated by veterans.''

The door opened and Blane came in. He glanced at Kenley, then turned an icy glare on Dave. His fists were planted on his hips, and he looked ready to fight. ''Explain.''

It was hard to mistake the cold tone of his voice, but Dave didn't seem to notice. ''I thought it was time to show her where you spent your Wednesdays.''

''You were out of line.''

''So sue me. Now if you'll excuse me, I'll let you two battle this out.''

Blane's lower jaw worked angrily as he watched Dave leave. Without so much as a glance in her direction, he walked behind the desk, rubbing his forehead as if trying to hold back his temper. "I'm sorry. He shouldn't have brought you here."

Despite herself, Kenley felt her heart go out to him. He did look bad—tired, older and somehow defeated. "Why not?"

"Because you don't belong here. This is foreign territory."

Kenley stepped closer to the desk, her blue eyes clouded and troubled. "Dave said I'd have all my questions answered, if I came here. What is this place? What do you do here?"

Blane sat down. "We help people. Veterans mainly, the ones who served in Nam. We give them training, group therapy, help with paperwork from Uncle Sam, sometimes cut through the red tape and make sure they get all the benefits that are due them. A hundred other things."

"You mean you're part of the Veterans Administration?"

"No. We're a private organization, but we do work with the VA closely. They do a good job, but get bogged down with government regulations and policies. Now that the VA has its own Cabinet post, it'll probably get worse. We're outside that. We can accomplish more where it counts—on the streets with the guys."

"Why keep this such a big secret?" she asked softly. "Why be so mysterious?"

Blane tapped a pencil thoughtfully. "In the beginning it wasn't important. It didn't involve you or your fight for D'Evereaux. Plus, it's an old habit. We faced a lot of opposition when we started. People didn't understand that veterans of Vietnam needed a special kind of help. Then public opinion started to change. The truth about the war came out and delayed stress was the focus of every talk show in the country. Even TV shows started to show the Vet in a better light." The disapproval in his voice was obvious.

"Isn't that good? I mean didn't that make your job easier?"

Blane entwined his fingers, searching for the right words to explain, to make her understand. "The media attention was helpful to a degree, yes. But they zeroed in on the wrong things. Suddenly everyone wanted to jump on the GI bandwagon.

"We had over twenty centers by that time and the press wanted to turn me into some sort of hero, a savior of the war-scarred soldier. They treated the centers like some religious cult, and me like some knight on a crusade."

"But what you're doing is noble," she said softly, dazed by the things he was telling her.

"No!" he shouted. "I'm just a guy doing a job that needs to be done. We aren't noble, any of us. We all did things we weren't proud of over there, myself included. But we're not freaks, or candidates for a celebrity telethon. Isn't it bad enough we had to fight our war in front of the dinner table every night? Now they want to watch us heal in prime time as well?"

"Is this what your father disapproved of?" she asked suddenly, beginning to grasp the problem.

"He couldn't see why I would give up an established career with him to start a business that in his eyes was little better than running a soup kitchen for freaked-out GIs." He sighed deeply. "My wife wasn't fond of the idea, either."

Kenley felt the old knife twisting. She understood now what he meant when he'd said his wife didn't like his avocation. "This is why you traveled so much." It was a statement more than a question.

He nodded. "Yes. We have forty centers around the U.S., and it takes about four months to get one operational."

"How do you manage it all? It must be an awesome task."

"I don't. Not literally. I set them up, get them running. From there on, it's mainly the vets who run the business. It's a franchise-type setup. Guys who have been helped come back to teach, train, or just volunteer. Sort of a favor-for-a-favor plan. No one gets rich, but no one gets lost in the shuffle, either.''

It all started to make sense now. He'd been struggling against his father and public opinion, not to mention losing a wife over his unusual occupation. She'd totally misread everything about him.

"Why didn't you tell me?" she asked, her voice barely a whisper. "I would have understood. I wouldn't have turned away like your wife."

Blane stared at her levelly, his eyes challenging and filled with doubt. "What is it?" she asked, unable to read his message.

"Do you remember what you said to me during the storm, what your first words were when I told you I'd been in Nam?"

She struggled to remember, but it all seemed lost in a haze of pain. "I said, I was sorry."

"What else?"

She shook her head slowly, unable to call up her words, then, "I was shocked to learn you were one of those men who'd been there."

"To quote you directly, you said, 'You're one of those.' Hardly a resounding note of support."

She saw suddenly how her words must have sounded to him. More an accusation than an acceptance. She was so ashamed. All her ugly suspicions, the accusations. "Oh God, I didn't mean..." she turned away.

"It wasn't totally because of you." He added. "I had another reason. Remember me telling you I wasn't such a good judge of people myself? There was a woman, in L.A. I was out there several years ago scouting locations for two centers and she was the real-estate agent showing me around. We hit it off and became involved. At that point I was constantly being hounded by the press for interviews, features. They didn't care about the centers. They just wanted to make me into some sort of war hero. I was getting pretty fed up with it. Debbi had been pressing me to take some of the offers. She couldn't understand why I kept turning them down. Then I found out that she was an aspiring screenwriter." He took a deep breath and exhaled slowly, a grim smile on his face. "It seems she figured a story on me, a first-hand intimate account would be her ticket to a new career."

Kenley was one step ahead of him now. "And you were afraid that I might use you to save D'Evereaux?"

"The thought had occurred to me."

A fresh wave of shame washed over her and she realized that she could quite possibly have done the very thing he feared. She had been so obsessed with saving that house she would have done anything to protect it.

What a blind, selfish idiot she'd been—about Carla, about Blane's past. "Blane, I..." What could she say to him to erase the things she'd thought, the things she'd done?

Now that it was all out in the open, Blane felt strangely numb, empty as if none of it mattered anymore. He watched as Kenley withdrew, pulling herself in tighter, shutting him out. "Kenley, you know that there's nothing between Carla and me. She's been coming to the center for a long time. I gave her a job with Crawford Plastics so she could support her family after her husband was laid off. I was going to tell you everything at dinner that night."

Kenley turned away. She felt so worthless. She'd suspected Blane at every turn, accused him of deceitful things, of treachery, and he was still able to speak to her in a civil, understanding tone. She wished he'd shout at her, call her names, anything but be nice. She didn't deserve any kindness.

"As far as D'Evereaux is concerned..."

Her humiliation grew. She couldn't stand to hear about that now. What did the house matter? Alva was right. It had become an obsession. "Don't. Please. I don't want to hear about it." She couldn't look him in the eye, couldn't stand to look inside herself. All she wanted was to get away.

Blane felt a knife twist in his gut at her reaction. True to form her first thought was for D'Evereaux. Fine, then he would give her what she wanted. Rising from the chair he walked around the desk and stopped at her side. "I think we need to settle some things. I want you to come with me."

Too dazed and humiliated to refuse she nodded, turning her steps toward the door. Like some mechanical doll she followed him outside and got into his car staring blindly out the window as her eyes filled with tears. How he must hate her. He had tried to explain about everything, but she had been too consumed with her own insignificant concerns.

She wanted to hide from herself and the ugliness in her soul, to escape the hideous vision she'd just glimpsed of the real nature of Kenley Farrell. But there was nowhere to go. Like a wounded animal she hugged the door, longing to cry, but even the release of tears was denied her.

How could she have been so blind, so totally ignorant about the man she professed to love? Her wild imagination had cast Blane in the role of con artist and criminal, with no proof except her stupid fears and childish suspicions.

She could hardly blame him for not telling her about the centers. D'Evereaux had been the only thought on her mind; everything else would have been dismissed without a comment—the same way she'd reacted when he'd first told her he'd been in Vietnam: one brief, fleeting thought then back to her problems, her house, her petty insecurities. He had been concerned with repairing emotionally torn lives; she had been concerned with a house and her imaginary puzzle.

All the pieces came together now. If she had been the least bit open to his needs, she wouldn't have forced him to doubt her and withhold the truth, fearing her rejection. How could she have been so stupid? But even as she asked, she knew the answer.

Alva was right. She'd been playing games—horrible, selfish games—putting her desires above all else, looking at the world from only her own narrow perspective, being unwilling to compromise, determined to have her way at any cost. She'd been so quick to believe the worst about Blane, to jump to conclusions, deliberately looking for a reason to shove him into that well-worn cubbyhole marked "unsuitable."

She'd put so many men in that slot for so many reasons, all in a vain attempt to find the perfect man, a man totally unlike Russ or her father.

Somewhere she'd acquired the notion that if she picked wisely enough, delved deeply enough into their pasts, she could avoid the heartache of her mother and the marital mistakes of Lena. She knew now that was impossible.

Blane had told her to lead with her heart. Instead she'd led with her brain—her suspicious, cynical brain. Her heart had believed him, but that black curtain of fear had kept falling between her emotions and her logic, never allowing them to mesh with love and trust.

Everything had been so clear before Blane came to New Orleans. No, that wasn't true. She'd been discontented with every aspect of her life for months. Blane had only stirred the already muddy waters.

He'd looked into her eyes and sparked life in her soul; she'd just been too self-centered to realize it. From almost the moment they met, Blane had understood her much better than she understood herself. His insight had terrified her.

Suddenly it was very clear in her mind. The layers of self-doubt and fear lifted, the barriers crumbled. She could sort through the mistakes, unearth feelings and emotions she'd ignored. And what she found at the bottom of the pile, were two very real and enduring things: a belief in herself and an abiding love for Blane.

She realized now that all her petty fears about commitment had been crippling her, not sustaining her. She'd tried to hide behind her job and her independence, afraid to trust her own judgment and instincts. Instead of learning from her mistakes, she'd caved in to them. Now she knew her instincts were sound and valid. They had led her to Blane. He hadn't let her down. She had let herself down.

He had told her the secret to life was learning to roll with the punches. From now on that would be her approach. He had taught her to believe in herself again. Even if it was too late for their relationship, she'd discovered who she was, and that knowledge was her most valuable possession. She knew now she wouldn't be afraid to love anymore. And she did love Blane desperately, passionately. He made her feel cherished. He was all that mattered. If she couldn't have him, her life would be bleak and half of her would be missing.

Remove all the obstacles, Alva had said. The only one remaining now was herself. But how could he ever forgive her? Her callousness, her suspicions, her unfeeling attitude were hardly qualities he could respect, let alone forgive. But she had to try. She couldn't let him slip out of her life without a fight. She had created this situation; she could at least face up to her shortcomings and deal with the circumstances.

Somewhere in her dazed state she had assumed that Blane was taking her to The Shackleford House to talk. She blinked in surprise when she saw that he was pulling into the parking garage of the Ellison Building. Why had he brought her here? She glanced over at him but could read no answers in the grim set of his jaw as he got out of the car and came around to open her door.

Silently she joined him, feeling the knot in her stomach tighten as they rode the elevator upward and entered his office. Blane walked directly to his desk and sat down, slipping on a pair of reading glasses as he reached for a dark folder. She'd never seen them before. They gave him a distinguished, academic look but did nothing to diminish his attractiveness. Her heart pounded wildly. She'd finally plowed through all the roadblocks and knew what she really wanted, but it might be too late. Taking a deep breath she decided to face the consequences head on. "Blane."

Blane looked up from the documents he held. For a moment his eyes softened. He hadn't anticipated this response from her. He could see that she was hurting, taking all the blame on her shoulders. Reaching up he removed his glasses, laying them on the desk. He didn't smile. "I brought you here to clear up any lingering doubts and to set a few things straight."

Kenley's heart pounded expectantly. "Oh? What about?"

He rose and walked toward her, still holding the papers. As he drew nearer, she took in every detail hungrily. He looked incredibly handsome in the gray suit and crisp white shirt. His magnetism was in full force. Why had she thrown away the only thing that really mattered to her? Why had she not realized what she had until it was too late?

"I wanted to give you these." Silently he wondered why he hadn't done this before. He should have trusted his own instincts. They had told him Kenley would understand, and she had. Like her, his own scarred past had blinded him to the truth. But she was still here, still within reach and he wouldn't let her get away without talking everything out.

Careful not to touch him, Kenley took the documents he offered and looked at them twice before their meaning sunk in. "These are deeds. In my name." She looked up at Blane for an explanation.

"The first one is for a piece of land upriver a few miles. The other is clear title to D'Evereaux."

"I don't understand."

Blane sat on the edge of his desk, one foot dangling, his arm resting across his thigh. Kenley couldn't help noticing how the masculine pose heightened all his best features and her heart ached with love. She sent up a quick prayer that there was still some small shred of hope left for them.

"It was the only solution I could find that would solve both our problems, and I have you to thank." His voice was even, controlled.

"Me?"

"You gave me the idea the day you suggested I build my new plant somewhere else. Remember?"

Kenley lowered her eyes and nodded. She remembered only too well.

"I made some phone calls, talked to some people and made arrangements to have the plantation moved to the new site. It'll take about three months. I won't be able to help with the restoration, but I figured the society could work that out."

Kenley was stunned, almost speechless. "How...how did you manage this?"

"It wasn't difficult. I guess dismantling and reconstructing a 150-year-old house isn't that uncommon down here. That's why your restraining order fell through. I wasn't tearing it down, only relocating it."

The significance of what Blane had done was filtering through. "No, I mean the money. Where did you get it? This is a very expensive project."

Blane rose and walked back around the desk, his fingers tapping nervously on the inlaid top. "I sold my father's house."

Kenley felt a wave of deep regret. "Oh no, not Shackleford House. Blane, that was your home."

He shook his head. "No. It was my father's, not mine. Besides—" he grinned sardonically "—I got enough out of it to save D'Evereaux and Crawford Plastics. Not a bad trade."

Kenley focused on the papers in her hand, unwilling to meet his eyes and see the contempt that must be in them now.

Four months ago she would have given her soul for the deed to D'Evereaux. Now it seemed little better than an insignificant piece of paper. The sacrifice from Blane was more valuable. "Where will you live?"

He shrugged. "We'll find something."

There was an awkward moment of silence before he spoke again. "There's some paperwork you'll need concerning the move. I'm sure you'll want to supervise. I have one request, though. I'd like you to use veterans on the restoration whenever possible."

She nodded absently, still struggling to absorb it all. He had done this for her, sold his home to save an empty shell of a house. "Is this what you were going to tell me the other night?"

Blane chewed the corner of his mouth and looked beyond her when he spoke. "It was supposed to be a surprise, but . . ." He turned and walked to the window, leaning against the frame, his eyes trained to the activity below but not seeing it. "You know, you really did a number on my ego. I'm used to winning. I'm not very familiar with failure. But with you I seemed to make a mistake, no matter what I did. And in the end, I lost it all." He looked over at her, the shadows obscuring his eyes. "I never wanted to hurt you. I wanted to give you everything. I wanted to make you feel safe, loved. Moving D'Evereaux was a last resort. I was afraid if it failed . . . I couldn't bear to see the disappointment in your eyes if I destroyed something you loved so much."

Kenley ached with remorse. "How can you stand to look at me? I've been selfish and cruel. I believed terrible, despicable things about you. And then I discover you've devoted your life to doing these wonderful, noble things."

"Not noble, Kenley. I just provide a much-needed service."

"But what you do is important. More important than my petty concerns for an old building. I was just too stupid, too narrow-minded to understand. If I'd only trusted you." She met his gaze and her azure eyes were filled with regret. "I've made everything so much more difficult for you. I'm so sorry."

The look in her eyes gave him renewed hope. "Then you have no problems with what I do? No reservations? I won't give it up, you know."

"Of course not," she stated firmly. "Didn't you tell me the same thing? I know I've been a selfish idiot, but I could never ask you to give up the centers. It's too important. If I hadn't been so scared, so certain that you were out to hurt me I would have been able to help you, instead of ruining everything between us. I'm so ashamed of what I've done, the things I thought."

"Kenley..."

"No, let me finish. It was just easier for me to think the worst. I'm an old hand at rejection, you know. It's something I understand. I kept looking for a way to push you aside rather than try and deal with the new, frightening feelings you gave me."

Tentatively Kenley took a step closer to him. "You tried to tell me about putting things before people, that having someone to share with was all that mattered. The ride over here gave me a chance to take a long, hard look at myself and to think about some rather blunt observations Alva shared with me. I've made so many mistakes, but I love you. I realized it the morning before you and Carla went to D'Evereaux. I know it's probably too late for us, and I accept full responsibility for that. I've destroyed everything special between us with my suspicions and insecurities."

From across the room, Blane's brown eyes seemed to touch her. He held out his hand. Afraid to hope, but longing to touch him again, she went to him and put her hand in his.

"Forgive me," she said softly. "I do love you, very much."

"We've both made mistakes," he said. "We should have been honest and open from the start. Dave tried to warn me. He said I should tell you about my plans for D'Evereaux, but I wouldn't listen. You aren't the only one responsible."

"I'm sorry. I've made such a mess of everything." The tears started to fall down her cheeks, and she brushed them away angrily. "I swore I wouldn't do this. I told myself I would be strong."

Blane slipped his arms around her gently. "Strength doesn't always mean standing alone."

Kenley looked up into his eyes and felt her heart sing. "What now? I'm sorry, you're sorry..."

"If I say I love you and that I want to commit the rest of my life to being with you and making you happy, will you run away?"

She nearly went weak with relief and joy. She'd never really believed he would forgive her, that he still loved her was more than she'd dared to hope. "No, no never again. But I just don't want to make any more mistakes."

Blane laughed softly, his eyes filled with love. "You'll make plenty. So will I. There'll even be times when you won't like me very much and vice versa. But it won't change the love underneath."

Kenley smiled and held him close. "Love conquers all?"

He shook his head. "No. But it leads the way. It led us to one another in spite of fear, pride and a crumbling old plantation."

"I love you," she whispered against his chest, feeling as if she was only alive in his embrace.

"Will you give me back the deeds?" he asked softly.

"Yes, of course," she answered quickly, starting to pull away. But he held her firmly against him.

"No hesitation?"

"None."

He grinned happily. "You know, I can read your emotions so clearly. It's a very becoming trait. I think it's the first thing about you that I fell in love with. I only want them back to change the name. To Kenley Crawford."

"Oh, Blane, I don't deserve this. I'm not sure I deserve you."

He kissed the top of her head. "You may live to eat those words," he teased. "Oh, I should tell you that I finally located the file on D'Evereaux."

"Oh?" She really wasn't interested. All that mattered was the warmth and love she found here in his arms.

"Uh-huh. It was in my father's room beside his bed."

"Anything interesting in it?"

"No. Nothing conclusive, either. He'd scribbled a few notes to himself and one about me."

Curious, Kenley lifted her eyes. "About you?"

Blane nodded. "He wanted me to meet you, get to know you. He thought we might get along well together."

"The last time I saw your father, the day he decided to donate D'Evereaux, he said some odd things. I thought he was talking about the house, but maybe..." Her words trailed off.

Blane looked down at her quizzically. "Maybe what?"

Kenley shook her head, still trying to sort it all out. "He talked about making amends and needing new ideas and a new perspective." She looked up at him. "He said he wanted to correct a great many terrible mistakes." Blane gazed off over her head. "Do you think he felt you could help the company? Do you think he knew we'd fall in love?"

"I don't know. I don't suppose we'll ever know about that or about his real plans for D'Evereaux. All I know is that I'm very grateful he gave me the chance to find you. Very grateful." He pulled her closer, seeking her lips, and proceeded to show her just how grateful he was.

* * * * *

FOUR UNIQUE SERIES FOR EVERY WOMAN YOU ARE...

Silhouette Romance®

Tender, delightful, provocative—stories that capture the laughter, the tears, the *joy* of falling in love. Pure romance...straight from the heart!

SILHOUETTE *Desire*®

Go wild with Desire! Passionate, emotional, sensuous stories of fiery romance. With heroines you'll like and heroes you'll *love*, Silhouette Desire never fails to deliver.

Silhouette Special Edition®

Stories of love and life, these powerful novels are tales that you can identify with—romances with "something special" added in! Silhouette Special Edition is entertainment for the heart.

SILHOUETTE·INTIMATE·MOMENTS™

Enter a world where passions run hot and excitement is the rule. Dramatic, larger-than-life and always compelling—Silhouette Intimate Moments will never let you down.

SGENERIC